ANTONIA WHITE

was born in London in 1899, and educated at the Convent of the Sacred Heart, Roehampton and St Paul's Girls' School, London. She trained as an actress at the Royal Academy of Dramatic Art, working for her living as a freelance copywriter and contributing short stories to a variety of magazines. In 1924 she joined the staff of W. S. Crawford as a copywriter, became Assistant Editor of *Life and Letters* in 1928, theatre critic of *Time and Tide* in 1934, and was the Fashion Editor of the *Daily Mirror* and then the *Sunday Pictorial* until the outbreak of the Second World War. During the war Antonia White worked first in the BBC and then in the French Section of the Political Intelligence Department of the Foreign Office.

Antonia White published four novels: *Frost in May* (1933), *The Lost Traveller* (1950), *The Sugar House* (1952), and *Beyond The Glass* (1954) all published as Virago Modern Classics. This quartet of novels will be televised by the BBC in 1981. Her other published work includes a volume of short stories, *Strangers* (1954), shortly to be published by Virago.

Antonia White translated over thirty novels from the French, and was awarded the Clairouin Prize for her first one, Maupassant's *Une Vie*, in 1950. She also translated many of the works of Colette. Like Colette, Antonia White was devoted to cats and wrote two books about her own – *Minka and Curdy* and *Living With Minka and Curdy*. She was married three times and had two daughters and four grandchildren. She lived most of her life in London and died in 1980 in Sussex, where her father and many generations of her family were born and bred.

The Hound and the Falcon

THE STORY OF A RECONVERSION
TO THE CATHOLIC FAITH

ANTONIA WHITE

NEW INTRODUCTION
BY SARA MAITLAND

Virago

Published by VIRAGO PRESS Limited 1980
41 William IV Street, London WC2N 4DB

Reprinted 1983

First published in Great Britain by
Longmans, Green & Co. Ltd. 1965

Printed in Great Britain by litho by
Anchor Press, Tiptree, Essex

British Library Cataloguing in Publication Data
White, Antonia
    The hound and the falcon.
    1. White, Antonia   2. Converts, Catholic –
    England – Biography
    I. Title
    282'.09214   BX4668.W48

ISBN 0-86068-172-6

CONTENTS

INTRODUCTION

In a relaxed moment in this book Antonia White writes: 'No rationalising can be as beautiful as the Virgin pregnant with God.' If this phrase has any meaning at all to you personally – I do not mean Mary, or God, necessarily, but that a mythic, a spiritual, a divine image can be the carrier of ultimate meaning – then this book is about you: is about confused ambitious faith in an age when non-materialism has become discredited. If the phrase has no meaning then this book may explain to you why some of your friends, despite careful political training and otherwise raised consciousness seem to go on and on bitching about something and you are not sure what.

Antonia White was born in 1899. After the conversion of her parents she was baptised into the Roman Catholic Church at the age of seven and was educated as a Catholic and inspired by her passionately devout father. The 1920s (the decade of her own twenties) she spent in an emotional chaos which included nine months in a lunatic asylum; three marriages – two of which were annulled for non-consummation; and having two children in two years by two different fathers. In 1933 her first novel *Frost in May* was published, to considerable acclaim. It is an obviously autobiographical novel (like her other fiction) about her experience as an 'unsatisfactory' pupil in a Roman Catholic Convent school, confronting and being defeated by Holy Mother Church. Apart from being an impressive and moving account of adolescence and a stylish bit of writing the novel also reveals quite painfully the author's conflicts about the Church she had decisively left and yet continued to yearn for. This voice in *Frost in May* is not solely, or even predominantly, a nostalgic longing for the sweet security of childhood. It is something quite different: a note I have heard from other lapsed Catholics and nowhere else. The nearest equivalent, quite seriously, is the way that some women I knew in a Battered Women's Refuge, especially if they had been married for a long time, would sometimes speak of their husbands; with a knowledge that they had been hurt and would be hurt again which could not totally outweigh the passionate longing to be involved again in that relationship which was the source of all emotions -- positive as well as negative. *Frost in May* -- and this is not a criticism of its artistic unity -- has strong undertones of unfinished business.

At Christmas-time 1940, while she was working for the BBC in wartime London, Antonia White returned to the practice of Roman Catholicism. That, at its simplest, is what this book is about. In November of that year she received a 'fan letter' about *Frost in May* from a former Jesuit novice, now a married re-convert, considerably older than herself, whom she had never met. This letter, the personality of her Peter, and the emotional relationship they generated between them inspired the correspondence which makes up this book. Having some-one outside her normal social circle who was willing to take seriously and sympathetically the problems of faith she experienced, and who at the same time was resolute that 'the one Holy, Catholic and Apostolic Church' was the proper place for her to be, clearly stimulated her to tackle the unfinished business of *Frost in May*. It seems probable that with her strong sense of being hunted by God and haunted by Catholicism Antonia White would have eventually found some route back into the Church, but the emotional attraction and intellectual demands of Peter, plus I would think the pressure of the war itself, made 1940 the time for such a reconversion.

The Church that Antonia White left in the twenties and was reconsidering in the early forties was markedly different from the Roman Catholic Church today. For all that the restrictions and narrownesses of the hierarchy may annoy radical and progressive Catholics in the 1970s and 80s, the second Vatican Council of the 1960s did genuinely change the approach of the Church. Hans Küng and others may be 'disciplined' today for heretical writing, Father Tyrrell and many others were excommunicated, persecuted and denied Catholic burial only 70 years ago. While nuns today protest at being asked to return to the habit, the canonical regulations of 1917 imposed on them stricter enclosure and less autonomy than they had experienced at any stage of their whole history. The tension between the would-be liberals and the conservatives before the Second World War was more painful than at any other time in modern church history. There were a number of reasons for this, but basically the nineteenth century saw the rise of both political instability and of a new approach to theology, especially to biblical and historical material which dangerously threatened the traditional Catholic understanding of authority. A real power struggle emerged within the Roman Catholic Church between two groups – the traditionalist, pro-papal, pro-centralised-absolute authority and with a marked conservative tendency to 'keep the church out of political involvement' and, on the other hand, the 'modernists' who believed that the Church should respond to contemporary and local social conditions; should accept a (fairly crude) social evolutionary stand on politics; should show a deeper respect for historical and scholarly developments – including scientific discoveries; and should encourage personal integrity and autonomy. The English Hierarchy, only recently re-established and always nervous about its identity, was markedly conservative, but in Northern Europe and the USA the 'modernists' received considerable support from the local authorities and so became increasingly forceful and influential. In the earliest period modernism was consistently defeated by the conservative party: the declaration of Papal Infallibility in 1870 should be seen in the light of this debate. More particularly, in 1908 Pius X declared 'modernism' to be heretical. This meant that people who would not withdraw their 'modernist' views could be disciplined; their opinions could not be published by Catholic Presses, taught in Catholic institutions, nor read by the faithful. Many individuals were either excommunicated or left the Church.

Liberalism, of course, was not destroyed by this attack, the forms of which were often extremely savage. In a historical perspective, indeed, the progressives can be seen to have triumphed, because the Second Vatican Council, at least in the realms of theoretical theology, vindicated many of the radical ideas of the first half of the century; but for Antonia White and her generation of intellectual Catholics the problem was difficult and complicated. By intellectual taste and training she was definitively a 'modernist':

> Surely we want more and more people to be Catholics not from fear or habit but from unforced conviction? Is it a heresy to wish that the rulers were not inevitably fixed for all time in Rome and were a slightly more cosmopolitan body? Her rigidity has pre-

served her [the Church] in the past but surely the time has come for a little flexibility; for more understanding, more charity, more humility and less persecution mania.

and elsewhere:

I think the Church's view of marriage is certainly good and right (with slight hesitation about dogmatic forbidding of contraceptives) but wonder if she couldn't modify her rigour a trifle in the case of people unable to marry or unsuited to marriage . . . I can't help feeling a little might be left to individual conscience . . . surely there might be some loophole for reinterpretation.

Antonia White has little or no interest in the socio-political aspects of modernism, but her sense that the Church was depriving individuals of intellectual freedom is very strong:

The more good artists, scholars, philosophers, scientists and psychologists she can produce as well as saints the better . . . In broad outline she is always wiser than men, in detail I think not always. And I am sure that her honour can only be kept untarnished by admitting her errors, not denying them. If she is the city of truth she must admit to be examined in the light of truth in ordinary matters.

It's a sign of these extraordinary times that, if one reads anyone good, one always fears they've either renounced the Church or been condemned by it.

On the other hand Antonia White appears to take the indictment of modernism absolutely seriously. If she wants to receive the sacraments she must bend herself to one hundred per cent orthodoxy. Great sections of these letters are taken up *denying* the validity of her own ideas and inclinations; all doubts and difficulties have to be blamed on her own character or development, rather than facing the fact that she – and other intellectuals – might be right.

The Church's very lack of 'accommodatingness' is a strong point in her favour. . . It still did seem to me that the Church demanded the sacrifice of such intellectual honesty as one had. But last night it occurred to me that she demanded the sacrifice not of intellectual honesty but of intellectual pride.

Necessity for restraint, incessant vigilance, mortification and redirection of one's natural impulses . . . seem to me not only necessary but natural and wholesome.

I am under marching orders now and in a regiment that will keep me going when I want to fall out. Naturally good and unselfish people seem to do very well outside the Church, but the best place for aggressive and egotistical ones like me is in it – *well* in.

It is not surprising that under these conflicts Antonia White feels the Church 'sitting on her brain like an octopus' and that her feelings waver between love and intense revulsion and repugnance.

As a sacramentalist Christian myself I have little difficulty in understanding why Antonia White wanted to be back inside the practising life of the Church. What is more interesting is why she was unable to accept comfortably an identity with the radical, critical Catholic school. Those were the writers she read and admired: Spinoza, Santanos, Bernanos, Tyrrell, Von Hügel (some of them 'in' and some 'out', but all witnessing to a new way forward for the Church). Those were the directions in which all her sympathies lay: but she was unable to identify with this group. It is this tension that makes the book so fascinating and also makes a solution to the dilemma impossible.

There seem to be a number of reasons why Antonia White could not make this leap. Firstly she does not have that high estimation of her own worth that makes it possible to assert oneself and one's ideas over against a beloved authority. This seems to me an important point: it is fairly easy to summon up the energy and courage to struggle against a designated *enemy*; it is far harder and requires a deep sense of oneself as intrinsically lovable and worthwhile to engage in struggle with someone, or something, that one acknowledges one does indeed *love*. Antonia White loved the Church – she felt continually attracted to it, yearned to return to its practise, and moreover she believed that it represented something of crucial importance to a full view of the human condition. But although she attempts to stress that it is important to love or 'at least to tolerate ourselves', she is fundamentally unable to do so:

> I am tormented sometimes by miseries and scruples and by the awful old fear that it is all my fault if I can't see . . . that I am fundamentally perverted.

> None of us likes to dwell on the doctrine of hell and yet there is, for us, some fearful inevitability in it.

You must forgive me if I am being silly and priggish. I am both, often, and I am also cruel, vain and fond of power of any kind.

It used to frighten me, even as a child, because though I did practice quite fervently, I was terrified that God would demand too much of me and I should fail.

Antonia White's own personal history cannot have helped her to form a strong and loving self-image. But her problem is compounded by the very low opinion she had of femaleness. This book is punctuated with passing references to women (not individually but generically) as stupid, incoherent and sinful, while masculine qualities are perceived of as good:

I was impressed oddly enough by a life of St Thérèse of Lisieux . . . I felt that here was a really heroic and austere soul, holding on in spite of darkness and fear – a very masculine soul under all the frills. . .

Her most explicit reference to the inferiority of women comes in an expression of Catholic orthodoxy for her time:

It is a profound truth that makes Eve the *Channel* of the fall and the Church's defects may be due to her femaleness. A woman is more corruptible, I believe, than a man because of the slower rhythm of her life, as still waters breed scum. And haven't you often noticed in men, that it is their female side that betrays and corrupts them? It is not for nothing that in no religion is God imagined as female.

Carrying this sort of self-image it is not surprising that Antonia White found herself continually attempting to placate and charm God; and that she lacked the interior resources to set herself against the beloved authority of the Church. Intellectually of course she can see and understand the problem:

I am so frightened of losing whatever I may have painfully found, and yet I know this fear of loss is itself suspect and one of my besetting faults which has so often prevented me from making the best use of my life and gifts. . . Too much stress was laid on fear in my childhood and my own nature was too responsive to fear, anyway. I think it was very much an amateurish way of getting rid of fear that made me so rebellious against the Church. Now that, through other circumstances, that fear has been lessened, I may be freer to love. I know that, humanly speaking, my greatest defect is lack of power to love.

But for all the rational talking, she frequently reveals that the fear and self-hatred remain embedded in her relationship to God and the Church:

> The hardest article of faith for me to swallow is that God loves human beings. That one fact alone convinces me that the gospel *is* a revelation for I don't see how one could ever arrive at such a conclusion by reason alone.

Contemporary Christian feminists attempt to confront the world and the Church in a strong conviction of their own – individual and collective – holiness, lovability and God-imaged-ness. Such a conviction is the basis for a radical critique of the Church. However it is not the only approach; another, used by many who know that religion won't leave them alone, is to take it 'lightly' – practice but not get knotted up about it. This attitude is described brilliantly by Antonia White herself in *Frost in May*, using the character of Leonie, and recognised by her as being a healthy way of going about the business of God. But it demands a quality that she herself is apparently totally devoid of – a high level of loving self-irony and inner confidence, plus an amused delight in ritual and cultic imagery. For some reason this approach offends convinced atheists and agnostics deeply, but it is a saving grace. But Antonia White cannot take religion like this because she has no sense of humour about herself and – riddled with guilt and awe – absolutely none at all about God or the Church. It is fair to point out that this tendency must have been emphasised by the war. The whole book is shot through with this reality: her children evacuated, her friends overseas or dead, and she experiencing the nightly horror of the Blitz. When she returned to the Church she discovered that the stiff conditions normally attached to the return of excommunicants had been lifted because everyone in London was regarded as being '*in extremis*' – in immediate danger of death. Throughout the period of these letters she is harried by the frightening, and also by the tedious aspects of the war – constantly engaged in hard, unsympathetic work, short of sleep, probably of food and always of money and time. That these stresses should simultaneously have brought her to a renewed contemplation of her faith and limited her resources of irony is not at all surprising. But I am sure that there was another and important reason why she had to take the whole thing so painfully seriously and that has to be sought in the relationship that developed between her and Peter, her correspondent. Although his letters are not included, some sense of him as a person emerges from her correspondence – and their increasing emotional involvement with each other creates one of the most fascinating tensions of the book. At the height of their involvement they both admit to 'being in love' and to feeling physical desire for the other. They discuss in all seriousness the reasons why they won't sleep together – despite the fact that they had never even met. But it would be totally untrue to present their whole relationship solely as a romantic or sentimental delusion.

We are not on the whole a generation, or society, of letter writers. Many people may really doubt the possibility of creating and maintaining a 'real' relationship entirely, or even mainly, by post. But this is of course a very modern view based on easy travel, the telephone and a broader social foundation on which to build more immediate friendships and connections. Elizabeth Barrett and Robert Browning, for example, witness that very real and lasting relationships can be founded on correspondence. My own experience is certainly that epistolatory-friendships have a very special quality: the other party cannot interrupt, even by apparent boredom, when one is 'speaking' – each individual has both to listen and speak longer to maintain the communication. The interruptions for work, making meals and popping out to buy cigarettes are eliminated and all the other relationships and activities of the correspondents are invisible – or only introduced as the writer chooses: there is a real concentration on the other person. Moreoever, what is said cannot be dismissed or distorted but remains absolutely available for as long as the recipient chooses to keep the letters.

It is probably only in the format of letters – not so 'serious' as a work of art (and it cannot be incidental that Antonia White was suffering from a writer's block during the most intense phase of the relationship) but more concentrated than conversation – that Antonia White would have been able to deal with so much conflicting material without burying her whole personality in a polemic diatribe. But there is a major disadvantage for the reader in this method of communication.

Antonia White's relationship with her correspondent – a man of obvious will and forceful character – inevitably seems to affect the content. I do, for once, believe that these letters were written without even half an eye to publication, and they are therefore meant for a single audience; an audience moreover who shared many of her interests, had a similar education and background and who wanted very emphatically for her to return to the Church. That audience – as 'lover', as a man old enough to be her father, as secure and determined Christian – summons up in the writer, despite her denials, certain responses of which one is the evident desire to please him. Because of this single audience she often presents things that we would like to hear more about in very limited ways. For example she breaks the news that she has been back to confession and communion like this:

> Over Christmas I took a step which surprised me . . . perhaps it will surprise you less. And I have to admit that I am still full of doubts about it and I hope you won't be too distressed if I don't continue in it.

It is not likely that his possible distress, or his level of surprise was really her predominant emotion at the time (what was?). But inevitably in writing to a single and personally involved audience she takes his reaction into account. There is a prejudice and this is intensified as she comes to think of him, in whatever way, as her 'lover'. This relationship adds to the difficulty of assessing the whole subject of the book. It is certainly an attempt to be honest about something that matters enormously to the author, but it is an honesty within a special context. Her confusion is part of that honesty and so is her feeling for Peter and her desire to love and be loved by him in a healthy and nourishing way. Because of all these conflicts it is hard to say whether the *Hound and the Falcon* can most genuinely be read as sisterly encouragement and sharing in the area of religious experience or as a cautionary tale. What is clear is that we get a self-portrait of an unusually passionate woman deeply engaged with a passionately important subject.

The contemporary women's movement has, on the whole, dismissed the whole subject altogether – and denies its importance. This dismissal is similar to that experienced by Antonia White herself:

In the last century it was mainly, for the ordinary person, a question of which church you went to. In this, in the sort of circles you and I have moved in, if you go to Church at all, you're considered amusingly eccentric, an ignorant fool, or a guilt-racked neurotic.

However there are a substantial number of women who – while accepting that all three of these accusations were quite possibly true – would still want to reply 'nonetheless it is matter of importance to me, and I'm not getting any input from my sisters.' We cannot come to terms with religion in isolation; the request for serious consideration remains legitimate because the questions raised are profound ones. In the USA a feminist critique of Christianity and other religious options has been developed for the last dozen or so years with increasing commitment and sophistication. But the basic position, laid out clearly by Antonia White in this book, remains; because of its emotional as well as its intellectual content it continues to demand a response:

> Whether or not the Church *can* be purged of those inessentials which are such a stumbling block raises so many questions that I should like to hear you talk about. I know that on many occasions when I have felt drawn to the Church again and have attempted, diffidently, to talk to priests, I have always had the feeling of being offered a pretty hard stone instead of bread.

but on the other hand:

> I don't think I have ever doubted, since I was a child, that there was a spiritual life and that it was profoundly important.

Sara Maitland, London 1980

FOREWORD

The man to whom these letters were written a quarter of a century ago has been dead several years and his side of our intensive correspondence between the autumn of 1940 and that of 1941 has unfortunately vanished. When this hectic exchange of letters began, we were strangers to each other. We met only once in the thick of it and once more when it had dwindled to normal proportions, but we remained friends to the end of his life and continued to write to each other at intervals until his last illness.

My first letter from 'Peter' (not his real name but one he liked to be called by) arrived 'out of the blue' in November 1940. It had been sent to me care of a publisher and did not reach me till three weeks after it was written. The name signed at the end of several pages of that beautiful script with which I was soon to become so familiar conveyed nothing to me, for I did not then know of the books he had written and did not move in Catholic circles. His reason for writing to me was that he had read my novel *Frost in May* and, guessing that it was based on my own experience as a child in a Catholic convent school, he was anxious to know what was my present attitude to Catholicism. He told me something of his own relations with the Church. A 'cradle' Catholic, he had been so devout as a young man that he had intended to become a priest and had even spent some years in the Jesuit novitiate before his superiors decided he had no vocation, either to the Society or to the priesthood. Subsequently he had married, had had a successful career in advertising and literary journalism, and for a period of thirty years had lapsed completely from the Catholic faith. Now, for some years, he had been back in the Church but, though *croyant* and *pratiquant*, he was troubled by many aspects of Catholicism. So much so that he was thinking of drawing up an 'indictment' based on his own and other people's difficulties in adhering to their Faith in view of the Church's rigorously repressive attitude towards so much in contemporary thought and opinion.

At that time, having 'lapsed' completely for fifteen years, I did not see myself ever returning to my former belief. In my innermost mind, however, I had never ceased to be concerned with the problem of religion and this letter brought it right to the surface. I answered it at length and as honestly as I could. Within a week or two, 'Peter' and I were launched on an intensive correspondence which lasted for a year and in which religion remained the constant theme, though it was interwoven with another, that of the relationship which developed almost at once between two impulsive people who had never met and who had everything to learn about each other, including how much and how little they had in common.

Soon after this cross-fire of letters began to be exchanged, I did, to my own surprise, return to the Church: not, however, to find peace of mind. On the contrary, my old problems were intensified and I went on wrestling with them like a bad swimmer in a rough sea; now coming to the surface, now being helplessly submerged again before finding some spar to hold on to. How much 'Peter' contributed to my 'reconversion' I cannot tell. There were other forces, natural and supernatural, at work. What is certain is that he stimulated me into thinking, reading, trying to clarify my confused mind about the whole subject of Catholicism with a new urgency. And for that, as for so much else, I owe 'Peter', one of the most generous men I have ever known, an unrepaid and unrepayable debt.

People may well ask why one side of a private correspondence, which deals almost as much with the letter-writers' personal problems as with their religious ones, should now be printed. Is there not something rather distasteful in the publication, in one's own lifetime, of intimate letters to a dead friend, intended for no eyes but his? Such an objection may well be raised, and to say that the publication, almost in full, of this series of my own letters was not due to my own initiative does not dispel it. I could have refused the suggestion that they should be published. Since I did not refuse it, the responsibility for their appearing in print is mine. All I hope is that 'Peter' himself, had he still been alive, would have given this book his *Imprimatur*.

The chain of accidental circumstances which has led to its publication is long and rather curious. It began in the spring of 1942 with a chance suggestion that I should write something for Horizon about my return to the Catholic Church. It ended with a chance remark at a dinner-party in the summer of 1964 which John Guest of Longmans happened to overhear.

My first abortive attempt to produce something for Horizon took the form of a letter to Cyril Connolly which I never sent to him and which is printed at the end of this book as Appendix I. Dissatisfied with it, I decided it would be better to base my article on actual day-to-day records of the mental conflicts and oscillations which had preceded and followed my 'reconversion'. Reading over my journals for that time, I found disappointingly little about what had been my most intense preoccupation. Everything vital, I realised, had gone into my correspondence with 'Peter'. He had, I knew, kept my letters. He had also asked for his own back, since he had intended to make extracts from both sides of our correspondence to furnish points for his projected 'indictment'. I asked him to send me mine because I wanted to quarry in them for my *Horizon* article. When he returned them, I found he had already edited and annotated many of them with a view to making a book out of extracts from our letters to each other, a kind of religious debate by correspondence. This project, like the indictment itself, never materialised. His own letters remained in his possession and I think he must eventually have destroyed them; at any rate they have disappeared. With much labour, I pieced together from the hundreds of pages I had written to 'Peter' in 1940 and 1941, a sequence of short passages which gave a rough idea of my conflicting thoughts and feelings about Catholicism before, months after my return to it, I reached some kind of anchorage. When I showed this sequence to Cyril Connolly it distressed him so much that he could not bring himself to publish it in *Horizon*. He said it was like watching a person making desperate attempts to retain their reason and finally lapsing into insanity.

I put the rejected article away and forgot all about it. I also put away the vast bundle of letters from which I had quarried it. I had meant to return them to 'Peter' at once, but since he had no urgent reason for wanting them, and since he never mentioned the subject again, I forgot all about them and they remained where they were.

Eight years later, Father Philip Caraman S.J. asked me if I had any ideas for a possible article for *The Month*. Being invariably short of ideas, I suddenly remembered my rejected *Horizon* article and asked if he would care to see it. I dug out the now yellowing typescript and sent it to him. He accepted the article as it stood and it was published in *The Month* of August 1950 under the title of 'Smoking Flax'.

Fourteen years later still, one night in July 1964, I was having dinner with Neville Braybrooke and his wife. Among the two or three other people there was John Guest of Longmans. After dinner Neville, to whom I had been talking about Raïssa Maritain's *Journal* which I was then translating, suddenly said to me: 'I wish more of your own Journal could be published. I was so interested by those few bits that were.' Greatly puzzled, I said: 'It's true that I've kept a kind of journal for years, but no one but myself has read it and certainly none of it has ever appeared in print.' Neville then assured me that, years ago, he had read extracts from this 'Journal' in *The Month*—an account of my doubts and anxieties when I returned to the Faith. 'It was called "Smoking Flax" and it has stuck in my mind all this time.' I explained that it was, in fact, extracts from letters and Neville observed: 'Well, whatever it was, I think it's the most interesting thing of yours I ever read.' Overhearing this, John Guest said he would like to read 'Smoking Flax' and asked if I would send it to him. I promised to do so and did.

When he had read it he rang me up to say it had genuinely interested him as it touched on so many religious problems that were vexing people's minds today. He also said that if the whole of this correspondence existed, he would be interested to see it. The other side of it, as I had to explain, had unfortunately disappeared, but I believed I still had my own put away in some file.

I discovered the letters and sorted them out by dates. Reading them through after more than twenty years was a strange and, at times, embarrassing experience. It would have taken too long to go through them and 'edit' them and, after all, John Guest had only asked to see them. Even then, they would first have to be typed; my small writing, now overlaid with innumerable pencil and red-ink markings and comments by 'Peter' would have strained any eyesight. I got a kind friend to make a literal typed transcript of them which I sent to John Guest, just as it stood, not without considerable misgivings, both about their actual content and their inordinate length. The typescript of these letters, all written in the space of less than a year, in the intervals of a full-time job in the B.B.C. and against the background of the London blitz, amounted to over eighty thousand words—more than the average length of a novel.

Nevertheless, John Guest read the thick pile from end to end. When he had finished, he told me that, with some obviously necessary pruning, he thought that these letters ought to be published, just as they were spontaneously written, with all their flaws and discrepancies, all their confused feeling and thinking, all that they reveal, wittingly and unwittingly, of the character of this odd pair of correspondents.

Perhaps the only justification for their publication is that some people may find in them a reflection of their own difficulties concerning religious, and, in particular, Catholic belief and be relieved to know that others, possibly more than they think, share them. For, though 'Peter' is silent, I think at least some echo of his voice can be heard through the clamour of mine in the pages that follow.

A.W.

10 November, 1940.

Dear Mr T——,

Thank you very much for your extremely interesting letter. I only received it yesterday as I moved to London about three weeks ago and the friends to whom it was forwarded did not know my new address.

Your letter interested me immensely and I should like nothing better than to have a long talk with you and ask you endless questions. But I have just got a job with the B.B.C. and I only get a day and a half off every week. Travelling being slow and difficult at the moment, I do not see how I can go as far as Wales and back again between Saturday noon and Sunday night! I may have to go to Liverpool some time soon in connection with a programme, but my geography is so weak that I don't know how long it would take to get from there to Portmeirion.

All that you say revives the problems which have exercised me off and on for many years. I have not been a practising Catholic for nearly fifteen years. In fact, I recently discovered, when, on a sudden impulse, I tried to go to Confession not so long ago, that I had been excommunicated for ten of them without knowing it. This was for a technical breach of discipline which I had committed quite innocently. I *could* be reconciled, but to do so would apparently involve signing various articles of submission which, at the moment, I do not feel prepared to sign.

Nevertheless, if one has been brought up as a Catholic and for many years has unquestioningly believed in its doctrine and practised with some degree of fervour, the pull of the Church is very strong. It is like one's native language and, though one may have become denationalised, one cannot help reverting to it and even thinking in its terms. I still find myself automatically taking the Catholic point of view and defending the Catholic position and instinctively using Catholic imagery and terms in thought and speech. Yet it is very much a case of *Odi et Amo*. Often I long to embrace it again—even to practise it without literally believing in it—if that is possible. But I find it an impossible problem. To return and wholeheartedly embrace it again may be simply mental and emotional weakness, a desire for security—the instinct, that grows stronger as one gets older, to recapture the past. To remain cut off from it, sceptical and hesitating, may be, as the Catholics themselves would certainly say, a refusal of grace and a blind persistence in spiritual pride.

So much in the actual mechanics of the Church and its extremely intolerant attitude repels me, yet those defects *could* be regarded as trivial compared to its essential beauty and truth. At present, I think I feel piety towards the Church (or rather towards the Catholic religion) as a magnificent transcript of human experience and as a method of dealing with one's life rather than as a literal revelation of the supernatural. But I am afraid this attitude would be too heretical to allow one to be admitted into the life of the Church.

I have for some months been reading Spinoza and Santayana, both of whom seem to shed some light on what I am trying, perhaps hopelessly, to discover. I don't think I have ever doubted, since I was a child, that there was a spiritual life and that it was profoundly important. Nor do I believe that it can be lived without discipline and constant awareness and self-watchfulness. But whether the Catholic Church which was once the guardian of it for western people is still its guardian, I don't know. I do not trust either my mind or my heart enough to be able to lead me to such truth as I might be capable of knowing. I can only manage blindly and provisionally, trying to be honest and recognising my natural bias towards pride and laziness, trying to note the points of contact between experiences, of whatever kind, that seem to have a particular 'tone' which I can only call spiritual, and trying to connect them into some kind of very rough and amateurish map for my own guidance.

I am greatly interested in your 'indictment'. It seems to me a very courageous step! Also I should very much like to hear about Fr Tyrrell.* When I was a little girl, I remember hearing him mentioned as a brilliant but wicked man who had set himself up against the authority of the Church. I used to spend all my summer holidays near Storrington and I remember standing by his grave in the Protestant Cemetery and feeling a shock of horror and pity.

I do not think I have been unfair in my treatment of Roehampton.† I certainly tried to be impartial and to give as detached a picture as I could both of its extraordinary charm and its curious narrowness and rigidity. I do not think it *can* be denied that there was a good deal of snobbery there, not much among the children, but a considerable amount among the nuns. Mere wealth was despised, but to belong to an old Catholic family and to be wealthy enough to live a typical 'society' life were certainly advantages and children

* See Appendix II.

† Convent of the Sacred Heart, Roehampton, which he had recognised as the 'Lippington' of my first novel *Frost in May*.

who did not come from that social background were made to feel it in a thousand tiny pin-pricks and allusions. That may be a purely feminine thing and possibly one would not find it in a Jesuit college.

As regards the education itself, I think it was in many ways admirable (though naturally restricted on certain subjects) and gave one a much wider base on which to build than the examination-cramming system of such schools as St Paul's where I went afterwards. Many of the nuns were extremely intelligent and cultured women and were exceedingly critical and fastidious in any field such as music or painting where criticism could be safely exercised.

Whether or not the Church *can* be purged of those inessentials which are such a stumbling block raises so many questions that I should like to hear you talk about. I know that on many occasions when I have felt drawn to the Church again and have attempted, diffidently, to talk to priests, I have always had the feeling of being offered a pretty hard stone instead of bread. But there again, of course, if I had been humble enough to accept the stone, it might have turned into bread!

Again, I feel sometimes that the Church is wrong in trying to base so much on reason. Usually the reasons it gives are very easily destroyed or highly ambiguous and it might have been wiser to appeal to nothing but faith. But everything I say seems to point to a nature so obstinate that perhaps there is no place for me in the Church.

I know very well what you mean when you say that the 'Léonie'* attitude is fundamentally right. If so, I agree that it is not possible for English Catholics. We are too self-conscious and on the defensive to take our religion in the natural, easy, almost casual way continental Catholics do.

What happened to 'Léonie'? She married an Englishman and has two children. I have not seen her for many years; our lives are too far apart. When I last saw her, her peculiar ironic charm was as potent as ever.

What happened to 'Nanda'† is such a long story that I cannot attempt to tell it here. It is muddled, catastrophic, inconsistent and also very funny, but given 'Nanda's' nature, circumstances and upbringing, Nanda herself can now see that it was all logical and inevitable—and also wonder whether she has really become quite as sensible as she sometimes feels! Her legal description is 'feme

* A character in *Frost in May*, a highly intelligent and very witty girl of French and German ancestry.

† The character in *Frost in May* through whose eyes the convent school and its personalities are seen.

sole', she works at the moment in the B.B.C. where she is alternately bewildered and amused, and she has two charming daughters aged 9 and 11, neither of whom, owing to Nanda's hopeless uncertainty and unwillingness to commit herself or them, have even been baptised.

You will probably be surprised at receiving such a long letter but not more surprised than I am at writing it. I do not usually write long letters except to people I know very well, and then rarely. But your letter interested me so much and pressed so many springs that I have written pages. It would be far more satisfactory to talk and I do hope very much that some day it will be possible for us to do so.

Yours sincerely,
Antonia White.

23 November, 1940.

Dear Mr T——,

Thank you very much indeed for your letter. You must forgive me for not having answered before. I work very hard at the B.B.C., sometimes till 4 a.m., and it is becoming very difficult to keep up with one's private life, so you must forgive me if I am an extremely erratic correspondent!

I am very much afraid that, much as I should like to, it is not going to be possible for us to meet just yet. They are not sending me to Liverpool after all. All the staff who have gone at all far from London lately have had such disastrous experiences on their journeys, ten-hour delays etc., etc., that they are keeping us near home and arranging to have long-distance jobs done by people on the spot. It was very kind indeed of you to invite me to your home and I do hope that one day it may be possible for me to accept your invitation.

I do feel just a little disconcerted by P.S.3. Frankly that is one of the things I have against the Catholic attitude—this suspicion of a trap or a devil's lure in every situation. I wrote you a long letter— a *very* unusual thing for me to do—simply because yours interested me very much and touched on many things in my mind. I am afraid most of the people who are kind enough to write to me about *Frost in May* get a polite acknowledgement and nothing more. But because two people happen to find that they have several points of common interest, is that any reason to be alarmed? Why be so much on the defensive? If you knew the miseries I go through trying to write one page of 'a work of art' and how I dashed off a tremendously long letter to you at top speed without stopping to think, instead of being alarmed, you'd be amused. Oh dear, if 'works of art' were written so easily, I'd have a shelf of books to my credit! So *please*!

Of course, if you build up a romantic picture of me, all 'niceness' and 'interest', you will be horribly disappointed when we meet. But if you think of me as a dangerous woman and an intellectual seducer, you will be equally mistaken. I am hot-tempered, obstinate, aggressive and—I hope—middling honest. There—that's off my mind.

As to 'choosing' a confessor, I've never done such a thing but simply walked into any confessional box where I happen to be and taken my chance. Very occasionally I meet priests socially but I hardly ever talk to them about anything but secular subjects. I feel I know all the things they would say to me. The simple and saintly ones simply cannot understand what worries one and, oddly enough, I feel far more respect for them and far more humble towards them than to the brilliant ones who dazzle you with philosophical arguments and who seem so anxious to prove that they are every bit as worldly as you are.

I tell myself I won't go back from fear; I will only go back from love. But it must be love from one's whole nature. I know what a little way reason can take one, yet there is a discipline even in using that small part of a feeble and feminine reason and not surrendering to an emotional pull and old associations, even though it means losing a great deal of richness and magic from one's life. No, I *don't* feel one loses it. The older I get, the more extraordinary and beautiful the whole spectacle seems to me. The Catholic Church is one aspect of it but I should hate to be cut off from all the others. The natural world is full enough of mystery and beauty and if the universe proves to be indifferent to man, at least man has this curious and precious power of being able to contemplate it.

Poetically true and deeply true psychologically I *do* believe the Catholic religion (if not the Catholic Church!) to be. But *literally true* . . . I find it hard to believe. I think religion oversteps its function in claiming to be literally true. It seems to me a religion should be a *method* of exploring the realm of spirit. Whether the Catholic is the best one for people of this time in the west, is another question. I think one is hampered without a religion but possibly even more hampered with the wrong one.

When I do talk to priests—never, of course, getting as far as this —but stammering out a few of my difficulties, they invariably try to knock me down with arguments. Their invariable assumption that

5

they must be right makes the argument as meaningless as most discussions are. And I believe profoundly with Keats that 'Man should not dispute or assert but whisper results to his neighbour.' That is why I am so much more moved by any simple priest who leads a dull life without any of the ordinary pleasures and who says: 'The theologians are too clever for me. I only know that I believe in God and love Him.'

I very much liked your note on Fr Tyrrell. I should so much like to hear you talk about him.

By the way, I mentioned your letter to a great friend of mine the other day and asked if he knew your name. He said he thought he did and then remembered he had seen it mentioned in connection with Eric Gill. I believe you wrote an article on him?

If you really mean it . . . you can be of use to me in a most concrete way. I am suddenly faced with a huge programme for S. America to celebrate the fourth centenary of the Jesuits. I have snatched all the books I can find but I have very little time. What I want to know is: (a) How do the Jesuits stand in S. America today? Have they many houses and are they on the whole in good odour politically? (b) Do you happen to know if there were any Jesuit geographers and explorers in S. America? I have got plenty of material about the Paraguayan missions and the 'Jesuit State'. But if you could answer (a) and (b) offhand (please don't bother to hunt up anything) I should be most grateful.

I am very tired and must stop. It is silly how much one wants to sleep these days. I wish the day were thirty-six hours long.

Good night, and thank you again for your letter.

Yours (how does one end a letter?!),
Antonia White.

29 November, 1940.

Dear Peter T——,

I am afraid I shall always have to be in your debt about letters. My life is just one long rush these days with very little time to myself. It is a kind of nightmare trying to catch up with things and I am sure you will understand. I come home very tired; sleep is usually rather broken by the noise outside and the job is exacting. Meanwhile unanswered letters pile up. I *must* write often to the children who are both away from me just now and, besides letters from friends, there are all the tiresome business ones to be dealt with, for, being on my own, there is no one else to deal with them. And, as I am vainly trying to write a book too (I have done just six pages in as many weeks), I am sure you will forgive me if I write seldom and meagrely. I daren't get that hunted feeling of never catching up or I shall collapse. I never seem to have time nowadays to read or think or just *exist*.

It was very kind of you to take so much trouble about the Jesuits. You shouldn't have bothered to send a telegram. I have got to do two programmes as, instead of taking 'either/or' they took both suggestions. But the first will be fairly simple, just on St Ignatius and the second, the Paraguay mission one, can wait till after Christmas.

Your letters interest me very much and you can be assured that I read them several times, even though I don't *answer* them! They raise so many points that I could only answer them by talking to you and I do hope very much that will be possible long before the war is over! I wish you did not live so far away. For the first year of the war (and for the first time in my life, since I've worked for my living since I was 16) I had no job and could so easily have come over to Portmeirion. At the moment it just isn't possible. It's a nuisance having no leisure, but I do like having a job again.

You must forgive me for not knowing your name since it's obviously a much better-known one than mine! I should be very much interested to read your autobiography. If I can find a photograph, I will send you one. But I hardly ever am photographed and all my things are in store. But I will hunt around. I've got various papers in friends' houses all over the place since I haven't had a home of my own since the war.

I do feel I would have to know you better—to have seen you and talked to you—before I could tell you about my life. It's a long story and a queer one and I'm only just beginning to understand it myself. Now I do understand it fairly well and see that the struggles and difficulties were inevitable. If you have a double nature, you cannot expect a peaceful life. After an unconscious struggle of about fifteen years and a very conscious one of five, I have managed to reach a sort of equilibrium. I have had a bad enemy in myself to fight and a real terror to overcome. But I have been very lucky; the fear no longer oppresses me and the enemy is encamped at a (comparatively!) safe distance. I have been over the edge of something terrifying and it has inevitably altered all my ideas of what a human being is.

If you want me to feel confident with you, don't try to 'convert' me. Remember that, for many years, people of all kinds have been trying to do that. I suffered much from my father's coercion and also from the fact that I had to disappoint him bitterly by going my own way instead of his. I loved him dearly and he died feeling that I had failed him in every important way.

One of the things I find hardest to bear in 'Catholic apologetics' is the way they put up an argument you have never used and proceed to demolish it. Why should there be no alternative between the 'blind dance of atoms' and the Catholic conception of God and the universe? I find no difficulty in believing in God but I prefer Spinoza's conception of God to the Catholic conception of God and I find Spinoza's life considerably more edifying than most of the lives of the saints. Frankly, I detest most of the saints. I hate their morbid preoccupation with sin and guilt, I hate their smug intimacy with what they call God, and I hate their anxious, niggling concern with their own salvation. The only saint I have a whole-hearted respect for (and that probably because I only know one thing about him) is St Charles Borromeo who was asked, during a game of chess, what he would do if the last trumpet sounded and who answered: 'I should go on playing chess.' There are very few 'pious' writings I find as moving or as nourishing as some parts of Keats' letters. Of course there are wonderful cries in the saints and in the devout books. There is nothing more beautiful than St Augustine's 'Sero nimis te amavi' or that wonderful passage about 'the bitter and blind bawlers . . . who, being famished, do lick their very shadows' or the passage in the *Imitation* 'The lover flieth, runneth, rejoiceth . . .' and 'Thou must be naked and carry a pure heart to God if thou wouldst attend at leisure and see how sweet the Lord is', but these cries come in some form from every genius and spiritual man, Christian or non-Christian. The only pious book that never sickens me is the New Testament and, however alienated from the Church I feel, I find more and more in it every time but it does *not* lead me to the bosom of Catholicism.

I would rather worship a God who was indifferent to me and destroyed me (since my destruction is a manifestation of his law and power) than one who kept a petty personal account of my sins and virtues and was jealous and revengeful and 'suffered' if I did not love him. At least St Francis Xavier had the grace to say: '*Oh Deus, ego amo te, Nec amo te ut salvas me.*'

I went to Mass at the Carmelites on Sunday. Yes, I tried sincerely to pray. I was moved to be back in the church I used to go to as a child, to find everything unchanged. But it is very hard to know just how much value that has. I think one must be what one was intended

8

to be, no matter how tempting and desirable it may seem to be something else. Of course I long to be part of something as one may long for a language and a fatherland. But going very slowly and in the dark, following false lights and wrong paths, I *do* find here and there, in the past and present, enough hints to know that I'm not entirely alone.

I have written more than I meant to and too much about myself. From what clues I can gather from your letters, our experiences overlap in many ways, but I think our natures are very different and therefore need different food. No amount of affection and good-will can short-circuit those differences. I always feel I am being discourteous if I don't agree entirely with someone else's point of view! Yet not a single one of my friends, even my most intimate and respected one, holds exactly the same opinions (if you can call them opinions!) as I do. So I REFUSE to enter into controversies, partly because I am incompetent, partly because I don't think they're fruitful. This doesn't mean I don't like hearing what you think, because I do. Only it's no good asking me questions because I shall either not answer them or answer them very indirectly. More likely still, I shall, as I have tonight, just ramble on about what *I* think!

Oh dear, I must resist your lure and write some business letters. If you have a photograph to spare, I should very much like one.

Good night.

Antonia.

P.S. Of course I was impressed by your saintly humility! !

P.P.S. I think it highly improbable I shall ever be on the Civil List. But the B.B.C. has notified me today that it will contribute £20 towards my burial expenses if I am killed in 'discharge of my duties'.

6 December, 1940.

Dear Peter,

I am very sorry you are ill so I will answer—or rather write—even though you tell me not to!

Your last letter touched me a good deal and I am truly grateful to you for not forcing the 'conversion' issue. This at once puts me very much more at my ease with you. Any sort of coercion, even the kindest and gentlest, always makes me feel like an animal in a trap and I'll bite my own paws off to get out.

I am sorry you 'don't like yourself at all'. Because I do think sooner or later one has to learn, at least, to tolerate oneself. Can't you extend your 'tolerance' a little further? It's only since I've managed, with considerable difficulty (and, even now, not consistently!), to regard myself without passionate self-loathing or passionate self-adoration that I've been freed from this insatiable thirst for love, admiration and reassurance which makes one's life a perpetual defence against loneliness and destroys all one's independence. I couldn't have done it without a good deal of help (which I resented acutely at the time!) but, being faced with a much worse alternative, I *had* to submit to a pretty rigorous mental discipline for four years. The net result of this is that I do know a little about myself, as one might know a little about the engine of a car, and roughly what I can and cannot expect of the machine.

This being so, of course I am flattered and pleased and touched by all the things you say. But I have to remember that they do not necessarily apply to *me* but only to your image of me. And your image of me consists not only of me, but of you.

I am sorry that I can't live up to your physical image of me! For though I am definitely fair, I am not tall and I am plumpish. I think I was what you call 'pretty' when I was a girl; at least I was certainly treated as if I were pretty. But I never had fool-proof good looks as I should like to have had but only the intermittent kind that make people look at you with interest one day and completely ignore you the next. Ever since I grew up, and even to this day (I am 41 now), I am usually taken for considerably more or considerably less than my age owing to this peculiar variability which affects not only features and shape of face but actual colouring of skin and hair. Someone who knew me very well once said to me: 'I have seen you vary in the course of a day from a daughter of the morning to a debauched Roman Emperor and back again.' But as I get older, this wild fluctuation becomes less marked and I think I am tolerably recognisable from day to day. Also if I am serene and fairly hard-worked (the two go together; if I have too much leisure I disintegrate and become melancholic) it shows in my face. I can't describe my face except to say I have a fair skin, a high forehead and an obstinate chin.

There, now you know a great deal more about what I look like than I know about you. What else to amuse you while you're ill, though I hope you'll be well again by the time you get this? I like clothes and all feminine nonsense though I like occasionally to run wild and get horribly untidy. I love cats of all kinds from kittens to tigers and passionately admire, though I am frankly terrified of, horses. You, as a hunting man, will despise me for this! Both my children adore horses and, though they get little chance of riding, are fearless riders. The only physical thing I've ever wanted to do very much is to ride. But it's no good. I don't understand horses and they know it instinctively. I can't even give them sugar properly. If I were left alone with a horse, I should be terrified, whereas if I were left alone with a lion I should be cautious but confident because I *do* know how felines like to be treated.

I like working with men and talking to men, but for ordinary chit-chat and companionship, I prefer women. And naturally I like being admired, flattered, made a fuss of, and listened to by men. I like being extremely gay and extremely serious, I like small gatherings of people and hate large parties, I like interminable conversations over a dinner-table and I like to spend a certain part of every day entirely alone.

Well, see how your invitation to my egoism has been answered! I'm afraid I'll always fall headlong into that trap.

I'm glad you agree with me about St Aloysius and the Little Flower. Well, of course, you don't quite. I daresay the biographers are very much to blame. But I feel there must be some foundation in the saints' own writings and letters for the extraordinary acts and attitudes attributed to them. I suppose one tends to forget that a saint is a genius and there are unpalatable, even horrifying things in the life of every genius that ever lived. One judges a genius, not by how he behaves, but by what he reveals, and maybe that is how one should judge the saints.

My beloved Keats' life was squalid enough, and much of his writing vulgar and poor but all that is irrelevant beside the things he saw when his genius was on him.

'Bitter and blind bawlers' is from St Augustine's *Civitas Dei* which I haven't read for many years.

Since you like 'cries', here are two more for you; they aren't exactly 'cries' but they are things I recur to often. This one is Dostoievsky: 'Love in action is a harsh and dreadful thing compared with love in dreams. Love in dreams is greedy for immediate action, rapidly performed and in the sight of all . . . active love is labour and fortitude and for some people too, perhaps, a complete science.'

The other is from Rilke. All my books are in store so I can't write you the passage that comes before. It is a wonderful description of a blind man in the street: 'My God, it struck me with sudden vehemence, thus then art Thou! There are proofs of Thy existence.

I have forgotten them all and have never demanded any, for what a formidable obligation would lie in the certainty of Thy existence! And yet it has just been proved to me. This then is to Thy liking, in this dost Thou take pleasure: that we should learn to endure all and not judge. What are the grievous things and what the gracious? Thou alone knowest.'

But, if I go on quoting things I like, this will turn into an essay instead of a letter!

As regards your 'mystifying experience', why not enjoy it? I have only one criterion for 'love' of any kind—if it increases the life of the two 'lovers' it is all right, if it narrows or destroys it, it is all wrong. I promise nothing and offer nothing. Take what you find and be your own judge. You will soon know in your own life and in your relations with other people whether the 'mystifying experience' is productive or destructive.

I've written a few other things, some of which I wouldn't mind you reading. But I'm bad about writing and have a definite jam in my mind about it which *may* be permanent. I have a superb collection of beginnings! I do hope I live to be very old, otherwise I'll never get my work done! When you consider I wrote the first two chapters of *Frost in May* when I was 16 and the rest when I was over 30 you'll see how unresponsive and slow the machine is. As regards actual words committed to paper, I suppose I write about 150,000 a year in ephemeral journalism of every kind.

By the way, congratulations on being a dramatic critic for twenty-one years! I forget if I told you my own career on *Time and Tide* lasted six months.

Your brisk handling of the Jesuit situation produced immediate results. A certain Father Christie sent me a packet of useful notes. I have of course thanked him and now thank you once more.

Oh dear, how amusing it will be when we finally meet and exchange the story of our lives! By that time our lives will be almost interminable, my minute physical description will be out of date and we shall have to shout them into each other's ear trumpets. You will know me by my snow-white hair and hawk-like nose and I shall know you by the angelic detachment of your expression and the almost imperceptible limp caused by a fall from a horse not yet foaled.

Still, seriously, I should like to be exposed to the full blast of your 'charm'. Why despise it? It is so useful. I used to be able to manage it myself, before I became so frightfully sensible. And if, after enquiring for eight weeks from seven departments, I can persuade the B.B.C. to give me a window pole so that I can just once open the window, I shall be convinced I still possess Charm to an inordinate degree. A dear old man, one of the original carpenters of the ark, has gone so far as to procure me a 'nice little pole' and he assures me that all I now need is a 'nice little 'ook'. If I ever get that 'nice little 'ook' there will be no holding me.

Really, Peter, I can hardly call this a letter. It is what an American friend of mine calls 'going into a narcissistic huddle'. But if you will lime the twig, it's no good complaining that there's a bird stuck to it.

It's very late and I always write nonsense when I'm sleepy—and not only when I'm sleepy.

I've a sneaking suspicion that I watch the posts too. Get well, and be happy.

In order that you shouldn't have to tire yourself with puzzling over cryptograms, I am

Yours affectionately,
Antonia.

P.S.   I am sending you back the first letter you returned to me with comments because you said you wanted it back. I had been going to destroy it because one's own letters look so strange.

Wednesday, 11 December, 1940.

Dear P. T.,

At last I have a moment to write and thank you for the book and the photograph. This is the tenth letter I've written today and, apart from one to Susan,* the only human one.

The last two days have been a little confused. I arrived on Monday to find we had been well and truly bombed out of the B.B.C. and all our offices uninhabitable. I managed to rescue all our stuff from a litter of dust and smashed glass and evacuated myself and secretary to Linden Gardens, where my sitting-room now looks rather worse than the bombed (or rather blasted) office. I was very lucky not to be there when it happened. A land mine fell, luckily not on the B.B.C. but just in front, wrecking several houses in Portland Place. Every window is smashed right down to Oxford Circus. It really is astonishing what blast can do—ceilings and doors torn off right

* My elder daughter.

13

inside the building. Several people were hurt and I think some killed but we don't yet know who they all were. Also there was a fire and a flood so that the people broadcasting on Sunday night were standing ankle-deep in water with more water pouring through the ceiling and the possibility of the building collapsing on top of them. Luckily the pumps worked well. You can imagine the indescribable muddle we are in now with no offices and a temporary headquarters at Bedford College which has one telephone line.

I was exceedingly interested in your book. Naturally, from my point of view, it left out much too much and, as you say, it was written quickly and 'to order'.

But it was very interesting to see at how many points our lives have touched or had certain affinities. For example, Crawford's. I was head woman copywriter there for nine years and knew Ashley Havinden and McKnight Kauffer very well. By the way, I entirely agree with everything you say about advertising. I am very glad to be out of that racket which I drifted into by accident when I was 17. Francis Meynell was my publisher for a time (officially, anyway) when Desmond Harmsworth melted into the Nonesuch. I am also interested in printing . . . or rather in types. The note-heading on your first letter told me that you were. Again, you had a house and six acres in Sussex. I have a house and *one* acre in Sussex where my father's people have lived for nearly three hundred years. (It's a *small* house!)

You knew Francis Thompson for whom as a child I had such a passion that I would have given a finger to have seen him once. I knew all the long Odes by heart when I was 11 and believe I still do. And so on and so on.

Naturally I pounced on the photograph even before the book. A *very* interesting head and handsome, sir, too. But I searched in vain for a full face because you only get the outlines in a profile and not the face and the look presented to you.

I really have tried to find one for you but I can't find anything at all recent or even recognisable but I'll try and get my secretary, who's just got a new camera that she's longing to try out, to take a contemporary snap. I look very queer in photographs which is probably why I hate being photographed and don't keep the pictures if I am taken.

You have certainly had a difficult life, in spite of the successes. Arriving in the world after training for the priesthood can't have been much fun. I would like to have met you before you had that well-cut suit. I do understand your passion for clothes. I notice most of us who were at Roehampton have or had it. Years of blue serge,

14

stiff high collars, long skirts (at 9 !) and no looking-glasses make you much vainer than nice clothes do. I notice that my two daughters who have always had gay and comfortable clothes don't care a fig what they look like and only examine their faces with interest when they've lost a tooth or have a particularly impressive bruise.

Yes, I'm glad I've read your book. Though it gives quite a different impression from your letters. I've an odd feeling that, at some time, you made yourself a 'character' and had to live up to it and that the book is, partly at any rate, the surface story of that 'character'. The things that seem permanent are your impetuousness and freshness (English, not American sense !), because those come out in your letters too. Although you are legally older than I am, you sometimes make me feel much older than you ! I almost feel as if I wanted to spare you any real knowledge of the grown-up 'Nanda'. Not in the ordinary sense of shocking you by anything I have done —much of which is the usual muddled drifting and entanglement of most women of my generation—but by something in my nature which is tough, harsh and, to many people, repellent. For myself that harsh streak is the only thing I value in myself and the thing that gives me any hope of some day doing some good work. But for that, I am just one of the thousands of men and women with a touch of talent and a feeling for beauty and all the rest. I haven't used it yet mainly because I haven't had the moral courage and have stuck to the safe, pretty way.

The few things you say about Fr Tyrrell and the things you quote whet my appetite for more. When I begin to read again, I want to read him. I know I should have loved him, though I've no doubt he could be maddening. But he has that mixture of warmth and hardness that I most admire. And what sense he talks about writing and how admirably he writes.

I feel sorry for the Jesuit who taught you philosophy ! At this very moment, when I'm not caught up in the net of the B.B.C. (or writing to P. T. !) I'm puzzling over the difference between 'essence' and 'existence' . . . and enjoying puzzling. And you, horrid little novice with your infectious high spirits and exuberant boyish fun, would be bombarding me with rhubarb cubes and putting soot and dead mice in my bed. As a punishment, I'll tell you what 'existence' is. 'Existence is such being as is in flux, conditioned by external relations and jostled by irrelevant events.' I'll tell you what 'essence' is when I know myself, but at the moment I am too much jostled by irrelevant events to get it clear !

One thing I do understand about your life and that is what you call 'neurasthenia'. And I know the acute misery of it. I am very lucky for I have been cured . . . or as nearly cured as anyone can be. I don't want to talk about it because, just at the moment, till I know you better, I don't want to talk about my 'beast in the jungle' which anyway seems to have retracted to a safe distance and only comes back as a mere ghost in nightmares. The only thing which is still tiresome is having to immerse oneself in a meaningless activity like the B.B.C. because one is still frightened to be too much alone or to have too much leisure. But if I'm not killed, I may eventually convince myself it's not necessary to keep banging gongs and lighting fires to keep the beast away. Goodness knows, I don't want to die yet, but I am much more afraid of the beast than of death. If I could come to terms with the beast, real terms, I would be an artist instead of a Clever Little Thing. Once I was right in the power of the beast and it was terrible and wonderful. But that was a sudden stroke and I had no time to think. It was afterwards, feeling the very slow approach of the beast, over years, that was hard.

I talk in all these riddles about 'the beast' because you may possibly guess what 'the beast' is or was. But don't puzzle about it.

If only I had the courage to write about what I have seen and known, without self-pity or self-flattery, and above all, without explanation, it would be worth reading. I hope I may do it some day. I have been given such wonderful material and I'm so afraid of spoiling it. It only has any importance if this particular truth is a general truth.

Oh dear, I'm sorry to wrap myself in a fog like this. Words are intractable things unless two people happen to speak the same language. I feel you are more innocent, more warm-hearted than I am. I think what I am after—in writing, anyway—is something Francis Thompson put very well in *An Anthem of Earth*:

> *Dissolution even, and disintegration*
> *Which in our dull thoughts symbolise disorder*
> *Find in God's thoughts irrefragable order*
> *And admirable of the manner of our corruption*
> *As of our health.*

My letters are getting too long. I ramble on and think aloud and talk too much about myself and too little about you.

I hope soon to have a letter from you which, as usual, I shall read several times and then 'answer' all askew.

Sometimes I wish immensely we could meet and talk. At others, I think things may be better as they are and that, if we met, there would be too many 'irrelevant events'. I only ask one thing, that you

16

should write just as you feel—or as nearly as you can—and not say anything just to please me because you feel you ought to say it, or because you think I expect you to say it. You will notice that my 'one thing' includes about half-a-dozen and is therefore a typically feminine request.

The only thing that worries me, dear Peter (for I do feel very affectionately towards you), is whether I am meat or poison to you. Because I do know from experience that I am definitely one or the other to anyone who gets at all involved with me. I may be stimulating to you or just upsetting and disturbing and I do beg you, in the coldest, most unromantic light (if you have one!) to consider whether I am useful or a hindrance. If the latter—then cut me out and don't think that I shall be offended. I shall understand perfectly.

Now I *must* go to bed.

Good night,

Antonia.

Friday.—I'm so sorry—I said I'd enclosed the letter and I hadn't. So here it is.

As a postscript to the letter in the other envelope, I do wish I'd known Fr Tyrrell. I have been reading an odd book by an ex-Jesuit, Boyd Barrett, called *The Jesuit Enigma*. It is interesting but so full of bitterness that it rather defeats its own ends. But, full of bitterness as it is, his admiration of Fr Tyrrell is unqualified and the few things he quotes from Tyrrell are so good that I think you are right when you say I should have loved him. I have often been in Mulberry House where he died, for it used to belong to some cousins of my father's. And Meg Tyrrell, who was, I think, his first cousin once removed, was a great friend of 'Léonie's'. I often met her and was very fond of her. She was a most charming and gifted creature who died tragically young at the birth of her first child. Long before I knew Meg, the name of Tyrrell always had a fascination for me and I told you how I stood by his grave when I was a child. I used to pray for him in those days because I was so distressed about his being buried in unconsecrated ground. I don't suppose I can honestly 'pray' for anyone now, yet sometimes it is impossible not at least to 'commend' them, as it were, from one's own feeling if not from any hope that it can make a 'difference'. Again, good night,

Antonia.

Dear Peter,

Writing letters to you is rapidly becoming a vice. If I'd written as much on a book or a story I would have quite a decent pile of MS. by now! I've had more time than usual this week as we're so dislocated by being bombed out and, whenever I've a spare moment, I seem to get out a block and start a long letter to you. Tonight the 'excuse' (for one's always got to have an excuse!) is that I've got a streaming cold, the sort that makes you feel physically and mentally dusty, as if you'd had a bath in glue and then been air-brushed with fine grit. So I can't settle down to work, can I, Peter? And 8.30 is too early to go to bed, isn't it, Peter? And the posts are so bad at the week-end that if I don't write tonight, it will be so long before you get it, won't it, Peter?

I think you have a good deal more self-control than I have. I am rather scolding myself at the moment, for various reasons. Partly because after all these years I still find it hard to shake off the idea that, if I enjoy doing something, it must be wrong. Incidentally, why is the 'more expansive' the 'less valuable' part of you?

There are other reasons. Like you, I'm afraid of self-deception. And when someone shows signs of genuine affection for me, it's hard not to respond frankly and freely. But I know myself pretty well and I am selfish, impulsive and very ready to be caught up in a dream. It is only in the last few days that I have become a little uneasy because I find myself constantly thinking about you and sometimes feel you almost physically present. I think you will understand what I mean by 'uneasiness' even if I don't put it into words. Because we live far apart, have never met, are very different in some of our ways of thought does not mean that we cannot, consciously and unconsciously, exercise a very strong influence on each other. It may be good, it may be bad, but it is a force to reckon with and a delicate mechanism to balance. I am making a considerable act of faith in you in saying even as much as this, for I run the risk of your thinking 'the poor deluded woman must imagine I am in love with her'. Very well, I must run the risk then. But I do believe you will understand. I feel, in your letters, that you are offering me some part of yourself —it is difficult to define—but something in which the heart and imagination play more part than in the ordinary 'friendship' which can exist between people of the same or opposite sexes. Oh dear, it is so difficult to talk, knowing nothing of your circumstances. But if it is so, I do want to feel very sure that I am not taking something which belongs by right to someone else. I am just an emanation on paper, something new and, as new things are, stimulating. But I've never shared even an hour of your life, never stood by you in dullness and difficulties and so have all the advantages of the 'illusion'. You must forgive me if I'm being silly and priggish. I am both, often, and I am also cruel, vain and fond of power of any kind. I don't believe in giving things up for the sake of giving them up but I do believe in giving them up if they cause unnecessary pain to other people or interfere with things which are permanently important.

I'm not a saint and I'm not a stone and if I've led a very quiet and 'spectatorish' life for the last year, it's probably as much due to having met no one who interested me specially as to any sudden accretion of wisdom or detachment. I felt stone dead except for a faint glimmer in the mind until I came back to London in October. Then the excitement of being in a job again and the slight danger which certainly whets one's appetite for life made me begin to feel alive again. Then your first letter came and now, for the last few days, I have had that slightly feverish, dreamy feeling, a symptom we must both often have experienced in the past!

If I were as honest as I would LIKE to be, I would have hunted up some appalling snapshot of myself and sent it to you. Instead of which, I wished I could find some wonderful 'studio portrait' only just not too flattered to be recognisable and showing Miss White at her very, very, very best. The one I did find is rather out of date—about two years—and I should think it's a fair average. I hope I can look better and I know I can look a lot worse but when I'm lying down and thinking of nothing in particular I should think this is tolerably recognisable.

Lots of things I should like to ask about your book—or rather about your life. You say nothing about your childhood, your real, before-school childhood. How I should like to have heard you sing, and how I envy you for being able to sing. I love music and have no more voice than a cockchafer. Taken all in all, I love Mozart most, which simply means that I can listen to Mozart with joy in any mood. Then you can use your hands; your backgammon table and chessboard are admirable. Mine are only useful for stroking cats. It takes me an hour to darn a stocking and every time I cook the dinner, I burn my fingers. I want to know more about 'my Sylvia'. That one story of her bearding the editor establishes her as a remarkable woman for I know what moral courage *that* takes! I remember, when I was at Crawford's, a week before Susan was born I rang up and said I didn't feel so good and need I come in? A shocked, a piously shocked voice the other end said: 'But, Miss White, *whatever happens*, Crawford's work *must* go on.'

I was interested in what Helen Parry Eden said about *Frost in May*. As to its being distorted, people who were at Roehampton with me didn't think so and I deliberately left out some things which, though they happened, *would* have given a distorted impression. Out-of-date it should be, since it covers the period 1908-14. And yet, last year I met an Old Child of Roehampton aged 23, an ardent Catholic and a great lover of the school, who said that remarkably little had changed there in 1935. Even in my day Tunbridge Wells* was always said to be much less strict and was almost certainly much less snob-bish. The Catholic papers did not think it unfair; the only paper that said 'Such a school can only have existed in the disordered imagination of the novelist' was the Protestant *Church Times*.

No, I cannot truly say that I think the Catholic Church is the 'biggest thing in the world'. What the Catholic Church symbolises and once perhaps symbolised better than anything else in the west— I might say that was the greatest thing or one of the great things. And I do not *want* to 'hate' Catholicism. I fear it sometimes—which is always the real base of hatred—and I genuinely dislike many of its manifestations and its effects on human beings, or at least on the ones I have known. I admit other things can have as bad or much worse effects. I know it is pure heresy to say that Catholicism is the right religion and practice for some people and not for others. But whether from 'invincible ignorance', 'spiritual pride' or selfishness and moral instability, that is what I do feel and have felt for a long time. One difference between us, I think, is that, though you are very good and reticent about it, it pains you that I am no longer a practising or believing Catholic. Whereas I don't want to change you from a Catholic into anything else.

As to 'simple faith in God' I don't know that I ever had it natur-ally. I was taught there was a God and of what kind and I believed unquestioningly what I was told. Now I am feeling towards a faith in God which *is*, if you like, simple, but it is in a different God, per-haps. If I have a sudden emotional impulse or even a 'certainty', I accept that and don't deny it but remind myself it may be an illusion. If I feel like praying, I pray, nearly always the same prayer, the 'Our Father' which seems to me the best of all prayers. But, to use Catholic language, my 'devotion' would be to the Holy Ghost. And I think the Holy Ghost is Spinoza's God, not the Father who dis-penses favours and punishes sins, nor the Son who sacrifices himself and relieves the burden of human guilt, but the Spirit that illuminates and informs the universe and who is worshipped in spirit and truth. Blake makes Voltaire say that he blasphemed against Christ

* Another Sacred Heart convent.

but that we blaspheme against the Holy Ghost in condemning Voltaire.

By the way, did you know that Voltaire wrote this? I didn't till I came across it the other day:

O Dieu qu'on méconnait. O Dieu que tout annonce,
Entends les derniers mots que ma bouche prononce—
Si je me suis trompé, c'est en cherchant ta loi:
Mon coeur peut s'égarer, mais il est plein de toi.
Je vois sans m'alarmer l'Éternité paraître;
Et je ne puis penser qu'un Dieu qui m'a fait naître,
Qu'un Dieu qui sur mes jours versa tant de bienfaits,
Quand mes jours sont éteints, me tourmente à jamais.

You ask me to send you things I've written. This is difficult, because all my possessions are scattered. The thing I like best I have no copy of and I don't want to show it to you yet because it is connected with 'the beast'. What you probably would like to see is the endless 'notebook' I have kept since 1921 and which no one has ever seen in full and never will, I think. But I may do something about it one day and transcribe parts of it—much is repetitive and dull—as I don't think I can write a straight novel. I am sending you the only poems I ever wrote and which I wrote suddenly about three years ago.* It's in a queer little magazine,† not a bit the kind I write for as a rule, but Fredi Perlès begged me for them and I couldn't refuse. I'm afraid they're all a bit mystifying without the key, especially *The Crest* which is entirely made up of private images and means nothing except to the two people concerned. But to them it *does* mean something and is not just an arbitrary collection of images. *The Double Man* is straightforward; an epigram on one particular person but applying to any number. *Epitaph* is also mysterious and written about a woman friend of mine who died in terrible but inevitable circumstances. You can also take it as being an epitaph on myself too, had I killed myself at a certain time of my life. But this would involve too much explanation. I send it you as it stands. If I were re-writing it, I would probably cut out the four lines before the last stanza as I think they are overstrained and too adjectival. The poem is much better without them. As so often happens, I thought they were the best when I wrote them because they came easily. Now, as you see, they are the worst.

Peter dear, I must stop. There are always a thousand things more

* See Appendix V.
† *Delta*, edited by Alfred Perlès and published in Paris.

I want to say but I've been writing to you for two and a half solid hours. To pacify the Paper Controller I've written on the back, but, even so, this letter is getting 'inordinate'!

Mentioning the notebooks made me turn up one of them. Rather oddly, it opened at a bit about this question of belief in God. This was in 1935.

Do I believe in God? I must behave *as if* I did not trust in any future salvation and yet aim always at that difficult, detached interior life; I must not allow myself to think of a merciful God. We are not strong enough to bear much violent happiness. One must learn not to let either misery or joy make one callous and isolated. Love is never lost unless one consumes one's own love.

Five years ago, as you can see, I was in a state of considerable tension. I probably would not write just that today.

About the same time I tried to formulate a prayer for myself. Again, I would not put it quite the same way today. But I put it in here to show you that my feeling about the Church doesn't, I think, mean that I don't care and don't want to find out.

Let me not be afraid of going into myself or going out of myself. Let me be content to be anonymous, despised, intermittent. Let me not be puffed up by my suffering or ashamed to be happy. Give me grace to wait, always to wait, to expect nothing and to be ready at any moment to part with all I have. Take away from me the desire to be loved and admired and give me instead the power to love without desiring to possess. Give me eyes to see with, remembering always that the eye sees nothing but what the light that falls on it permits it to see.

Well, I can't live up to that, as you know. But it is still what I want. And when I want it enough, it will be answered.

It is very strange. I write to you more intimately, I think, than to anyone I have ever known. I don't understand it. I am proud, obstinate, cynical and critical and yet I say things to you that I cannot say to people I have known and cared for for years.

I say too much, perhaps—but it is such a pleasure to talk to you.
Good night, my dear.
Antonia.

My dear Peter,

Posts are getting much worse, which since I became an inveterate post-watcher is serious. Your last letter took three days and mine four.

The one I got today, with the photographs, I kept re-reading incredulously since it seemed as if you must have got my second one. It answered so many things I wanted to know and had asked you in that letter. This is 'correspondence' with a vengeance if you can answer a letter before you receive it.

I should have begun this letter half an hour ago (and I shall almost certainly be tiresomely interrupted) but I have been poring over the photographs, puzzling and comparing. How sensible to send me lots. I am keeping all the ones you allow. I wish I could do the same but I have very few and goodness knows where they are. As all my papers and belongings are either in store or scattered between Sussex, Wiltshire, Chelsea and here, it is impossible to find anything. I can't even find any snaps of the children and I have lots and long to show them to you. I shall just have to appear in person as soon as I possibly can which I long to do. It's just this silly time business. My two days' Christmas leave I must tack on to a week-end with the children for I haven't seen them properly for months. Since I came to London in October we've been separated, Susan at school in Salisbury and Lyndall with her father in the country. It will be my first Christmas away from them for they are going to stay with Tom (my ex-husband) and his new wife. Then they go to Sussex for three weeks where I hope to join them for week-ends.

But the fact you are near Bangor raises a faint, faint hope. The B.B.C. has a branch there and if I could only contrive to get sent there for a few days on business, I could run over and see you. The other faint hope is that I should wangle a 'consultatory' visit re my second Jesuit programme. How long does the journey to Holyhead take roughly?

The photographs are fascinating, and puzzling too. You certainly are a handsome and striking man and admirably built. I am much too short and plump for my own tastes and would like to be 5 ft 8 instead of 5 ft 3, so I can admire your good proportions . . . not without envy ! I really only look well in long sweeping frocks (though thank goodness I haven't got fat legs) and a rather eighteenth-century cut of dress. We are about as contrasted as two physical types could be except that we both have the same rather Roman type of profile, though yours is infinitely better than mine. But what strikes me so much is the look of strain, suffering, even bitterness in nearly all the full-face ones. This is not the impression I get from your letters, but perhaps the conflict which shows in your face has been resolved since these were taken. Even in the very young face there is that peculiar strain. Have you noticed how very different the two sides of your face are if you cover one half at a time? And that slight downward turn of the lips becomes a deep line as time goes on. If I had not read your letters, I should be more than a little frightened of you for you look as if you had the devil of a temper and could be pretty ruthless too. None of this comes out in the book or in your letters and may be merely a trick of the camera or you may set your face in a special way when you look at it. Modelling of forehead and nose *very* good—you look as if you had a musician's forehead. I suspect your profile should be seen in repose, your full face animated and talking to get the right impression. But such a mixture, my dear Peter, poet, idealist, dandy, successful man of the world, a touch of actor perhaps, and more than a touch of priest. And in the Pegram drawing, a gentle, sensitive, almost too unworldly young man! Compare that with the Orpen drawing and I defy anyone to solve the puzzle. My dear, I am surprised you are satisfied with four, no five women friends besides your wife!

Not being one hundred per cent woman, I can't rely on female intuitions about you. But I can see why we have a curious fascination for each other. I have done a great many odd things in my life but I have *never* fallen in love by post before. It is lucky that we have both acquired a grain of sense and luckier still that we both have people who love us, put up with us and believe in us. My parallel to your Sylvia is the mysterious Eric who is my devoted and extremely critical and absolutely irreplaceable friend, or rather phenomenon.

Oh dear, once I start the story of my life it is endless. You shall have it all one day. It seems such a l-o-n-g life. I ought to be 80 by now. But I suppose that comes of being married three times between 20 and 30. This is the bald synopsis.

I married first when I was 21—a young man the same age, very sweet but hopelessly reckless and feckless and an incurable drinker. That marriage was annulled both by the State and by the Church. The, I can only call it obscenity, with which the Church conducts such things gave me my first real horror of it as an institution. It was far worse than the civil case and that was bad enough. While I was waiting for this case to be wound up, I had a sudden and completely unexpected mental smash and was put by my father into a public asylum. I was 23 and in those days no one attempted to discover the causes of insanity or tried to cure it. That, as you guess, was 'the beast'. There is no doubt about the insanity but it had causes and was neither mental deficiency nor a hereditary disease. Ten months later I recovered with equally dramatic suddenness and was de-certified. No, I wasn't about in Fleet Street from 1916-25. I did not go into advertising till 1924,* a year after I came out of the asylum. In 1925, being pronounced fit, told I had had 'brain fever', that it would not recur, that it was all right for me to have children, I married the famous Eric whom I had known already for six years and certainly never thought of marrying. I had simply admired him as the strangest, most intelligent, most amusing person I had ever met and I think I married him because I was so surprised and too much overwhelmed by the honour to refuse. I still maintain that marrying Eric was the most sensible thing I ever did in my life though a psychologist might have thought the opposite. I am not, and never have been, 'in love' with Eric nor he with me, but we have the strongest, most indestructible bond two people can have, one which has survived the most difficult and fantastic situations and will sur-vive anything that can happen to either of us. We are extremely un-like—he is almost all pure intelligence and wit, the most civilised, balanced and lucid person I have ever met, whereas I am half a romantic barbarian. Any intellectual training I have had is due to twenty-two years of slow patient teaching from Eric and my function is to be a kind of medium between him and the outside world which he finds more difficult to deal with than I do. I can't describe Eric because he is indescribable. Because, with all this luminous and steady play of mind, he is the gayest, lightest creature imaginable and every-one who knows him, from the heaviest hearties to the most captious 'intellectuals', adores him. Fr D'Arcy whom he meets sometimes at the Grecians, which they both frequent, once said to him: 'You have only one fault, you want to anticipate the beatific vision.' Eric has never been a Catholic nor is he likely to become one. I don't deny that it would probably influence me very much if he did become one. But he is no way to blame for my giving up Catholicism. He never tried to stop me from practising (we were married in a Catholic Church), never mocked my religion or tried to reason me out of it. On the contrary, he encouraged me to tell him everything I could about it and listened with the greatest interest. But if I had ever met a Catholic who was as true, as good, as incorruptible as Eric, with so clear and so fair and so rich a mind, I should have been much more convinced of the truth of the Catholic belief. I have met saintly Catholics, brilliant Catholics but never one with this peculiarly free,

* Not into an agency, that is. I'd done free-lance advertising since I was 17.

wide-ranging and yet disciplined mind nor one who could act towards other people with such understanding and delicacy and pass off what was really a heroic act with such amusing, dry grace.

Forgive me for writing such a panegyric of a man whom you don't know but Eric is so very important to me that you can't know anything about me without knowing something about *him*.

Well, of course, the inevitable happened. I fell in love in the ordinary way and very soon found I was going to have a child. Eric begged me to wait a little, but being impetuous and very much in love, I wanted to marry my lover and live an ordinary 'natural' life. The lover went off to America, where I was supposed to join him after the baby was born and marry him if the case were successful. The lawyers would not let me sue or be sued for a straight divorce but, mainly from professional excitement, made me bring a nullity suit against Eric which I won. I could not face going through the ecclesiastical courts again, so, according to the Church, Eric is still my husband. In the end, I did not marry Susan's father but Tom Hopkinson who has just been made Editor of *Picture Post*. Lyndall is his child, but he is just as devoted to Susan who was a year old when we married. To please his father, who is an Archdeacon, I was married in a Protestant Church. Had I known then (as I discovered ten years later) that this meant excommunication, I should certainly not have done it but insisted on a registrar's office.

Everything went well until I began to develop rather alarming nervous symptoms. I imagine I became intolerable to live with. At the same time Tom fell seriously in love with someone else. We separated—temporarily as we thought—and during that separation I discovered I was menaced with a very serious form of insanity which this time would almost certainly be permanent. Eric stood by me magnificently—encouraged me through nearly four years of treatment (knowing what I did not know till later—that the doctor was very dubious about the possibility of cure and that at any moment I might go hopelessly insane or kill myself). Well, the wonderful thing happened. I am quite possibly entirely cured and at any rate I shall probably have several years of freedom from 'the beast'.

I divorced Tom two years ago and have now been living on my own for more than five years, usually with the children. Tom has married again, still loves and misses Susan and Lyndall and is still my friend. We have shared too much and been through too much to disappear out of each other's lives but I should have been wiser to resist the temptation to marry him.

Well, there is the outline of the queer and funny story. And it's all played out against a background of work, for all through I kept on at jobs and except for the first year of the war I was never out of a job, or not working as a freelance, for longer than a month. Hardly anyone except Eric, Tom and a few intimate friends knew that all this mental trouble was going on, so you see I'm a tolerably good actress off the stage. During one of the worst, not *the* worst year, I was making £1,000 a year at J. Walter Thompson's so it shows what a lunatic can get away with in the advertising world! So don't you go and give me away to any employer, past or prospective, for I have and always shall have a living to earn!

The war broke out just when I'd pieced my life together again, had arrived at some mental stability and was doing very well as a free-lance journalist. Home, jobs, money went literally overnight. I spent an uncomfortable but very instructive year as a P.G. in other people's houses, got a job by accident in the B.B.C. two months ago, and that, dearest Peter, is ALL.

All for the present, too. I have given you enough to digest for the time being. It's not the letter I meant to write and not the answer to yours. I will write that soon but now I *must* go to sleep. All the answer you shall have now is 'I understand'. I am very happy about our queer situation.

Thank you very much for the Fr Tyrrell photographs. He does not look as I imagined, but oh, I like his face.

I love the snapshot of you and your wife.

By the way, how do you know I'm called Tony? I can't have been so careless as to put it in *Frost* surely? If so, I've never noticed it, nor has anyone else. I haven't a copy here. It gave me a sweet shock when you wrote it.

Very much love and forgive a corkscrew answer.

Tony.

Thursday morning. Your other letter came this morning and for some reason makes me rather doubtful about sending this. I suppose I shall send it as I am scribbling a postscript in the buffet at Waterloo while I wait for Susan's train to arrive.

Having already said so much to you, I suppose I may as well take the risk and let you see what I have written here. But having given you one shock with my face, I hesitate to give you another with my personal history. But if you can't 'take it', well, you can't and I shan't be altogether surprised. I would very much have preferred to tell it you rather than write it, but the possibility of our meeting is so vague that I felt the time had come when I ought to tell you something about my life.

I think there is no doubt that your dream image of me does not coincide with the real creature and that I should be a disappointment to you, not only physically but in many other ways. All the same, I should like us to meet, if only once.

As I had no preconceived image of you but have gradually pieced notions together from your letters, your book and your photographs, I *can't* be disappointed because I don't make up my mind beforehand as to what I expect to find and I delight in surprises and inconsistencies in my friends' characters.

I do realise that we are very different, in tastes, gifts and type of mind. That should be valuable but it needs a good deal of patience and adaptation.

Friday evening. I have still not posted the letter, but shall tomorrow. I felt I needed time to think. Your last letter made me feel I was not sure I wanted to tell you all this nor that you wanted to hear it.

On re-reading the letter very carefully I decided to take the risk. Sometimes you rush me a little faster than I feel quite ready for. And your last letter definitely made me feel I was piling up on you like a life-work and exhausting you with my long letters.

Usually the slowest and meanest of correspondents, even with my best friends, I have gone to the other extreme lately with you. But you must take the blame for writing me letters which I want to 'answer' (if you can call it 'answering') at great length.

Difference of history, character—and of a generation—do mean, I'm afraid, that both of us have to do a great deal of explaining which wouldn't be necessary if we were able to meet.

I don't think my poems are either 'brilliant' or 'obscure'. I was only trying to say in images something I felt very deeply and by no means letting off fireworks in the dark. *The Crest* is obscure— for reasons I gave you—and should really never have been printed since it was written for one person and one definite occasion.

You talk so much about 'love' that you make me nervous and analytical. You seem to me to be saying 'our relation is *this*, but it mustn't go beyond *that*' or 'it is *that* but must give way to *this*'. In fact, my dear Peter, you explain it so much that you have me much more fogged than I've ever had you fogged by my 'metaphysics'!

I don't personally feel it needs all that explanation and analysis. In fact I've always found it dangerous to talk too much about any feelings of that kind. What its nature is will emerge from how we behave to each other and react to each other. How can—how dare you say to me 'You cannot take the place of my Sylvia'? As if I'd ever given you the least provocation for saying such a thing! How could I suppose, not being an infatuated schoolgirl, that such a thing was possible? Not being a blood-sucker, how could I dream of wishing it? I'm sorry, but I can't say 'I love you' yet. I mean a lot when I do say it and the older I get, the less likely I am to say it, even if I feel warmth, sympathy and desire towards someone. Heart, imagination and blood can all be touched but that is still 'love in dreams' and not 'love in action'.

I hope we shall go on knowing each other better and getting lights from each other and caring for each other. But if this were my last letter to you and you found that all I have told you about my life is (together with my face!) too disillusioning . . . well, I won't finish the sentence. If you do answer this my 'address' name (to answer a question direct for once!) is Miss and not Mrs. I keep Mrs Hopkinson 'legally' because it's simpler for the children but in work and to most of my friends I'm A. W.

Good night, dear Peter. I hope you have or have had a happy Christmas. Remember cats have rough tongues, sharp claws and easily arch their backs.

Yours very affectionately,
Tony.

P.S. On a sudden impulse I am sending you *The House of Clouds*.* I'm afraid it must be a loan as it's out of print. Even this copy is only borrowed. I lent my own last copy to someone who promised to return it in two days. That is fourteen months ago and I have not even their address.

22 December, 1940.

Peter dear,

Your touching little letter arrived today (yes, on a Sunday!) and made me feel remorseful for being rather sharp at the end of my last one. I'm afraid this won't arrive in time to reassure you but I'm writing at once.

Really, my dear, I do think you're worrying over nothing. The only way I can think of to clear things up a little is to tell you what I feel about it. It has been rather hard to understand parts of your recent letters because you seemed so nervous of saying too much or too little and therefore it wasn't easy to know just how you meant

* A short story about madness, originally published in *Life and Letters*.

me to take it. If I've got it all wrong and put things too crudely, forgive me.

The 'intimate respected friend' I told you of was Eric. I explained about Eric in a long letter which I expect you have by now. I was married to him for five years and he is still the most important person in my life.

Of course, I have had lovers 'in the ordinary sense'. But on my side there was much more emotional attachment than physical attachment. Actual sex became a kind of ordeal mixed up with all sorts of terrors and feelings of extreme guilt. Now that the mental knot has at last been untied, I am a perfectly 'normal' woman. And, ironically enough, since I became 'normal' I have led a practically celibate life. But now that I am no longer frigid and can feel natural desire, I don't feel any distress—or no unbearable distress—if for one reason or another it isn't possible to gratify it. As you say, what the body cries out for is not necessarily the best thing for it (or rather for the whole person) and in your case you have voluntarily accepted a limitation which I wouldn't want you to break down. Even if you were tempted to, you would almost certainly be very unhappy afterwards and would feel you had lost far more than you had gained.

My own point of view is different but it probably leads to the same conclusions. If you had not accepted this limitation and if, when we met, we felt we both wanted that particular expression, I certainly would not hold back. I don't think now, as I was taught, that the sexual act is wrong. But from experience I do know that it can be 'pure' or 'impure' even between the same two people and that it is a good thing in some relationships and bad in others. But the natural impulse behind it, when it springs from attraction and affection, is a good thing and it's perfectly possible to express it in other ways. One may be 'chaste' not from love of chastity in the abstract (which is so often the 'fear of life' you talk about) but because chastity is necessary or expedient in a particular case. An athlete may give up drink not because he thinks drink is 'bad' but because he wants to run faster. And the fact that he *does* run faster is compensation for not having the drink.

While we're on this vexed subject, I'm inclined to think priests probably take a more reasonable view of it than nuns. Though your Jesuits seem to have been even more curious in their behaviour than the Sacred Heart nuns . . . or at least *as* curious. But a woman who takes a vow of chastity gives up two of her natural functions instead of one and therefore is probably apt to be unconsciously more bitter about it.

Oh, I wish you wouldn't be so much on the defensive. I think now that it is yourself you fear and not me. But the more you can trust yourself and not be frightened by the contradictory feelings you have about me (for they are contradictory, aren't they?) the more I can trust you. You don't have to make an artificial 'best self' for me . . . I'm much more likely to love the real one. And, for goodness sake, don't worry about *me*. I'm very tough.

Such a man for getting into *states*! You're worse than I used to be.

Your pretty line about 'May' and 'December', ought, I fear, to be . . . say September and November. You make me feel quite dashing when you call me a 'vile modern'. To the real 'moderns' I seem the dearest old-fashioned auntie. I stop somewhere about Proust, Joyce and T. S. Eliot and am as dated as the long waist and the cloche hat. Yes, dear, I quite understand the lines Fr Tyrrell quotes and even have the impudence to like them. Whose are they? My guess is Alice Meynell.

I must break a lance for the poor old moderns though. I know very well four or five poets ranging from 21-25. They read Tennyson, Shakespeare, Milton, Pope and Coleridge. They read Dickens, Trollope, Carlyle and P. G. Wodehouse. They love their wives. I will not say they are models of prudence or that they are dazzling economists. And until the war they were all convinced they were communists. Really, nearly as much trouble has been taken to convert me to communism as to bring me back to Catholicism. A lot more, in fact. The hard benches I have sat on! The 'demos' in the east wind! Once they even got me to walk in a May Day procession. But as soon as I've struggled through the Marxist catechism, they've all become liberals, labourites, conservatives or bomber pilots.

I admire your political zeal, but haven't any political vocation whatever. I read a bit of history (and about time too!) and I go slowly on with my old Spinoza and Santayana with a bit of Plato and Aristotle thrown in. But I don't feel convinced enough about anything to want to try and convince anyone else.

Your Agenda Club was a very interesting piece of work. And I'm sure it *wasn't* a failure. I like it because it's the English way of doing things—part of the national genius and something the people who try and impose abstract systems on us will never understand. You don't know what work it did or what influence it had. All sorts of changes now afoot may have come out of it.

I enclose a charming little note from Fr Christie. Is he a friend of yours? I must say the Jesuits do have nice manners.

Well, good night, dear Peter. I hope your holy plot with the Anglican Bishop succeeds. I have finished Jesuit script (I) which I should blush to show the Jesuits for the B.B.C. has a hideous standard of 'artiness' as opposed to accuracy and it resembles nothing so much as Savonarola Brown's great Tragedy! But it's awfully eulogistic. I have promised to do a long short story for *Horizon* by 15 January. As I've been contemplating it for five years and have written exactly seven hundred words of it I shall be in a Petrine State.

In case you feel I'm piling up a horrid overdraft of letters for you, this needs no answer except (I hope!) a sigh of relief. I feel twice as fond of you since your last letter.

Happy New Year, dearest P.

Tony.

27 December, 1940.

Darling Peter,

It was so lovely to come home cold, very tired and suffering from B.B.C. accidia, to find a letter from you. With Christmas and everything, I hadn't hoped for one tonight.

I have already said I'm sorry in my last letter for putting out the claws. I have also been punished, for my black kitten, in a fit of terror, flew at me this morning and scratched me well and truly. Milly doesn't look like growing into one of my historic cats like Mr Pusta and Fury, in fact she is only mine by courtesy and belongs to the house. She is the plainest of little black alley-cats born during an air-raid and brought up on a fountain-pen filler. But any cat is better than no cat and she is affectionate and painstaking.

Over Christmas I took a step which surprised me . . . perhaps it will surprise you less. And I have to admit I am still full of doubts about it and I hope you won't be too distressed if I don't continue in it. In my own mind I don't feel it to be more than opening a door . . . and I can't say whether or not I shall use the door. And if I don't use it, it may be cowardice, obstinacy . . . or what I take for honesty. I had meant to go to 'Midnight' Mass on Christmas Eve in any case . . . not from real devotion or as an act of submission to the Church, but let's say from sentimental reasons. I have always loved Christmas, and going to Mass and hearing the first *Adeste fideles* is part of it and is too much stamped on my mind, or feelings, not to feel Christmas Day very empty and meaningless without it. Well, I went to the Carmelite Church (I always went there as a child) on the Monday, just to find out what time Mass was—they can't have it at midnight because of air-raids. I wandered into the church and on a sudden impulse—one of those automatic ones over which one seems to have no control and which later appear to have been either foolish or extremely relevant—I found myself among the people going to Confession. I felt a fool, a hypocrite, but in a few minutes there I was in the confessional without the least idea of what I was going to say. The priest was a very good and kind man, very different from the Oratorian (no doubt good in his own way!) in whose confessional I found myself in the same automatic way eighteen months ago. I managed to blurt out some kind of story and to explain I had been told I was excommunicated. He said he was not sure that this was so, but he would find out. I went back the next day and he told me that he would see the Vicar-General on my behalf and that he thought I could be reinstated without the alarming conditions which the other priest had said were essential. Apparently we are all supposed to be in danger of death these days, so they're not so strict. Then, much to my surprise, he heard my Confession, gave me absolution and told me I could go to Communion on Christmas Day. I felt numb and strange, with a curious mixture of joy and terror. But I got up early and went to Communion on Christmas morning. A very blind and doubting Communion, like two photographs taken on the same film . . . old memories of what Communion had once meant and questioning whether or not this could now be the same for me. But there was a sense of peace and relief and 'home again'. I do not yet know whether the Vicar-General will agree with Fr Hugh's recommendation as he hasn't been able to see him yet.

Naturally I am now very much preoccupied with the question of whether or not I honestly want to become a practising Catholic again. I can only say 'I don't know'. Having been brought up a Catholic I can see how this episode can be interpreted as a great grace, perhaps as a direct answer to your prayers for me . . . or to the prayers of other people living or dead. I can also see that it may be mere laziness of mind, desire for security, affection for the past or plain weariness. I still find it very hard to accept unquestioningly all the dogmas of the Church and the process of reason on which she bases them. I have been trying to read Fr D'Arcy's *Nature of belief* and find it very confusing. He is a brilliant dialectician and I am not trained in dialectic and yet I cannot help feeling that he makes assumptions and sweeping generalisations and distorts what other writers and philosophers have said. I feel he is, as all the Catholic apologists are, out to prove a case, apparently by methods accessible to all, but that, being convinced beforehand that his case is un-assailable and his conclusions are divine revelations, it can only convince those who are convinced already.

God knows I am ignorant and I don't want to be obstinate but it is difficult to accept some things which seem to run counter to everything ' reason' and experience seem to affirm. I know Catholics will say my reason has been perverted, but so many people far better and wiser than I am have the same difficulty in accepting Catholic reasoning as valid.

I feel on surer ground when I read St Francis de Sales. I think I can truly say that I do believe and have always believed, even in my most anti-Catholic moments, in the possibility of a spiritual life and that a spiritual life must involve a certain method and discipline. Reading that particular saint, I feel what I'm afraid I don't feel about all the saints: 'Here is a truly spiritual man, towards whom I feel humble and loving and who has not only vision but a kind of divine common sense and I will take more from him on faith than I can take from the brilliant dialecticians and theologians who brow-beat my feeble reasoning faculties.'

Because I am interested in 'metaphysics' it does not follow that I have a head for them or can move easily or confidently among abstractions. All that I feel I can grope after and occasionally grasp is something which appears to me true and revealing and which I find now here, now there, in my own experience, in works of art, in things said by spiritual teachers and sometimes by philosophers. I have never stopped loving the gospels, even when I have doubted the Catholic interpretation of them and even if I don't stay in the Church, I don't think I can ever lose my reverence for them. But I am a very long way from either faith or even reasonable certainty.

Yes, do pray for me, dear Peter, and thank you for having prayed for me. I have prayed for you, too, in my very halting way. Since you truly believe in God and can therefore approach Him better than I, tell Him I am stupid, obstinate, and prejudiced (which He knows already!) and that He must make things very clear to me and show me a little at a time what I *can* grasp. As you can guess, my other side immediately says: 'If there is a God, all-knowing, all-powerful, He knows this already and nothing can change His designs towards me or any other living creature.'

To you, I must seem to be accepting a grace as ungraciously as any creature could. To myself, I am following an impulse which may be foolish and lead me nowhere but which may bring me some light to co-ordinate so many other impulses and hazy beliefs. I am so frightened of losing whatever I may have painfully found, and yet

I know this fear of loss is itself suspect and one of my besetting faults which has so often prevented me from making the best use of my life and my gifts. I do know there is only one thing for me and that is to be drawn by love and not driven by fear. Too much stress was laid on fear in my childhood and my own nature was too responsive to fear, anyway. I think it was very much an amateurish way of getting rid of fear that made me so rebellious against the Church. Now that, through other circumstances, that fear has been lessened, I may be freer to love. I know that, humanly speaking, my greatest defect is lack of power to love. And I need so much to love so as to be able to use my aggressiveness creatively instead of destructively.

This time you can indeed accuse me of not answering your letter! But not because I did not read it with much tenderness and gratitude.

I won't write more now because I want to go to Benediction. How strange that must sound to both of us.

With love,
Antonia (or Tony).

30 December, 1940.

Dearest Peter,

How sweet of you to send me your beautiful snuff-box. I do realise how much you will miss it and I can only say that it will be most carefully kept and very much treasured. I have it by me on the table as I write and it is so nice to have some concrete evidence of you here with me. Thank you very, very much.

I wish I had something really nice to send you of my own. But I haven't. I have so few things about now, everything is scattered or in store and anyway, except books, I have very little 'portable property' and what I have has been given to me and I don't quite like to give it away. So it will have to be something new. Of course I will get you any books you want, if you will tell me what they are. I can't choose myself as I haven't enough exact indication of the work you are doing. Apart from work books, have you got the Nonesuch *Blake* and *Donne*? Or *Keats' Letters*? And would you like any or all of them? Please let me know soon.

Your snuff-box has an exquisite smell. Is it the ghost of some very delicate snuff?

Now I am going to make a truly heroic effort to *answer* your last letter for I deeply sympathise with your confusion about what has been 'answered' and what hasn't!

I do appreciate very much your attitude about Eric. But there is nothing for you to be jealous about—and I mean that. My relation with E. is really 'fantastic', much more so than my relation with you. It is a phenomenon, there's no other word for it. All our friends are puzzled and amused by it, wonder why we don't get married again, but don't really understand it. I suppose he's the only person to whom I've ever freely given 'authority' over me—which he consistently refuses to recognise or assert! If you want a portrait of Eric and myself, look up Alice and the caterpillar. Eric is the caterpillar. For over twenty years, even in our first five when we used to meet once a year and go to a concert, I have consistently opposed him, argued with him, done the opposite of what he suggested and, except in one case, he has always turned out to be right. He never says 'do this' or 'don't do that' but always 'Try it and see. But I *think* you will find that this or that will happen if you do.' And it *does.* Yet his whole method is to try and make me, not dependent on him, but independent of him which, as you must know, is not what people who love one usually do. If I say to him '*Ought* I to do so and so?' I always get the same answer: 'I've spent more than half my life trying to expunge the word "ought" from your vocabulary.' And I have to admit it isn't out yet . . . as you can see!

Well, I won't go on boring you about Eric. I do wish you could meet him. He said you had a fine Henry Jamesian type of head. But if you don't like James as much as we do, you mayn't be complimented. By the way, 'Nanda' comes via Henry James and Eric because he says I'm like Nanda in *The Awkward Age.* This, however, I consider too flattering though of course I'm pleased. But how you're going to meet Eric I don't know. He's the most elusive man alive and since his branch of the F.O. has been evacuated I only catch a glimpse of him about once a fortnight. It's agony to him to write letters and I don't think I've had more than twenty from him in all these years and those extremely short. But you've been generous and understanding about Eric as I was almost sure you would be. In fact you've been Erician, if you don't mind that as term of praise! Perhaps I should say Petrine.

If you have had some experience of the beast—and I'm not altogether surprised, for our lives have so many extraordinary points of coincidence—you have all my sympathy. I am terribly sorry if *The House of Clouds* distressed you. I would not have sent it if I had thought it would. I didn't know for certain about your beast then and I forgot that there is, I think, a rather important difference between us. I can only deal with a difficult or painful situation in two ways—by facing or being made to face the full horror of it and then getting it into its right relation or by expressing it in what one loosely calls 'a work of art'. The second is really an extension of the first and one which I have not been able to use nearly enough, because I'm not yet able to write freely. A great deal of the trouble crystallised round the actual act of writing. It would be too long and boring to go into all that now. I can write what I really feel in notebooks and in letters to rare people like you, I can turn out any kind of journalism as a dressmaker makes dresses to any pattern, but of 'real' work I've done very little, as you know.

The House of Clouds was written in 1928 (asylum was 1922-23) and gave me no pain whatever in writing it, in fact it took the 'haunting' away. At that time, I sincerely believed the beast would not recur. It did not really begin to recur obviously till 1933, after *Frost in May* had been published. And for a long time, I did not think it was any more than tiredness, nerves and general strain. But when it came to delusions, a depression so deep that even now I don't like to think about it and violent suicidal impulses (one very nearly successful) something had to be done. The first people I went to were no good—like your bad psychiatrist. Eventually I was sent (I need hardly say by E.) to a good man. I had nearly four years of the strictest, severest Freudian analysis. You may not approve, but I can only judge by results. I went sceptical and hostile, and remained so nearly all the time. It was the most difficult and painful thing I've ever done and I used to think I would rather be raving or dead than continue. But all I can say is that, bit by bit, the intolerable pressure yielded and gradually the dark things cleared up until, though of course I'm still often moody, indecisive and depressed, I did get some sort of clue to the trouble and more stability than I've ever had. There is nothing in the least sensational about analysis. It is simply a slow, dull, patient process of unravelling threads which have got tangled and it doesn't hand, or profess to hand, you the key to life on a golden plate. The net result is as if, before, you had been swimming with your feet tied together and now you are swimming with them free. But swimming is still difficult and where you swim is your own affair.

About your chimney disaster—that avalanche of bricks and soot in the drawing-room—you have my unbounded admiration. How I wish I could deal with such things. I could organise a corps of sweeps and builders, write the most lucid articles on how to deal with the situation, but could do nothing in practice but look helpless and get covered with soot. What a man to be wrecked on a desert island with! My admiration outruns my grammar.

As regards my 'material' I don't think you should worry. One thing I have been pretty sure of for a good many years is that my job in life is to be able to give a form in writing to certain experiences. The expression may be direct or indirect and I may be able to do very little and perhaps not for a long time. It's a kind of testimony, if you like, and difficult to make both honest and at the same time a work of art, something consistent with itself and complete and not just 'reporting' or 'a slice of life'. It has to crystallise out very slowly . . . but all the elements have to be there, the 'bad' as well as the 'good'. I feel very strongly that 'good' and 'bad' are very much relative terms and that we tend to judge them from our own point of view of what we fear and desire as human beings. We call cancer or toothache 'bad' because they hurt us and yet the laws of the growth of a cancer may be wonderful if we could consider them in as detached a way as we consider the growth of a flower. I don't have the same difficulty that I used to have about 'evil' and pain and all the things which seem so difficult to reconcile with the idea of a benevolent God. I find it far harder to see the Catholic point of view of a universe created by a 'good' God and interfered with by the devil. I feel the Catholics give the 'devil' far too much power, because having said God is a transcendent, immutable spirit they immediately go on to attribute to Him all sorts of human qualities such as the power to be hurt, desire to revenge, etc., and thereby get involved in all sorts of difficulties. But I do believe the laws of nature are the laws of God (whose else can they be?) and that nothing in them should fill us with horror, though we may shrink from them as human beings. I am not a scientist and so can never discover any of these laws as they apply to stars or plants or animals or metals and may not have the wit to appreciate or understand them when discovered. But I can in a small, dim way see them working out in the lives of human beings. You may call me a perverse and crazy pantheist but if by 'pantheist' you mean that I think everything that exists in the universe *is* God, I am not one. But if to believe that everything in the universe is an *expression* of God and that God is to the universe what the soul is to the body, immanent in it and yet able to transcend and survey it, then you can call me what you like . . . pantheist or anything else. I would say too, with Spinoza, that some things are more perfect expressions of God than others as *King Lear* is a more perfect expression of Shakespeare than *Love's Labour's Lost*.

But there I go again, speculating in what must be to you a wild and unorthodox way, when you don't want to hear my speculations anyway!

We are, yes, 'in the same boat'. But I'm not sure that we shall follow the same route. I'm more likely to jump in the sea and flounder about in the waves or I'll rock the boat so much that you'll throw me overboard.

About your sister—that's interesting. I presume she left the Benedictines as you say she had hard trials as a wife and mother. Breakdowns very often happen because one's chosen the wrong kind of life and perhaps she needed the trials of a wife and mother and not the other kind. It often works the other way, people unsuited to marriage break down after marriage. 'Madness', apart from the manias concomitant with diseases and injuries to the brain, is nearly always connected with the emotions.

I am glad my letter made you feel happy. Goodness knows I want you to be. You must forgive me if I'm nervous of being loved —certainly not because I don't like it but because it is a kind of responsibility and I feel I may disappoint you so badly, by what I am and what I do. I am too fond of you ever to *want* to hurt you and yet I feel that I inevitably may. I can't be anything but myself with you and that self is so inconsistent and contradictory. I would like to be all you think me—or would like to think me— and I know only too well that I am not. And please brush me away ruthlessly if I get in the way of work. I'm so pleased and excited that you seem to be working well for I do think it's almost the most important thing there is.

As to seeing you—oh dear, it does look difficult at the moment. Perhaps I will be able to take a few days leave in the spring. I do long to see you and talk to you. It is maddening that you live so far away. I suppose you can never come to London? You would let me pay your fare, etc., if you could come, wouldn't you?

As to the sexual act being wrong in the eyes of the Church— well, it's all very puzzling. I have never yet read any Catholic book which did not say that the sexual act was a sin except in marriage and for the purpose of procreation. The priest to whom I went to Confession the other day was emphatic on this point and so has every other priest always been. How this squares with the actual practice of Catholics, married and unmarried, I frankly don't know. Some of the practising Catholics I know are 'chaste', some are not and I don't know what the attitude of the latter is.

And, from my own experience, I know that it enriches some relationships and destroys others. I cannot believe the act is in

39

itself sinful but that, like most other things, it is good in some relations and bad in others. I respect your loyalties and feel that it is much better, and more for our real happiness, to help each other to abide by them.

Don't be too 'perplexed', dear Peter. The rules of our game may not be formulated but they will formulate themselves. Don't over-strain yourself by being *too* unselfish; let's just take each situation as it comes and try to deal with it fairly by each other.

I'm answering in the wrong order as usual but I *am* answering as best I can. Please don't worry over unhappiness I've had in the past. I assure you it was inevitable, very much my own fault and, though I'm glad it's over, I'm glad I had it. I need to have things pretty forcibly demonstrated to me before I really grasp them and I usually prefer to burn my hand rather than to take it on faith that I *shall* burn it if I pick up a hot coal. There are obvious draw-backs to this but some advantages. Sometimes you find that both the sensation and the results of the burning are not at all what people told you they would be and, if you have an inquisitive nature, you find this interesting.

I'm amused at your strain showing itself in wild spending and wild lovemaking because it's so like me. In fact I know that sudden irrational attachments and a disposition to spend money I haven't got are warnings to me to be careful!

I know you'll find this nonsense. But just because we're so much alike and have had so many of the same difficulties, I think we must be extra careful with each other. You may think me a horrid prudent kill-joy but I do think there are possible dangers for both of us and that we must keep an eye on them. Which does not mean we are not to have much joy from knowing each other. I think you'll find over and over again we shall come to the same conclusions for different reasons.

I do think your Sylvia must be a remarkable woman. I must say, of many imaginary conversations I should like to hear, one between her and Eric would come high on the list.

Annulment. I'm sorry but I *did* find the Church more horrid than the State, though heaven knows that was bad enough. The State was searching, but impersonal. I don't think I'm exaggerating, but there seemed to be a definite element of *gloating* in the other. Very excusable, no doubt, but exceedingly unpleasant. Also the financial side was a little queer.

Please, darling, don't worry yourself about raids. I expect I'll last quite a long time. And if I don't, well I don't and you mustn't worry about *that*, or not too much. I truly don't think I'm exposed

40

to any more risk than millions of other people. No use to pretend I wouldn't be frightened if the house caught fire or the roof fell down. If you were here you'd put the fire out and prop the roof up. My landlord has taken every conceivable precaution though I'm afraid I don't sleep in his beautiful shelter and it will be my own fault if through love of comfort I am destroyed in my bed. So far I've been very lucky, missing both the B.B.C. bombings and the one at Eric's house. But I somehow feel it's more likely I'm intended to moil and muddle along for some more years till I'm fifty or so instead of being suddenly eclipsed. My troubles don't usually come in one sensational explosion but in naggings and turmoils over a number of years. So let me turn this anxiety round and beg you not to go impaling your face on bayonets or getting shot by parachutists.

I assure you I am only loved in the strictest moderation by Susan and Lyndall. They had an afternoon's riding as part of my Christmas present, so I was certainly loved for an hour or two! I wish I could have seen them. Susan, usually as obstinate as her mother, *always* considers the horse is right and that it's her fault if she falls off. Horses are a mania with her. I wasn't allowed to send a certain handkerchief to the wash for weeks because Pygmalion, an enormous and much revered horse, had blown his nose on it! But she's a wonderful child though by all the laws of morality she oughtn't to exist at all.

One thing I can never compete with—though I can admire it—is your 'sociological' side. I love individuals and can't cope at all with groups. But I like knowing all the details of your life and it gives me an absurd pleasure to know that you had to have a bath at the end of your last letter because you were still sooty from chimney-sweeping.

As to all I wrote in my last letter—dear Peter, you will have to be very patient about that. I have been reading books by Catholics since and though two are by very good men (one by someone whom I knew as a child and had the deepest respect for, Archbishop Goodier) and one by a saint, I still cannot conquer my strong repugnance to certain things in Catholicism. Perhaps I misinterpret them, but over and over again I have felt this strong attraction to the Church, always followed by an equally strong repulsion. It is not that I 'hate' the Church but I always have the feeling of being trapped and not released and I long to get into the fresh air again, however strong and uncomfortable it is and however secure and peaceful the Church seems. I know it will be a real sorrow to you if I don't 'persevere' and a great joy to you if I do. It is asking a great deal of you to bear with my uncertainty in this but remember that you have a deep conviction which makes you able to bear with doubts and difficulties and I have not. My sudden move was not the result of such a conviction. I have told you how it came about . . . almost automatically and against my will. And I know my 'blindness' and lack of faith may be entirely due to faults in my character—obstinacy, terror of committing myself wholly to anything, intolerance of anything which claims unquestioning obedience and asserts supreme authority. I know it's the most heretical thing to say but I cannot help feeling so deeply that God is so much more than the Church and can lead people by other ways. If I could really feel in my bones that God said 'The Church may conflict with everything you feel and think but your discipline is to accept that and make the best of it', I would do all that I could to accept it faithfully and stifle my rebelliousness. I know how terribly impatient I am. If you pray for me, pray for what I most need, patience and perseverance and the gift of real hard work. Pray that I may find a path and have the courage to pursue it even if it leads me into all sorts of difficulties and that I mayn't reject the path because so many people have followed it or because it seems to me too lonely and dangerous. I like to hold your hand, even if we're walking in different directions!

Well, darling, this is a long letter. But don't say I haven't faithfully tried to answer yours even if I've dashed off on my usual tangents all the time. Soon I'll have to deny myself the pleasure of spending my evenings with you because I must make an effort to do this story. The sad thing is I'm afraid you won't like it. It would have been such pleasure if you would have liked it. But I must write what I have to write and take a chance on what people think, even the ones I most care for.

I've missed out the poor old 'moderns'! You see I'm being morbidly scrupulous! I am substantially in agreement with you and find most of the new poets tiresomely obscure. The chances are that most of them are nothing; how many good poets are born in any generation? But I think one must be just on the careful side when trying to judge genuine new experiments. I am all for tradition but repetition and tradition are not the same things. I believe all true works of art in any age have something in common but the appearance of a new method is always difficult and may seem at first nothing but incompetence or a petulant rejection of the past. You remember your own change of attitude towards Gauguin. Wordsworth would have been abhorrent to the eighteenth-century poets, Mozart was considered a cacophonist by his contemporaries. Which does not mean that any neurotic young man writing in *New Verse* is a Rimbaud or a Baudelaire. But when it comes to serious artists like Joyce or Proust who have put their whole life into their work, I think one must at least be respectful and try to see, without prejudice, what they are trying to do. Sometimes things which are beautiful and wonderful seem to reach a point where one can no longer see them . . . they are too much overlaid with custom and associations. Then they usually go underground till someone rediscovers them and reinterprets them. I almost wish the Church would go underground, or that someone would change one's angle of vision so that suddenly it appeared full of force and freshness again and including everything instead, as it seems to the doubter, excluding so much. I hope very much you will do your 'indictment'. I cannot help feeling that an honest attack might be so much more stimulating than so much specious defence. When you say 'The Church is a bitch but I love her' I feel so much more that one *might* love her than when she is praised as something above all error. I should very much like to read Michael de la Bedoyère's *Christian Crisis* that you mentioned, if you feel like sending it.

It's 11.30 and I've been writing to you for three and a half hours! The dossier I'll fill in another time. It's a very good bit of detective work and reconstruction. I'm glad to have yours. I like to have dates and to know what you were doing and when.

Good night, my very dear Peter, and thank you truly for all your love and for all you give me. You are the best and most generous of friends. Be happy and stay happy and don't get ill—I am worried when you are ill.

I *do* like having your snuff-box. But you shall have it back if life's a misery without it. Tell me soon about the books you want. I'm going away from Friday to Monday to be with the children, then to horrid Evesham for Tuesday and Wednesday week. But I shall call in here on Tuesday in case there's a letter. Your photographs, etc., haven't arrived yet.

I *must* go to bed. So I'm going, carrying your snuff-box with me. So good night and a kiss.

Tony.

Goodness, I've just realised the SIZE of this letter. Do you mind? It's more like a memorandum. If I ever promised *anything* I'd promise the next should be short! But you see what comes of 'answering' a letter. Just try yourself and see! Sylvia must think we're both crazy. It won't even go into an ordinary envelope. There's 'excess' for you! But 'The road of excess leads to the palace of wisdom.' Not my own. Love. T.

My dearest Peter,

I have just got your letter and can't resist writing at once. I'm going away for four days tomorrow to Sussex to be with the children and posts will be bad, etc. In fact I *want* to write to you and am not so far advanced in mortification as to put it off!

Your letter was very good and very understanding . . . and very helpful too. I think I can reassure you. Naturally at first I went through every tangle of self-cross-questioning until I was worn out. I have learnt to be very suspicious of these sudden pulls for I have had them very often before and they have always been followed by reaction and hostility. But this time I had gone further and tentatively begun to practise again. So I expected a still more violent reaction, and got it. I did all the silly things I know one shouldn't do; read, or rather devoured far too many unrelated things by Catholics as if a few hours' reading could solve the problems of a lifetime, until I was in a state of mental and emotional exhaustion. Finally, on New Year's Eve, I went to bed very early and read a chapter of Santayana's *Realm of Essence* to clear my head and calm my mind. And, somehow, by seeing it from a different angle, I saw how the Church and its particular method fitted in with all I have been reading and trying to puzzle out all these years. I don't say there can't be other languages and other methods, but this is the language I know and everything I feel and need can, I think, be expressed in it. I do know that, for me at any rate, there must be something which can be *lived* as well as *thought*. And the great merit of the Church is that it does organise all one's impulses and give one a method both of disciplining and expressing them. Anybody who loves form as I do is not horrified by having limits imposed on them because the limit is the artist's greatest boon. But one has to concur with those limits and not feel that they are arbitrarily imposed. I think, once those limits are accepted, the other difficulties are purely practical. If you decide you're making a chair, there are plenty of practical difficulties about making it but not the agonising confusion (usually ending in doing nothing at all) of not knowing whether you're trying to make a chair or a table. I don't regret my long period of chaos, because, given my nature and particular difficulties, I don't think it could have been avoided. Nor do I suppose for one moment that I shall continue without lapses in serene submission!

I felt New Year's Day would be a kind of test. The Christmas magic was over and the violent struggle between acceptance and rebellion had left me numb. I was so tired and really needing sleep that I did not wake up in time to go to early Mass. With an office day ahead I had quite a good excuse for not going to Mass at all. But I felt, I suppose from old training, that this was just the time, when to go to Mass was just a routine duty, to make a small effort. So I went and was glad that I did. I thought: 'Is this mental dishonesty?' But, as you say, one would have to be a specialist in a hundred subjects, and have a mind clear and subtle enough to grasp the content of every philosophy, to know exactly where each went wrong or contradicted itself and might spend one's whole life in making up one's mind, even if one had such a mind and it were trained to the last fraction. Which doesn't mean I shan't try to go on cultivating what mind I have. But I think I can do that much more productively with a background of some sort of harmony and organisation of all the rest of one's nature. At present I only want to go very quietly and humbly and just try not to be so impatient and so arrogant and so bad-tempered.

I was rather worried about having to tell Eric all this—I can't write to him as I do to you—and I was afraid he'd think I had just been weak and lazy. I saw him last night and he took it wonderfully. In essence what he said was: 'I'm not surprised and I think it's a very good thing. I've always thought that when you'd got free of all the terrifying associations it had for you, you'd be able to practise your religion again. And the fact that you seem to be able to is, to my mind, a proof you're cured.' So that was a great relief. You mustn't think I feel I have to get E.'s 'permission' to do anything, but since he knows me so well and we are so devoted to each other, it's only natural I should be pleased if he thinks something I do sensible. I asked him if he had ever felt the need of an organised religion for himself and he said 'No'. Actually he has an organised philosophy and a way of living which is very definite . . . if ever there was a Greek born out of his time and background, it is Eric. But he said it would not in the least surprise him to find himself a Catholic. (It would certainly surprise me!)

Your advice to me is very good and shows you really understand these things. And it fits in with what my own impulse suggests, namely to go slowly, say short prayers and read only a little of what I really find nourishing. I like your 'Notes' so much—it has all the things I love in it—or rather, nothing that I do not love.

So many lines of Francis Thompson keep running through my head, especially

> All which thy child's mistake
> Fancies as lost, I have stored for thee at home.
> Rise, clasp My hand, and come.

and

> And some have eyes and would not see
> And some would see and have not eyes
> And fail the tryst, yet find the tree
> And take the lesson for the prize.

Please, dear Peter, in your prayers remember a certain Fr Hugh, a Carmelite. This priest, whose face I haven't even seen, has been so patient and so courteous that, whatever happens, I shall always feel grateful to him. He has taken great trouble to get this excommunication revoked and done it with so much delicacy, imposing no conditions on me except to try and practise my religion. When I came back today for the final verdict his first words were: 'Thank you. It was good of you to come.' Which made me feel very small but in a pleasant way. I feel if I'd met anyone less good than that man at that particular moment, I would have been driven away again and it would have been a very long time before I made another attempt.

Oh, I know I shall have endless doubts, reserves, difficulties and rebellions. But I think you will know the extraordinary pleasure of simply being able to say, when people ask you what you are: 'I am a Catholic'.

Forgive me for writing, as usual, a long letter. I value your love and friendship so much and so much enjoy talking to you. However much we may disagree, we *can* understand each other . . . and I am happy to feel us both in the same camp again, having got there by routes so much alike and so different.

You have been so patient with me, taking all my hints and adapting yourself to me. You have done so much in all this by not 'disputing or asserting' but 'whispering results'. I find all this extraordinary interpenetration of minds and apparently trivial circumstances rather wonderful. Perhaps you will find, as you look back on your life, that you have achieved all the things you wanted to do but by the most unexpected and roundabout ways.

Darling, I probably shan't write much about religion in the future. One delightful thing is that we can now take it for granted and there is no need for you to feel anxious or for me to be analytical or assertive or on the defensive.

And please don't worry about my 'delicate health'. I am awfully tough as I keep telling you. Now is the time for me to prove to you that I can stand strains which would have cracked me before. And remember that it was science that made it possible for me to get enough control of what one might call the 'physical' side of the mind (this is a metaphor and nothing to do with brain cells!) to be able to accept the other. I don't say religion couldn't have done the same but there are cases where religion has become so much entangled with other fears and so symbolical of them that the person cannot use it.

These endless letters are only substitutes for talking to you which isn't possible yet and a clumsy substitute too. Don't get awful scruples about 'answering'; everything gets 'answered' in time. I know you well enough now to take your love and interest for granted and though I love having letters and should like twenty pages a day, we live in time and I am *not* to interfere with your work! Soon I'*ll* have to do some work and then maybe my letters will be short and irregular. But for you, my dear, I say what you once said to me: 'Don't write unless it's a *rest* to write.'

I like the new photographs very much, especially the working ones and may I please keep them?

I will be able to go to my cottage this week-end and rout up some of me . . . to give you some more shocks! I have found one of the actual 'Nanda' in a school group of 1913 which will make you laugh. The more I look at photographs (I found some at Eric's last night) the more I wonder how I've ever hoodwinked anyone at any period of my life into thinking I was good-looking. But I'll send you a real packet next week *and* dossier with corrections and embellishments. So that you will then know *all* about me physically, morally and mentally and this correspondence may then cease (or not!).

Your packet arrived yesterday. I liked Fr Tyrrell's letter and his Susan-like drawings. I wish you had kept the others. Sylvia as a child is simply enchanting—exactly how I should imagine Swift's Stella looked. And I love the one of her sitting in the window. It's no good, Peter, you haven't picked a beauty this time! I shall just have to impress you by Solid Merit!

I think you made rather an effort to tell me about 'Stella'. I don't very well see how you could have acted otherwise and it was a generous and impulsive thing to do. But for Sylvia . . . well, I think it was an act of heroic virtue!

Now really, darling, ENOUGH. I must go and cook the dinner. If you haven't time to write, don't. But remember when you 'mortify' yourself in the matter of letters, you also mortify this innocent, deserving and impatient party. Just in case you'd forgotten!

Tony.

Ashurst,
Sussex.

4 January, 1941.

Dear, dearer, dearest Peter,

I really have *earned* the right to spend a little time with you and oh, how I've longed to. Alas, it's still only on paper. I'm down in Sussex for the week-end with the children and as my own beloved little house is let, we have to stay in a horrid, cold, untidy, waterless, communal 'guest house', the only one in the village. This is the first minute of privacy I've had and will be the last because last night we had all to sit together and, though I longed to go into a corner and write to you, I felt it would look rude and stand-offish and my inclination was to be both. Only you will understand that, having begun again as a Catholic, this was just one of the gritty bits one has to try to put up with for the sake of something else. Two of the boarders turned out to be Catholics too, so that was just an extra reason for making an effort to be chatty and polite. Your spoilt and eclectic cat finds it very hard to submit voluntarily to boredom but I knew it would please you more to know I'd tried to be affable to people whom I care nothing about than that I'd written you a letter. Next irony, the Catholics having promised to take me to early Mass have now decided not to go till eleven and this time I did really want to go to Communion. I thought 'Shall I make a huge effort and go for a cold dark walk, three miles each way?' But then I remembered that by the time I got back it would be long after their breakfast-time and over-worked landlady would have to get breakfast specially for me. So I decided I must go at eleven, miss Communion and break into my last morning with S. and L. You'll be amused to hear me reasoning in the old (pre-Peter) way. But anyway Our Lord can say to me: 'Having waited thirteen years or so to go to Communion you can wait a little longer—for other people's convenience instead of your own.'

Darling, I don't need a hair shirt! If you knew how hard it was for me, not to 'mortify' myself but just to behave like a normal decent human being for one single day (I haven't managed it yet!), you'd be amused and—I think—reassured that I'm trying to be very practical about it.

Don't worry, for I do believe 'all is well'. 'Strenuous peace' is exactly right and what I've wanted. Some of my resistance up to now has been due to my extreme stubbornness, some to a genuine desire not to give in from fear, laziness, or a wish for security. It's not easy for me to hold things in suspension; my tendency is to make a hasty decision and then regret it after. That's why I was suspicious at first this time. I thought it all happened too easily and carelessly to be sincere. But, since I've committed myself, I feel very differently and the conviction feels quiet but deep. It is as if the whole meaning of life had been restored to me and the missing piece fitted into the puzzle. What you say about taking it as a whole is absolutely right. You *have* insight into these things. In your first letters I thought you were just using the arguments I have heard so often though I was impressed by the fact that you had been out of the Church for thirty years and had been back for five and were still critical of certain things. It is the fact that you have been away and yet thought it worth while returning that made me listen to you, half unwilling, where I would not listen to the 'faithful' who seemed to have no troubles or the converts in their first glow of fervour. I have to admit I thought at first, sympathetically, but critically 'This man perhaps feels he has failed in what he wanted to do; he is getting older; he has cut a figure in the world, but is now bored and disillusioned and he wants peace' —things which I could equally truly say of myself and which my 'acquaintances' and even most of my friends will certainly say of me.

It is strange how *The Hound of Heaven* which impressed me so much when I was eleven that I immediately learnt it by heart has worked out almost line for line in my case. It used to frighten me, even as a child, because though I did practise quite fervently, I was terrified God would demand too much of me and I should fail. And I thought it meant giving up everything I cared for, renouncing all human pleasure, all love of human beings, all delight in natural things and in art and poetry unless they were directly 'religious' and 'edifying'. That is still my worst bugbear—the saints seemed so terribly dreary and inhuman—and there seemed no model for the 'in-betweens' who want to love God *and* all the delightful things of life too. And, as I grew up, I naturally made straight for the world of painters and writers. I was soon bored with what's called 'pleasure'—though I enjoyed it in fits and starts—simply because I didn't find it very amusing and much preferred hanging round the studios and talking about painting. And I used to get mad at the usual Catholic notion (judging by the Catholics I met) who thought a bad poem by Fr Faber was 'better' than a good poem by Coleridge because it was more edifying. Well, I can sort all that out now and even in my rebellious days it was always a comfort that Dante and Giotto were Catholics and that Cézanne went to Mass every Sunday. And I still think it's a sign of the vitality of the Church that she should produce good art as she did in the great days and that it's most encouraging that she's beginning to again. Cézanne, Mauriac, Claudel and the man who wrote *Journal d'un Curé de Campagne** are all excellent signs. The nuns always used to point admiringly to Chesterton to comfort me, but, though Chesterton was witty enough, I couldn't feel he was a very adequate substitute for all the non-Catholic writers of the nineteenth and early twentieth century.

Forgive this long digression. I am not so worried about that question now. You must remember I have met very, very few 'intelligent' Catholics and I made a bee line for intelligence, charm, and capacity for good work in any art, wherever I found it. I almost wish there were a kind of lay order that really mixed with the world in a way that even the Jesuits cannot. For people are usually shy and un-natural with priests and, in any case, don't normally run into them unless they move in Catholic circles. An order of men who were conspicuously good at their work and of women who were charming and attractive as well as 'good' seems to me quite a useful idea in the modern world. You like crazy notions, so I present it to you and almost believe you've got enough vitality and pertinacity to organise such a thing, given half a chance.

In the last century it was mainly, for the ordinary person, a question of which church you went to. In this, in the sort of circles you and I have moved in, if you go to church at all, you're considered amusingly eccentric, an ignorant fool, or a guilt-racked neurotic.

Oh dear, I do agree with Fr Tyrrell that it's time Catholics gave up the weapon of the sneer. For it does seem a favourite and they don't by any means always use it with grace. If they would only put the positive side instead of treating their opponents and critics

* Georges Bernanos.

with such contempt, I can't help feeling that many people, now repelled by their tone, would at least listen instead of arching their backs. I know that will amuse you too—to see the old advertising blood warming up again!

However, darling, I say this with all respect. I am at present engaged in studying the product and *not* in planning a selling campaign!

As usual, I'm not 'answering' properly. But I'm tired and writing in considerable discomfort—a bad light and a room so cold that even with a fire, a corduroy coat, a huge tweed cape and fleece-lined boots I'm still cold and my hands are pale mauve and my nose pale pink and I wish I had a fur face. Being a Cat through and through, I hate cold and discomfort and also hate being away from my own basket. This does *not* apply to The White Cottage. Oh, I do want to come there one day and see you, and wonder when. I cheated a bit in my conversation last night by asking the couple if they knew the best way to get to Portmeirion and they produced maps and I gloated over them and had to be told six times how to say 'Pen-ryn-*doy*-dreth' just because I wanted to linger over something connected with you. I even asked them if they knew you, just for the pleasure of saying your name. So, my dear, if you think I haven't got all the lover's usual manias, you are WRONG.

Dear Peter, I think I didn't put it quite right when I said or suggested I had no capacity to love for I don't think that's so. It's more that I'm afraid—or have been afraid—to love. It's always seemed to me that the more I cared for someone, the more likely it was to be disappointing or disastrous. And it did work out like that until I felt the mere fact of loving anyone was a guarantee that I should lose it or destroy it. Well, I think you have managed to break that spell.

I am writing in bed now by light of one candle on wrong side. Forgive if illegible. Now—until a little while ago—I should have wished for nothing so much in imagination as to go to sleep in your arms. Yes, 'chastely'—though I still hate the word and the necessity to use a word at all—but in your arms and feeling you close. Now is that 'wrong' or isn't it? The thought of having to have hair-splittings and scruples about one's very thought of love is repellent to me. I am willing to make our relationship anything you choose—in the framework of what we are both attempting to practise. This is both trusting you and putting a good deal of responsibility on you. Foolish perhaps to discuss it since we cannot meet. And yet I feel it's important to have some sort of attitude even in our minds and thoughts. It's queer to hear you asking me

51

to 'have the courage of our opportunity' because this is the sort of situation in which I've always taken the wildest risks—and most of my hardest knocks.

We have decided not to be 'lovers' in the modern sense. But where does 'love-making' begin and end? I can't help thinking of you as a man as well as a character and a spirit, and if you were a woman, though you might have had just the same character and outlook, I should not have the same warmth of feeling for you though I should want you as a permanent friend. It is a form of love-making, as we both know and realise, to write to each other. We know we are physically attracted to each other without ever having met. It sounds absurd—but I know it is so in my case— I think even without having seen a picture of you I would know you in the dark by touch. I had an odd dream about you the other night. The man I dreamt of was someone I had never seen and who stood nearly all the time with his back to me and yet it could have been no one but you and I knew it in my bones. In the dream I had great difficulties in getting to you, running through the snow so that I was too much out of breath to speak to you when at last I caught up with you. Then you turned round and I just saw your face—like a blend and transfiguration of all the faces you have presented me with, young and old, and really like a vision of your *true* face—before I walked straight into your arms. This was the first and only dream I have had about you and it was happy and beautiful.

Dearest, I am tired and will stop now though I want so much to talk. No, I just want to put my head on your shoulder and there would be no need to talk. I haven't even finished the difficulties about us. You know them. Tell me your answer.

Good night and bless you, my love.

Tony.

A.W.

Some dates may be wrong but they're near enough

b.1899   31 March.
1906   Received into Catholic Church after my parents' conversion.

52

1908-14	Convent of the Sacred Heart, Roehampton. Prizes all up school for English, French, German, Christian Doctrine, Latin, Literature.
1914-16	St Paul's Girls' School. Left against my father's wish because I was offered a job. (Lazy. Prizes only for English and French essay.)
1916-17	Governess for six months in Catholic family—six months mistress in a boys' school, teaching Latin, Greek, French.
	Started doing stories for papers and writing advertisements as a free-lance in 1916. Had a regular contract £250 a year from Dearborn's (Beauty preparations) which went on till 1921. I earned very little by teaching and in Government offices.
1918	Clerk in Min. of Pensions & Exchequer & Audit.
1919	Sent myself to A.D.A. (now R.A.D.A.), met Eric.
1920	Touring provinces as *ingénue* in *The Private Secretary* ! !
1921	Married R.G.W.
1921-Nov. 1922	V. bad time. No money except my £250. R. getting odd jobs driving vans for Lyons or on stage and always losing them. Only had one or two odd Stage Society parts for Komisarjevsky. Looks, brains and nerves all in total eclipse.
Nov.1922- Aug.1923	Asylum (Bethlem).
Aug.1923- June 1924	Not allowed to work. A few stories. Took a Spanish course at London University. Saw more of Eric and went to Italy with him and another man. Marriage to R. annulled.
1924	Crawford's: first junior, then head woman copywriter. Married Eric, lived in Paulton's Square, Chelsea.
1928	Half-time arrangement with Crawford's. Did six months as assistant to Desmond McCarthy on original *Life & Letters*. Met S.G.
1929	Susan born 18 August. Marriage to Eric annulled. My father died.
1930	Left Crawford's office but remained on 'retainer'. Journalism for various women's papers, *Sat. Review*, etc. Married Tom Hopkinson.
1931	Lyndall born 23 July. Six months in Harrods Advertising Dept (Hell !).
1932	Back on Crawford's regular staff.
1933	F. *in* M. published. Left Crawford's for good. Fashion

	Editor of *Daily Mirror*. Also Dramatic Critic *Time &* *Tide*.
1934	Return of Beast. Left Tom and lived alone in bed-sitting-room in Oakley Street.
1935-36	Lost *Mirror* job. V. ill. Free-lancing. Took job at £2 a week lecturing on Greek drama at St Denis' London Theatre Studio and writing scripts for students. Went to Spain.
1937	Copywriter at J. Walter Thompson. £1,000 a year. (Most A.W. ever made and she'll probably never make it again!) Divorced Tom.
1938	Fashion Editor *Sunday Pictorial* and free-lance advertising for Pritchard Wood, Graham & Gillies, etc., etc. Also free-lancing for *Picture Post* and various papers.
1939	War and all jobs gone. (During last five years had contributed to various anthologies, such as *Best Short Stories*; also to *Clarion, New Statesman*, etc., etc.)
1939-Oct. 1940	P.G. in other people's houses, wrote a play (v. bad) and about one-third of two novels.
Oct. 1940	B.B.C. and made acquaintance of P.T.

Lindon Gardens.

13 January, 1941.

Dearest Peter,

Yes, indeed you have said what I wanted you to say and would have liked to say to you. I agree with every syllable, even to your saying that we should not spend a night together 'platonically'. Something Chesterton said—I read it when I was a child—has always stuck in my mind: 'The Church has always loved red and white. She has always had a healthy hatred of pink.' We have our passion and we can recognise it and use it . . . in other ways. And though, God knows, I am weak and lazy and self-indulgent, I am not frightened by the mere fact of things being difficult. I have always respected the hard core in Catholicism which is probably why I would never be any other kind of 'institutional' Christian than a Catholic. In every art and every person I have ever cared for

54

there has been this streak of harshness. It is in nature too and God made a far more wonderful world, with tigers in it as well as lambs, than the humanitarians would make. To feel at one with you in my mind and heart does truly mean more to me than to be lost with you in a physical embrace—and yet I am glad that we have this tension between us of normal and passionate human beings.

But oh, how I wish our revered instructors of Catholic youth would be a little more sensible in their sex instruction or lack of it. The whole subject was so muffled and hedged round with horrors and pruriencies that one came to think 'impurity' was in a special class by itself . . . almost worse than the sin against the Holy Ghost. Like you, I didn't know those famous 'facts of life' till I was eighteen (and reacted with the same shocked incredulity) and I remember suffering agonies of shame and remorse and dreading going to Confession because, when I was twelve, a schoolboy kissed me at a party and I *enjoyed* it! If they would only tell us that love and desire (apart from lust which is usually cold and self-centred) are the physical type of our hunger for God instead of treating them as hideous manifestations of our fallen nature. I remember I was afraid to be fond of people in case I should be tempted to throw my arms round them or kiss them. We were not even allowed to take each other's arms at school. Can you wonder that so many girls from convent schools 'go to the bad'? Thinking that perfectly innocent things are wrong, they feel they might as well be hanged for a sheep as for a lamb.

I am reading von Hügel's* letters to his niece with such passionate interest and pleasure that I have almost to deny them to myself or they'd distract me from my dull, necessary work for the B.B.C. What a grand old man he is, how broad, how deep, how solid. And a wild man too, with a fierce, melancholic nature to curb. He is like a spiritual Beethoven, even to the ear-trumpet. Oh, he is so good. Thank you for putting me on to him. He welds together and lights up so many things I have been groping after. How I agree with his insistence on training. Thank God, I was trained as a grammarian by my father who was a classical scholar and in a love of history and the importance of 'disintoxication' by Eric. If I can fit it in with other things, I should like to follow book by book the reading programme he laid down for his niece. Such good things he says. About waiting for the 'second clearness' in writing. Journalists can only wait for the first, shallow clearness (you and I have this in abundance and can write very glibly from the top layer of our

* See Appendix III.

55

minds). Then comes the stage of darkness, obscurity, confusion. It seems to me many of the moderns who worry you by their obscurity may be writing in this second stage and not waiting for the third, the crystallisation. I think it is definitely true of Dylan Thomas who is a very sincere, richly gifted but exceedingly obscure poet.

What von Hügel says of writing certainly applied in my own case, and possibly in yours, to religion. My 'first clearness' in my youth was too glib, too neat, too second-hand. Then came those long years of confusion, rebellion and disintegration. And now my second clearness begins . . . almost in a new dimension. There will always be difficulties and I am busy now preparing for them, for this is a time for me of so much grace and sweetness that I know it will not go on indefinitely. I bought my books, the New Testament, the *Spiritual Combat* and the *Imitation*, feeling so much like a soldier buying his equipment! One has one's new uniform and weapons, all smart and shining, and knows how stained and battered they are going to get with use. Now one is in parade dress, everyone is welcoming and congratulating one, but soon it will be battle dress, wounds, weariness, terror and boring routine. My first passion was to be a soldier and I used to sleep with an old sword by my side. Well, I am under marching orders now and in a regiment that will keep me going when I want to fall out. Naturally good and unselfish people seem to do very well outside the Church but the best place for aggressive and egotistical ones like me is in it . . . well in!

I must tell you a little about Fr Hugh. I saw him face to face for the first time because I wanted some practical advice about the children. He is not, I think, a 'learned' man but he radiates holiness and that really unself-conscious type of goodness which accepts its own goodness as carelessly as a really beautiful woman accepts her beauty. I feel such a deep respect for this man and respect, dear Peter, is even harder for this captious cat to feel than love. So I am sure that God led me to this particular priest and that it is unnecessary for me to hunt up any more brilliant or sophisticated director. I don't think I've ever felt perfectly at ease with a priest before and I do with him. He is so frank and so human—and so humble. He said: 'I feel ten years younger since you came to me that day. I was beginning to feel tired and no longer friends with God and then that happened to me to show that there is a real point in being a priest.' I don't think anything ever touched me more or made me feel more humble. The idea that this man who has denied himself everything and devoted his whole life to God should have been helped by my coming to him that day shows me the extraordinary beauty of this interpenetration of souls and lives in the

Faith. It has always fascinated me in ordinary life and in the artist's world and here it is still richer, deeper, more complex and more simple. Then he told me that, at intervals, the same thing had happened, that through his instrumentality people had come back. And he said: 'I was sometimes puzzled that I should have been a channel of so much grace until a friend of mine said to me "God often writes with a blunt pencil"!' Now don't you think he sounds a truly holy man and right, not only for me, but for the children? I feel the friendship of such a man, who loves and understands children, will woo my two funny and beloved ones to the Church in exactly the right way. He told me he had prayed for me every day since I first came and he asked me to pray for him saying, with such sweet naïveté: 'I feel Our Lord is more likely to hear your prayers than mine. You see, He must be so *charmed* to see you back again that for the moment He can deny you nothing.' How sentimental that would have sounded had that man not been so true, so severe, so mortified under his sweetness. That is what I love in the Church —the rose and the thorn as God made it in this world. He said to me that dryness would come and I know it will and I must weather it quietly as von Hügel says. Never before did I see the importance of being in an organised body and having true friends within that body. It is like mountaineers being roped together. If one slips, the others can pull him up.

I love your prayer for us and echo it with all my heart. We *have* been trusted with something wonderful and something difficult. Thank you for all you give me and for all you hold back. If one is impulsive, it is not easy to hold back. But I know you restrain from true love and not from coldness, fear, or dread of committing yourself. Now I do feel we have hold of each other's hand and yet we both love something much more than each other.

I see dimly what eternity means—another dimension in which there would be space and time to contemplate God. Eternity meaning mere duration would not be *long* enough to contemplate God. It is as if we were preparing to enter another element and had to adapt all our organs to it by discipline. That makes an easier picture for me than 'mortification' as *deadening* of the senses. If they'd only called it 'vivification' instead!

As to my being a saint—no, no, *no*! I don't think I'd ever have the capacity for that. I'm too self-indulgent, compromising and sensual even to *wish* to be one. But I am beginning to respect the saints, 'worship' them even, and most certainly to find nourishment in them. Yet even the deepest and most beautiful things said by the saints seem to me pale compared to the slightest word of Our Lord.

For they *are* human and what one dislikes in them or misunderstands may be due to their humanity. Being human oneself, one does not see them as God sees them. One must be humble and respectful towards them as God's friends and emissaries but I have so often turned from them wearied and unrefreshed. Whereas every time I read the Gospels, I may be puzzled or frightened, but I always find some light, some stimulus. Every time I read any chapter, I find new meanings, new depths—in my most sceptical and rebellious days, I could never find a book that compared with the New Testament for beauty and profundity.

The two verses of the *Dies Irae* you quote* are the ones I like best. It is odd how I constantly found myself singing them in days when I was very far away from the Church and wanted to banish all memory of it from my mind. The other hymn that haunted me was 'Adoro *te devote, latens Deitas*' which I have always loved— it is so good, a sort of *the*ological syllogism in verse and yet so full of feeling. I love the sobriety of St Thomas Aquinas. I think if I had to choose patron saints I would choose him and St Augustine.

How I do talk! But I couldn't not answer your letter at once. Even now, it isn't 'answered'. What you say about the Church and writers is excellent. We don't want to be 'backed up', but we don't want to be tripped up, either. I would say the two 'physical' causes of my alienation from the Church were (1) its attitude towards sex or rather the version of its attitude which reached me and (2) the fear that, as a writer, I should have to write nothing but 'safe' books. I can't help feeling it may be a pity that the education of girls is entirely entrusted to nuns and not partly to priests or Catholic laymen . . . or laywomen. Anyway, I'm pretty sure women need *some* male teachers.

Saint, no, NO. But to find a vocation where I can use everything I have been given instead of dissipating it . . . ah, that I do long and pray for. First to have it shown to me; secondly to have the strength to follow it. And that, I know, you will pray for for me.

Heaven knows I long to see you. But I mustn't force it. What short holidays I get, I must spend with the children for I see them so little and there are double reasons now for seeing them all I can. Let's cheerfully wait till the opportunity comes naturally and I can

* Recordare Jesu pie
Quod sum causa tua viae:
Ne me perdas illa die.

Quaerens me sedisti lassus
Redemisti crucem passus
Tantus labor non sit cassus.

take it and not steal it as I'm so tempted to do. I know this is a sacrifice for both of us and yet we're so happily situated that we've nothing to lose!

I am sorry you've been ill, you didn't tell me before. Be good and take care of yourself, or let Sylvia take care of you.

At the moment I'm being pampered. Your lovely letter cleared up everything that worried me. And the little effort I made in the cold boarding-house was immediately repaid. The woman who seemed so boring turned out to have a beautiful voice and a real feeling for music and we had a pleasant evening reminding each other of all sorts of lovely songs from Mozart to Wolf. But I know I'm not being pampered for ever. I'm like a child being given special treats before it goes back to boarding-school and lessons. But it's delightful to know how sweet one's home is even if one is going to be homesick afterwards and bored with lessons and rebellious.

Two little things I wanted to send you. One from Keats—he said it when he was 23:

An extensive knowledge is needful to thinking people—it takes away the heat and the fever and helps, by widening speculation, to ease the Burden of the Mystery. The difference of high sensations with and without knowledge appears to me this: in the latter case we are falling continually ten thousand fathoms deep and being blown up again without wings and with all the horror of a bare-shouldered creature—in the former case, our shoulders are fledged and we go through the same air and space without fear.

Don't you think von Hügel would have liked that? And isn't it applicable to the spiritual life?

The other from Santayana:

It is only a passionate soul that can be truly contemplative . . . Everybody strives for possession; that is the animal instinct on which everything hangs; but possession leaves the true lover unsatisfied: his joy is in the character of the thing loved, in the essence it reveals, whether it be here or there, his or another's.

Now I must say good night and God bless you. I am so very happy and I hope you are.

Your loving
Tony—Antonia—what you like!

Dearest Peter,

I fear this won't be an 'answer' at all to your beautiful and very moving letter. I am tired and harassed by tiresome things that must be dealt with this week-end. But I hate to leave you too long without a sign of life. The B.B.C. is being rather difficult at the moment; the job seems so futile yet it involves more waste of nervous energy than doing some real work would. However it's very good discipline (I don't like being ordered about by people to whom it's awfully hard not to feel superior!) and I don't want to chuck it yet (a) because I don't like throwing up anything just because it's getting difficult and (b) because I can't afford to. I feel a bit overwhelmed tonight just because I've been working against time all the week; a rush of new work coinciding with the children's arrival and despatch to school and piles of unanswered letters, unpaid bills and unmended clothes heaping up on me like a life-work!

First of all, dearest Peter, of course you must keep the Coster photograph. I haven't a copy because they were taken for Penguin and I didn't order any at the time. I'm so glad you've found one you like at last.

All you wrote in that much-treasured letter nearly overwhelmed me. I feel shy and happy and undeserving and accepting all at once. We were sent into each other's lives so strangely that I do feel we have been given something mysterious and beautiful.

As to my return, yes, I am sure you were very much an instrument of it. I can't say the only one, though of course I can't know! So many other threads that I can trace were leading to it; so many others that I can't. But I feel very definitely that you *hastened* it. Your first letter, arriving just when it did, stimulated all those threads in me. And, becoming so quickly deeply involved with you, I became conscious all the time of the Church. Often rebelliously and critically, but there it was in my consciousness along with you. Instead of being something my mind picked up and dropped at intervals, there it was all the time in front of me. So that I think you were more than a 'signpost', more likely the match that lit the fire.

As to the children, Fr Hugh is being very understanding and doing all he can to back me up and smooth my path with less understanding ecclesiastics. They cannot be baptised as infants because they are 9 and 11 and would therefore have to be instructed. Since they are both away, one living with Tom and his wife in the country and one at school in Salisbury, this is physically difficult. Psychologically it is still more difficult. It is nothing to do with

Tom's being a good or bad Archdeacon's son that they were not baptised when they were little. The Archdeacon has wanted to baptise them for years but we have held out. Our position was roughly the same. Both Tom and I had been brought up in a strictly religious atmosphere and had been up to our early twenties, quite fervent in our respective religions. At the time we married both of us had rebelled against it and both had the same horror of children being *coerced* into rigid beliefs and practices. But we still felt that baptism was something serious and were not prepared to treat it, as many of our friends did, as a purely social business. We felt, if we had them baptised, we committed ourselves to bringing them up as Christians. We wanted them to choose their own religion when they were old enough to understand what religion was and we were quite prepared for them to become strict Catholics or Protestants or anything else that seemed right to them. We didn't force our own scepticism on them, we never prevented them from going to church or learning about Christianity, we never mocked at organised religion to them and we said we believed in God but we had no clear notion of Him ourselves though other people said they had.

Tom is a remarkable man with a poetic, almost mystical vein (I will send you two stories of his that I love) and a very strong sense of an unseen world. He is an exceedingly just and honest man, but, like all his family, extremely obstinate. Yes . . . more obstinate than I am ! And he loves those two children almost more than anything in the world. If he felt I was imposing something on them for which they were not yet ready, or which was alien to their natures, he would use all his very considerable influence with them against me and against Catholicism which would horribly confuse and distress them. And, truly fond as he is of me, he would feel *morally* justified in doing so.

Pray very much for me and them, my dear, that I may find the right way of handling this. It seems to me that I must go slowly and tactfully. From what I know of Tom, I think I must first convince him that this return of mine is real and permanent. He has seen me go through so many mental crises that he feels it may be a solution for me and a defence against the beast but no more. I have got to convince him, by being calm, gentle and considerate, that this is a change of nature as well as of conviction. He will respect that. I know he is activated by what he believes to be best for S. and L. If I can convince by deeds, as well as words, that this way is best, I think he will give in. I have told him that I shall answer their questions from the Catholic point of view and that I shall tell them something about my religion.

Already, of their own accord, they went to Mass and invited themselves to tea with our Sussex parish priest. Susan has met Fr Hugh and likes him and they were fascinated by the statues of the saints in a Catholic shop. Sue has gone back to school with St Francis (her own spontaneous choice not uninfluenced by the animals!) and Lyndall with Our Lady. They also have simple prayer books and like trying to follow Mass from pictures. God must want these two children. I am sure it will come right if I am patient.

Which do I love most? I adore them both and more as they get older (I was a hideously selfish and incompetent mother to them when they were little). Lyndall will always be loved everywhere, she is so sweet and sturdy and honest and funny. But Susan . . . well, she's just a part of me. I love her and fear for her because she's so gifted for good and bad and has such a proud, self-willed, passionate and critical nature. She is a born artist and a born thinker. Lyndall is still a *child* and will be for a long time. Susan, even when she was tiny, we both thought of as a *person*. Tom has a queer respect for her as well as love. Though she isn't his child, he loves her as much as Lyndall. If I had to part from Lyndall, it would be a great grief, but if I had to part from Sue, I'd never get over it. You don't get much idea of her from photos. She shuts her face up or simpers. You want to see her when she is talking or thinking . . . then she is beautiful. Lyndall has wonderful eyes and a wonderful mouth, but Sue has an extraordinary radiance—a kind of transparency when she is 'out' of herself. She is very fair, pure gold hair and white skin and oddly set blue eyes with black lashes. She is going to cause someone a lot of trouble one day—and herself more still. Tom is more sympathetic to the Catholic idea for her, knowing that she has the same sort of difficult nature that I have and has been speculative and interested in ideas ever since she could talk. But he feels that Lyndall only needs for the time being to be a happy, secure, loving and beloved little animal. Sue might be a saint. She has enough violence and intensity to be. But Lyndall, as a Catholic or anything else, seems pretty obviously destined to be a charming and devoted wife and mother. I don't think she'll ever 'go to the bad'. But Susan will go to one extreme or the other.

If by any chance I get hit by a bomb, I'd like you, dear Peter, to get in touch with her and keep an eye on her. One tiny story will give you an *aperçu* of her. When she was 4, she was sent home from the nursery school in disgrace. In a fit of jealousy she had run a penknife into her best friend's arm. She agreed perfectly reasonably that she had been very naughty but she was obviously interested in something else. I found her sitting up in bed, quite white with

intense thought. At last she said, with her 'Delphic oracle' look:
'You know, mother, it isn't loving people that makes you miserable
. . . it's wondering whether they love you.'

Oh Peter, will you forgive me for writing all about my children
instead of you? I always write to you what I'm thinking of at the
moment. It isn't that I'm not thinking of you, my beloved friend and
you know that, don't you?

I had a bad day of doubts and confusion yesterday. I had expected
it but it was strong. But I did not expect to find them all gone today
and I am so thankful. I know the light will be intermittent for me
and I must just try to keep quietly on in the dark spells. I know
this is my world and I must live in it more and more but there are
times when it seems unreconcilable with all one has experienced and
come to know of the natural world. But I know the two are locked
together at some point and not irreconcilable. I have found a good
book on von Hügel by a French priest (much about Tyrrell in it
and all in accordance with what you say of him) and it is most
illuminating and refreshing—letting so much air into the rather
stuffy pietism in which I was brought up. I am even coming to love
the saints!

I have ordered *The Realm of Spirit** for you and will send it next
week as a rather belated Christmas present. I have not read it yet,
because Eric who is an authority on Santayana and much influenced
by him makes me work all through the earlier ones first so that I
shall be properly grounded in the Santayanan grammar, as it were.
He says you may go wrong if you're not quite sure of all S.'s meanings or rather special senses in which he uses words such as 'essence',
'existence' and so on. But you'll almost certainly find it fascinating
and suggestive. He is not an easy writer in spite of the exquisite
smoothness and clarity of his style. I have been reading him on and
off for years and don't pretend to grasp him. Eric has studied him
closely for fifteen years and really knows him thoroughly. I find him
both stimulating and disconcerting. He is Catholic-trained though he
comes to very unorthodox conclusions; at least I fear they are unorthodox. And yet he makes me see the point of Catholicism more
than almost any other writer. I have more *reverence* for Spinoza,
whom I understand much better, but I am dazzled by this rainbow-
play of Santayana. He is for people who are by nature classical and
ironical, like Eric, and who can hold ideas in suspension. I am only
a romantic barbarian with a sense of form and I need something
tangible from which to start.

Now, dearest, I must stop. My duty letters aren't written and I

* By George Santayana.

am v. tired. God bless you, dear Peter, and thank you for everything. I can't write properly about *us* tonight.

Antonia (only for a change !).

Darling Peter,

I didn't mean to write to you tonight for I have some tasks, but I can't resist answering your letter at once. Yes . . . answering !

I'm very, very glad you wrote me my 'love-letter'. I don't seem to be able to write *you* a real love-letter, perhaps I'm shy, perhaps I can only say things by implication. But my dream about you had something of the quality of your 'waking dream'. And it left me with the same peace, as if now our knot was firmly tied. I just feel that for every extension of my love for you there *must* be an extension of my love of God and, at the moment, as regards God, I'm like a hunter on the trail. Now it is I who have to do the pursuing.

I love your vision of eternity and I am sure it was true. About Sylvia, I can't bear that she should suffer or feel she may suffer because of my existence. But I know that you will see that she has more, rather than less because of this. This *must* not mean 'infidelity' in any sense to her and I know you don't want it to. But if anything is hurting her—our too frequent letters or anything else—we must give it up. I often think of her; she is becoming a real person for me and I think she is a wonderful one. I have such an admiration for these naturally incorruptible people like Sylvia and Eric that I feel very critical of the ones who, having faith, yet fall so short of those two's natural goodness. Eric too says that he has never felt the faintest intuition of God. I can imagine few things more miraculous than *his* conversion. But we can only pray for them and meanwhile feel enormously respectful and grateful to them. I'm sure I don't know where either of us would be without them, probably in our respective strait-jackets. I would like you to give Sylvia my love if she doesn't think it impertinent. And please find me a book I can get for her that she'd really like. No wonder she's shocked at Keats' demands on Fanny. But if you're dying and she seems like life itself, you cling to her and nearly strangle her like a drowning man strangling his rescuer. They are terrible, those last letters; they really have the 'brassy taste of despair'. But how I love Keats and feel what a rich and profound spirit he had, with all that possessive passion of his.

I do feel very strongly that if one accepts nature as the work of God one must accept in it all that seems repulsive to us *as human beings*. I don't understand von Hügel's distinction of 'innocent' nature. I am perfectly willing to accept the doctrine of the 'fall of man', but, as far as I know, there is no official dogma of the 'fall of nature'. That nature became *hostile* to man after the fall, I understand perfectly, but not that nature itself suffered any corruption from man's fall. Of course we were told at school that there were no weeds and thistles or thorns on the roses before the Fall but this has always seemed to me a pious myth and a feeble one. I am sure we shall understand one day the marvellous interrelation of nature expressing God in a way we can no longer fathom; we are creeping back to it by science which, as I most certainly agree with the Baron, must not be treated as having no connection with religion, though religion transcends it. I am sure the more *facts* we know and do not blink can only in the end increase our delight in and adoration of God. Even in madness I had some apprehension of God and would not wish to have been without that experience. I am willing to have it again if God wishes me to, and I say this soberly.

I agree about the necessity of the frame for one's speculations and glimpses. And it is absolutely necessary too, to humble one's intellect, but not to ignore it. When I read difficult things now, I pray first to the Holy Ghost to make me understand it the right way. And in conversation I try to be truthful and not aggressive and to allow myself to be corrected with a good grace. This alternation of tension and relaxation seems as good for the mind as for the body.

I am pursuing von Hügel. I am reading an excellent book on him by M. Nedoncelle, a French priest. Thank God for an admirable book, unspoilt by the usual pettiness and bigotry of the sort of Catholic books I've read before. This man writes as reasonably as Santayana himself (and even mentions him respectfully) and his whole tone is so scholarly and so fair that I had to look for the *Imprimatur* to make sure that he wasn't a Modernist and a heretic! This is rather a sad criticism of what one commonly expects of *Imprimatur* writings and I only make it to you.

Your 'fatal tassel' story is really horrifying. I remember when I was about 14 living through months of terror because I thought I must have committed some appalling crime and was being turned into an animal for a punishment. I thought what was happening to me happened to no one else and I was full of shame and misery. I think the Church's *rules* about sex are probably all right (though very difficult to practise) but I hate the usual expression of them. There is so much more in sex than 'bestial appetite' and surely people should be taught to accept their human nature, understand it and deal with it rather than to treat it as a hideous phenomenon. I have to keep off pious books, admirable in other ways, that say 'I utterly despise and hate myself' for I think that's false. By all means let's say we're weak, liable to corruption, full of faults, but to *hate* one's whole nature is to hate the work of God. Of course we must try to get rid of our egotism and keep low and be sorry for our sins, but this bitter condemnation of those very impulses which have led us to God seems to me hypocritical and false. I want to love God and not to hate myself but gradually become detached from and indifferent to myself.

How I agree with you about taking back one's faith is to take it back transmuted to gold.

I don't know your statue. It sounds a very beautiful one. And I share your feeling about St Joseph who from being a dull neutral figure has become one of my favourite saints. I prefer him to nearly all the ones one can read about. It was really through St Joseph that I had my first strong drive towards the Church about eighteen months ago, though I couldn't follow it then and reacted violently. This is the story. Just before the war, I strayed into the Oratory one day and found myself stopping at the altar of St Joseph. I felt an impulse to pray to him, I don't know why, because, as I say, I'd never thought much about him. And suddenly I felt such a strong intuition of what that man was that I actually wept—which I hardly ever do. I have always wanted to be first and best in everything and I thought of this man, the support of the Holy Family yet always 'below' Our Lord and Our Lady, unknown and holding back always from this beautiful girl he had married as a man and not as a saint. And I asked him to make me content with being second and not first and just to get on with my own job without pining to be Shakespeare or Tolstoy. I feel sure he was a very good carpenter! And I felt he must sometimes have been tempted to be envious and jealous and self-pitying and assertive . . . just like me. Well, I didn't so much pray as simply remain in his presence. And eventually I was moved to go and ring the sacristy bell and ask for a priest.

That was the priest who told me I was excommunicated and was —well, on the surface—what you call a 'spiritual fascist'. He was so harsh, almost insulting, when I brought myself to blurt out my past, asked me why I wanted to return and did I 'expect to get an emotional kick out of religion?' Then he told me to read a certain book. I went out, feeling as if I had been slapped hard in the face but, trying to put down my pride and hurt vanity, I bought the book. It was one of the worst fifth-rate 'apologist' works, written condescendingly and exceedingly illogically and I'm afraid the combination of that and the priest's tone drove me right away. I felt my intuition of St Joseph was real and abiding but that the Catholic Church had no connection with the religion of the gospels any more and had become a mere collection of meaningless formulae like the formulae of the Pharisees. I don't say that priest wasn't a good and honest man according to his lights but I do think he lacked tact and discernment of human beings. Fr Hugh asked me in Confession just as searching and embarrassing questions but in such a different spirit.

Fr Hugh knows nothing about the complications and unhappiness in my life, only the bald facts as I have confessed them. My instinct tells me that is as it should be. He is too busy a man to be bothered with my soul-searchings and practical distresses of the past. Practical difficulties of the present are different. But on the rare occasions I see him outside the confessional we just talk about his gardening, the sacristan's wonderful embroidery, and, of course, the children. He loves children and understands them so tenderly. I'm sure his great cross in being a Carmelite is not to have children of his own. But I get more from hearing him talk about his life in his monastery than from anything I could say to him. It means more to me that he is tired from sitting up all night talking to the poor in the shelter or that he's got blisters from making up the furnace than if we talked about all sorts of 'deep' things. He is a holy man, and that is the important thing.

I don't believe the modern world has lost the 'deeper meanings of love' as much as all that. Some of it has and some of it hasn't. All the leaping into bed that used to go on in Bloomsbury and Chelsea was pretty trivial and meaningless, I admit. But even that was only an exaggerated reaction against the old taboos. And I think 'promiscuity among friends' was, at any rate, better than a man going to bed with a whore. At least there was some kind of mutual affection.

I still think, though officially I'm not supposed to, that a sexual relation between two unmarried people is not in itself wrong. I don't for a second deny that the sexual act can be sinful and often is. But this has nothing to do with whether the people are married or not.

And I don't feel that *we* ought to be lovers. I don't go back on anything I've said about that. It is much better for both of us this way, in view of what we're trying to do. It would be just greed for us who have so much else. If our destiny had been to meet long ago and marry each other, why then it would have been right. But we'd have been HOPELESS married!

But I'm sure you agree with me in your heart. You say yourself that you have known real richness and warmth in physical mating and so have I . . . very seldom, but sometimes. And I would never deny that and say it was something to repent and regret. Sex is not only rich and wholesome, but it's an opportunity for discipline like anything else. I will *not* deny what I have found good, no matter what the theologians say. It can bring two people to a harmony and understanding of each other which some can achieve in no other way. I don't say for a minute it's the only way. But I feel that, though the modern world has cheapened sex, the ecclesiastics have cheapened it too by throwing so much dirt at it. It's a sin to be greedy or to drink yourself into a maudlin state, but it's equally a sin to starve yourself and make yourself ill. And for some people I'm sure sex is just as much a physiological necessity as food and they become embittered and impoverished without it. Marriage—I mean ordinary family-raising marriage—is becoming more and more of a specialised vocation in the modern world. What about the men and women who aren't suited to it and are not called to celibacy?

I'm glad you've found priests so sympathetic. I can't say I have. Maybe they're more sympathetic to men. But as a young girl it used to cost me tremendous efforts to confess any 'sin against purity' because it was always the cue for the priest to begin what I can only call very prurient probing and questioning. They never did this about any other sin. They might have helped me a good deal if they'd probed into the occasions of my sins of anger, pride, jealousy, etc.

I do believe that, when the Church has enough really wise and understanding men in it, she will consider some possible mitigation of her rules about sex, some of which, like the celibacy of the clergy, are only a question of discipline. As it is, I suppose that knowing how full of occasions of sin and trouble sex is, she does right to make the rules strict. For the majority it is probably wise but the minority suffer agonies of conscience or else rebel against the whole institution.

And I don't admire chastity preserved from timid fear of con-tamination. I do admire it preserved for a *reason*, desire to move more swiftly in any sphere, spiritual, physical or mental.

I may sound unorthodox (and probably am) but I'm jealous of the

Church's honour, which is stained in one century by avarice, in another by cruelty, in another by narrowness and ignorance. I feel her children, while being respectful to her and honouring her for her true greatness and her divine patents, must work themselves to the bone—priests, religious and laymen—to keep it bright. The more good artists, scholars, philosophers, scientists and psychologists she can produce as well as saints, the better. I rejoice when she produces a von Hügel or a Nedoncelle. But one can be loyal to one's mother while criticising her and one doesn't abuse her to strangers. In broad outline she is always wiser than men, in details I think not always. And I am sure her honour can only be kept untarnished by admitting her errors, not denying them. If she is the city of truth, she must admit to being examined in the light of truth in ordinary matters.

Yes, the Communion of Saints is wonderful and I believe in it firmly. And there is a wide choice. I hope that by now there are plenty of uncanonised ones and that on All Saints' Day I can think of Spinoza with his thirst for the 'intellectual love of God' interceding for all those who, like him, are searching for God through the intellect alone.

I have copied two 'practices' from von Hügel, a chapter of the New Testament every day and a decade of the rosary. I think these will keep me in touch with the real life of the Church no matter how much I may become confused or rebellious.

Oh, how I agree with you about hating the 'Gardens' and 'Treasuries'. But I love all the old, solid prayers of the Church. And how I long once again to go through all the magnificent liturgy of Holy Week. Roehampton did at least encourage a solid taste and I have so much to thank Fr Goodier* for. There certainly was a deeply spiritual man.

I am so pleased that we have the same favourite prayers and hymns. I love too O Deus, ego amo te, Nec amo te ut salvas me which I used to sing even in the asylum. And I love being just one of the herd, one of the sheep, along with the old refugees from Gibraltar, the pious old maids, the young soldiers and sailors, saying the public prayers after Mass. I love the Church because one can be completely alone in her . . . alone with God, I mean, climbing the highest and loneliest places for which one has strength and yet one is also one of a crowd, in the valley, with the tired priest enjoying his cup of coffee after saying Mass and the women feeding the hens and the children running wild after keeping quiet for so long. I like

* Fr Alban Goodier S.J., afterwards Archbishop of Bombay, who was the school chaplain.

even to think of the Church as a solid old peasant woman, full of courage and vitality, very rough and plainspoken with her children, but infinitely tender when they are sick; unfastidious in her outward ways sometimes but never losing her inner dignity.

Yes, my very dear, I do want to do some work soon. And I'm afraid that will have to mean rationing letters. I so love writing to you that it will be a real deprivation. But you will understand, won't you, how it is? I instinctively write to you every time I have a free moment, but I don't get many with the B.B.C. work and very soon I must put myself under orders and spend evenings working. It's no good waiting till I 'feel like it'. I never do until I've started. Beginning any new work is agony to me and keeping on with it purgatory. I have to sit down with a pen and make an act of faith. So do please pray for me to start work soon even if it means fewer letters.

I believe heaven is a dimension, not a continuity. I don't want to think of us 'storing up good things in heaven' by going without them on earth. But simply of throwing ourselves hard on a trail, not much minding what we lose, if we get one fraction nearer that light and source of life. I want my very extravagance and hatred of restraint to lead me to God as well as my love of truth and order.

Of course I like all the things you say to me and even your praise of my 'beauty' which is a creation of your own mind and feeling and yet *makes* me beautiful for you as long as your imagination lasts. And I like the things you say about my character and think some are potentially true. But those are my court cards: the rest of the hand is pretty shabby.

Now, dearest, it's twelve as usual and I must go to bed. I do hope we're allowed to meet not *too* far hence.

Tony.

1 February, 1941.

Dearest Peter,

Thank you very much for the books, and especially your own little 'notes'. I long to borrow Tyrrell's *Nova et Vetera* and von Hügel's *Selected Letters*. I have one or two Maritains but have not embarked on them yet. I am trying St Thomas neat in Everyman as I always like to read the original before the commentators and interpreters. Hence New Testament before Saints etc. If I hadn't read (or rather *bitten* through) Spinoza myself first, I should have missed so much by only reading essays on him, even the excellent ones by Santayana.

Here are your letters. They're not in order but they're all there except the last few which I want to keep back to re-read and which are mainly 'personal' anyway. They should be a good gleaning for the 'Indictment' you were thinking of writing when we got launched on this vast correspondence. I am so glad you're thinking about your book. If I had leisure, I'd love to work with you. But I think now, when I've so little, that I must try to do something on my own. The book I have in mind (I've made several false starts on it in the last six years) will be 'unsafe'. It is an 'unsafe' subject the relation of a father and a daughter. But my return seems to have given me the right perspective on it at last. There will be no direct religious theme in it, but all by implication. And I want to bring in all the types of Catholic, good and bad, that one ordinarily meets. I can't help wishing for leisure or that my one year of leisure (last year) could have been better used.

My dear, I'm so moved by your wanting to send me your beloved statue. I accept it, and give it straight back to you with my love. I like always to think of that statue in your room.

I am sending you Santayana and the *Spiritual Combat*. The latter I think isn't really my book—not at the moment, anyway. The *Imitation* is.

Fr Hugh told me not to worry about S. and L. I thought perhaps I was being lazy and not doing enough. But he says 'Be patient and God will find a way.'

God bless you, my darling friend and keep you happy and help you to do your work, whatever it is to be. Don't be nervous about bombs for me. I rather suspect I shan't have a dramatic end just yet. It seems somehow more likely that I must have several years of drudgery and hard work before being allowed to die.

Now I must say good night.

Antonia.

P.S. *Important.* Remember when Santayana describes himself as a 'materialist' he only means he believes in the existence of matter as opposed to philosophers who think nothing but mind exists —such as Berkeley, etc. We shall both be new to this book. I have already found wonderful things in it in desultory page-cutting.

This is really a nickname like your 'Peter'. I was christened 'Eirene' but 'Peace' seemed a very inappropriate name for me. My mother always called me 'Tony' as a child and it gradually got lengthened into 'Antonia'.

1 February, 1941.

My very dear Peter,

You must forgive me if this is a very meagre return for no less than six letters. If only we could meet, so much ground could be covered in a few hours whereas, what with work and reading and thinking (and a certain tiredness as a result of all these things), I haven't time to answer or talk about the many points your letters raise though I *think* about them very much.

First, my dear, I don't know how to thank you or indeed to accept your lovely statue. I feel really overwhelmed by such a gift for I know what it means to you to part with it. I feel so unworthy of it—I mean this—and, for myself, I should have been so much happier if you would have kept it. I am so glad to have seen it and had it in my room but I truly wish you would let me send it back to you.

If, as I almost inevitably shall, I disappoint and puzzle you, it will distress me that you have committed to me something so very precious to you. Perhaps I am not generous enough myself to be able to accept such a gift without scruples and a kind of anxiety.

I have been in a state of considerable tension and doubt for some days. All my uncertainty and hostility is in a rampant state and I can only deal with it by trying to remain quiet and continuing in methodical practice and waiting for the storm to pass.

It is inevitable with such a double nature as mine. Tensions and contradictions of this kind are bound to arise and it may be more or less my permanent state and the particular cross I am called on to bear. Some people have to endure physical ill-health, others mental and psychological.

The cure, I feel, is patience in one realm, activity in another. I can only lay my difficulties frankly before God, asking for an increase of faith and love. I run round like a starving creature, trying to find some nourishment that suits me and that I can assimilate. But over and over again, trying in the saints and spiritual writers to find a light, I do find a light but along with it something abhorrent to nature. I do not mean simply that one should discipline one's natural impulses or try to become 'detached' or to love things in and for God, because for many years and from all sorts of sources I have gathered that and felt it was the right way, however difficult in practice.

But when I read, as I read today of St Catherine of Siena, that in crushing her natural affections, she turned from her mother's caresses 'with as much abhorrence as if they had been poison', I am deeply and instinctively revolted. And, in every saint or spiritual writer, I find this same thing and always have found it. It may be due to the vehemence of exaggeration but this element seems to be in all the saints, who are held up to us as ideals, and it seems to me morbid and perverse.

Again, the way in which God is repeatedly described as being 'jealous' of human affections and of having created the world solely for his own 'glory' . . . this seems to me to represent God as a selfish tyrant. That human beings, having a dim apprehension of God, should wish to purify themselves and to praise Him, seems to me only natural. But that they should represent Him as having the very characteristics which they would abhor in a human being and which they are trying to root out of themselves, seems to be horrible.

I do not want to be wayward and I am keenly aware of my own egotism, vanity, impatience and self-indulgence. And I do not mean to give up the practice of religion because that religion seems full of anomalies and repulsive elements. Also, I want to find the truth, or as much of the truth as an imperfect and limited creature can apprehend of the truth which is obviously the very smallest crumb. But I would rather have a crumb of real truth, however starved I felt, than a whole loaf of half-truth. I can only say that I want to be able to accept what is, however repugnant and painful, as opposed to what I would like to be, however delightful.

What von Hügel might call my attrait and what I might call my 'reason' often seem to be diametrically opposed. The feeling of something stronger than myself which calls me to follow the precepts of this religion may be an illusion but it is a genuine impulse in my nature. So, too, is the other, the desire to sift, compare and criticise. What is common to both is a kind of humility (tentative and easily breaking into pride and self-complacency) which notes all my faults and weaknesses (some at any rate, and it wishes to note them all) and makes me mistrustful of myself. Yet in this life one cannot stand still, one is always in flux and in spite of oneself must act, think, feel often instinctively.

I think all I can do is *practise* the religion and perhaps not talk about it too much.

Perhaps you will understand if I say that in some ways I am frightened of our friendship. Not because it is not dear and precious to me, for it is. But because I am nervous of the influence people can have on each other, especially people who, in many ways, are very much alike. I do not want to worry you with my difficulties, not because I think they can in any way disturb you, for I think that your faith and conviction are deep and firmly rooted. But I don't think it is good for you, having a nervous temperament like mine, to be subjected to that strain.

From my own point of view, I am just a little frightened that, in your zeal, you may try and force me where I am not ready to go and am perhaps not intended to go.

I read today von Hügel's and Tyrrell's letters. I was very much moved by this tragic and very beautiful story of a friendship between two profoundly spiritual and profoundly different men. Incidentally, I felt extremely sympathetic to Tyrrell, this swift, bright, heroic and tortured spirit. I admire the massiveness, the sweep and multiplicity of von Hügel. But, simply as a *nature*, I feel far more drawn to Tyrrell. And I cannot help feeling that the Baron, in his desire to impose his own activities on Tyrrell, in some way warped him from his true vocation. You see the same thing happening with von Hügel and his daughter Gertrude. The Baron is highly explosive material. Being a great solid mountain of a man, he can afford to be volcanic. I love and admire him immensely, but he seems to me to lack that tremendous courage of Tyrrell's, reckless and exaggerated perhaps, but how refreshing. It is amusing to see how von Hügel (though he is so touchingly aware of it and tries so hard to curb it) instinctively projects himself into other people. Admiring Tyrrell's enchanting style he cannot help saying what years of training must have gone to it (as they would in his own case!) whereas Tyrrell was surely a natural writer. But they were great men, both of them. The most beautiful thing of all seems to me that, when they had taken different paths and Tyrrell must perhaps have felt betrayed and deserted, he throws his whole heart into revising *The Mystical Element in Religion* knowing he can have no credit for it, since the mere mention of his name would make von Hügel's book suspect. That seems to me superb by any standard.

About your *Localism*. I shall read it with much interest. I will tell Tom about it for he most certainly was genuine in his 'reconstruction' number.* If you have a spare copy I wish you would send it

* of *Picture Post*.

to Cecil King at the *Daily Mirror*. C.K., who is the managing director, is a friend of mine and for years he has talked to me of just such a scheme as yours for decentralisation.

As to broadcasts, there are talks being organised by the religious section on the lines you suggest. Fr D'Arcy is doing one of them. This doesn't come in my department at all (we are almost too violently 'localised'!) so if you wrote to me, I'd only have to send it on to Talks. But you might write to Miss Wace, who arranges all the talks. (Bedford College, Regent's Park) and put your suggestion up to her. It would be grand if it came off and ah, how I should enjoy a 'legitimate' chance of meeting you.

Forgive me, dear Peter, for this very unsatisfactory letter. It does not mean I am any less fond of you, only that I am troubled and clouded. This does not mean I shall not go on practising. Pray for light *for* me and responsiveness *in* me. 'Strenuous peace' is one thing; tension, discord and strain another. But one does not choose one's cross, and that is probably mine. I believe there is an ultimate harmony of which one may only catch an occasional glimpse and I hope more understanding may confirm what I feel in my bones to be true; that nature and supernature are complementary and not antagonistic. There is only one love from which I need to be emancipated, the love of myself. For all other loves I need increase, not suppression. Ah, if you knew how much I wanted to find my *place*, however small and low, and the faith and courage to keep in it, which one can't do by standing still.

God bless you, my very dear and much-trusted friend. I am so grateful to you in spite of my waywardness and apparent coldness.

I have tonight anyway found much relief in the sayings of Abbé Huvelin on pp. 58-63 of *Selected Letters of von Hügel*.

And in an old hymn which I found in the introduction:

Veni Sancte Spiritus,
Reple tuorum corda fidelium
Et tui amoris in eis ignem accende,
Qui per diversitatem linguarum cunctarum,
Gentes in unitate fidel congregasti.

Forgive me if at present I don't send you any official 'difficulties' for your anthology. This isn't quite the moment for me to be critical. I must concentrate on swallowing the camel before straining at the gnat!

And just at the moment, apart from practical difficulties, I feel our actual lines of work should be separate. Perhaps you don't also, dear Peter, realise I have rather an exacting job at the B.B.C. (an incessant hair-shirt of tiresome details and practically no results of any value for a lot of grind and drudgery) and, being a slow worker in my own line, need most of my leisure if I'm to get anything done before I'm 50! It takes me literally years between thinking of something, even a story (the present one's been in my head for seven*) and doing it! So be patient with me. All honour to you for doing your book in *very* difficult circumstances.

I will get Sylvia's book as soon as I can. Waley is another taste we have in common . . . or rather, the Chinese.

Antonia.

I've answered so little—but will you let me hold the rest over?

P.S. Sunday 2 February. I feel much calmer and in 'better disposition' after going to Communion this morning.

This P.S. mainly to say I began your *Design for Transition* this morning and think it admirable. I will buy a copy and send it to King myself with a note. Why don't you send a copy to Allen Lane? It obviously ought to be a Penguin with a wide circulation.

One tiny comment on an old letter of yours. Don't get the idea that Eric's ban on 'ought' means that one should follow every impulse. Far from it. He simply means one should reason about a situation and try to imagine probable consequences of this or that act, especially on other people, instead of having some *abstract* notion of 'duty'. Also that one should try to discover the real needs of one's nature (and other people's) and not merely follow one's whims or any rule blindly taken over from convention and convenience and not really examined and accepted. In ethics he himself is certainly an example to most Christians; his only difference being that he arrives at Christian principles by reason and not by revelation! Reason and logic are *not* the same thing; the former being a human *function*, the latter a human *construction*. Sometimes you're so absolute in your alternatives. You obviously use 'modern' as a term of abuse meaning self-willed and rebellious. Why should one be 'ancient' or 'modern' in your sense? Why not *aspire*, at any rate, to be a rational creature?

Very much love,

Tony.

* *The Moment of Truth.*

My dear Peter,

I haven't written to you for some days, but I have been constantly thinking about you, waking up in the night to think, puzzle, try and clear my head about some things that have been worrying me. I have tried to drive them out or ignore them, but they come back too strongly and I feel there's no alternative to writing to you half-heartedly (or not writing at all) but to write as candidly as I can and ask you to forgive me if I put things crudely or unfairly. It would be horribly ungrateful to hurt you, after all your goodness to me, and, anyway, I feel too much real affection for you to want to hurt you. But, being the particular sort of creature I am, I can't feel at ease in any relationship when I can't be quite straightforward with my friends. There's bound to be a certain amount of 'fantasy' between two people who have never met and talked, and I can't help feeling that just a shade too much has crept in on your side. I do truly think that, if you met me, you would probably feel rather differently about me and that all sorts of things about me that would irritate or disconcert you would be more apparent than in my letters. And, no doubt, the things which irritate and disconcert me in your letters would be quite outweighed by new things which I would find to love and admire in you once I saw you as a flesh and blood person in action. The balance of feeling between us would then be redressed again. But for the last few days—longer, perhaps—I have been feeling the object of too much and too undeserved love and it is painful for me not to be able to give as much as I am given. I console myself by saying that what you love is at worst a figment of me created in your own mind, at best a potentiality. But, speaking selfishly, I would rather you had a genuine liking for me as I really am than a romantic devotion to some idealised version.

It is just because every letter I have ever written to you has expressed as sincerely as I could what I felt at each particular time, that this one may seem by comparison harsh and cold.

You may well ask what it is I'm fussing about. It's not easy to tell you. And I am trying to make all possible allowances (I ask you to make them too) for my hyper-sensitiveness to words and forms of expression, for my impatience and my natural aversion to people appearing to make too many claims on me or in any way to force me, even when it is done out of affection. I am not entirely obstinate, and anyone whom I really respect can influence me, teach me and curb me to their heart's content if they will use a little tact. And that, Peter dear, is what you don't always do. It would take too long to give concrete examples, for they are scattered here and there through all your letters. Sometimes 'mercurial T——' as Tyrrell calls you does dash rather wildly into places where people want to be alone or tries to rush them where they're not quite ready to go! Because something is vivid in your own mind, it is not necessarily so vivid in someone else's and between even the most sympathetic people there are profound and unexpected differences of modes of feeling and expression. It's natural for every human being to want to find another who is the exact replica of their own best selves. But if this were possible, love would be pure narcissism, literally loving one's reflection in a mirror. However, luckily, every human being is infinitesimally different from every other and these differences are part of the beauty of the scheme and to be discerned and cherished. So don't think I'm not sharply aware of a *beam* in my own eye as well as what seems to me a mote in my brother's! The only thing is that you haven't had much chance of seeing my beam (not having seen me in action where I'm, for the most part, deplorable) whereas your mote is probably more apparent to me in your written words than it would be anywhere else.

You'll say I'm still hedging—and so I am. I find it peculiarly hard to *say* just what is chilling me at the moment, though I *know* pretty well what it is. From the second letter you wrote me, it was quite apparent that you had already, in your own mind, put everything on a very personal basis between us. Whereas my first letter to you, knowing nothing whatever about you, was written entirely about *what you said* without much speculation as to *who you were*. You raised a number of points very near the surface of my mind just then and I simply went off like a gun without speculating as to who pulled the trigger. You wrote very much in the tone of an older person, taking care to point out that you were 'the safer and more respectful type of old gentleman' which should have put me on my guard! For, though deliberately 'safe' and far too 'respectful' as far as I'm concerned, 'old gentleman' is what you never can and never will be, dear Peter, if you live to be 99. And somehow, almost from the beginning, I found you implying that I was really in love with you but was too shy or too coquettish to say so. Remember your feeling had a long start over mine. You had already read my book and formed some idea of me as a human being whereas mine, being based on what I find of you in letters, miscellaneous writings, etc., ebbs and flows according as you present now this aspect, now that.

Please don't think I don't want our friendship to ripen into something so firm and strong that it will last the rest of our lives. If I didn't, I wouldn't be writing this letter. And I have enough indications that this is what you really want from many of your recent letters. All I say, as you so often have said yourself, is let us both be very much alert for self-deception. 'Platonic' love is very much more fertile soil for it than a simple sexual relationship. For whatever there is to be said against sexual relationships (apart from marriage) they certainly are a remarkably severe acid test and can reveal one's physical, moral and emotional shortcomings in the most vivid, if disconcerting, way. So, if you agree, let us exchange as much solid food as we can . . . but, when you spread the table, don't think I'm an unmannerly guest if I don't eat every single dish. I know that to anyone so generous as you this is hard. I am selfish (as you say you are too) and I have begun to learn from experience that genuine affection does try to give rather what the receiver needs than what the giver wants to give. Even generosity *can* be a subtle form of exhibitionism and self-assertion.

I won't bother about other tiny irritants . . . except for one which may be imaginary. In spite of all your annotations, I often get the feeling that you don't *read* my letters, or rather, that they recompose themselves in an entirely different form in your mind. Perhaps that is simply that you are busy when you write (as I am) and your memory plays you tricks. But so often I seem to have said something so loud and clear and weeks after you revert to the same point as if I'd never mentioned it. Or perhaps I say something and weeks later you bring it up with an air of revelation as of Moses producing an eleventh commandment. No doubt I do this too so call me a black kettle if I do!

But as to actual 'reading' one example will do. You wrote to me the other day: 'Why does Santayana call himself a convinced materialist?' In the letter I sent with the book I expressly wrote a postscript on what S. meant by being a materialist. I expect it's just because you're tired and overstrained, so be patient with my peevishness because I'm a little of both often.

And lastly . . . this will finish my scratching, which isn't wanton (as this cat's and other cats' often is) why do you keep telling me how intelligent you are? I think this means one of two things:
(a). you're a little doubtful as to whether you *are* intelligent;
(b). you suspect I'm not intelligent enough to perceive your intelligence.
My advice is (you've given me such quantities that I feel entitled to one modest admonition): 'In both cases, make an act of faith and forget it.'

I apologise about 'practice' and 'practise'. I *do* know the difference so it is not invincible ignorance but wanton carelessness.

You can now (if you've got so far) forget all that goes before and begin here.

About the obviously very exciting books you so sweetly offer to S. and L., may I wait a little longer before saying 'Yes' or 'No'? I can't tell you why I don't immediately jump at such a grand offer, especially as I covet the bird book myself, but it's something to do with You, Me and Them. Just for the moment, perhaps, I feel the Hopkinson family has been too much the receiver and too little the giver.

I have been reading Fr Tyrrell's letters and the first enthralling volume of the *Autobiography and Life** For one day I was completely obsessed by him. What a wonderful man he was and what an admirable writer. I am so glad you loved him. I want some day to hear from your own lips all that you can remember about him. I haven't felt so instantly and completely drawn to anyone since Keats. I find an echo of everything he thought, felt, feared, searched for in my own head, heart and experience. I admire this passionate strain-ing after truth in a man, on his own admission, adept in feigning; this devotion and self-sacrifice in a man so apt for hatred and violence. It is an amazing life, tragic and triumphant and inevitable as a Greek tragedy. I understand so well both this terror of committing oneself and terror of *not* committing oneself; the almost intolerable tension between the need for sincerity and the need for faith. Von Hügel, that great rock-bottomed old genius, solved the problem, but Tyrrell, with that extreme temperament, never could; always trying himself too hard and yet not quite having the courage to break a habit. The whole history of his relationship with the Jesuits is extraordinarily interesting and typical; the way he clings to what fundamentally could never suit his nature in spite of their quite sensible attempts to dislodge him in early years. He was, in a real sense, a martyr and I am sure every Catholic and the Church itself owes an immense and humble debt to him. And, though I find him personally far more attractive than von H. (for whom I have immense respect and affection) I think von H. was right and Tyrrell wrong in the long run. But I think von H. has much to answer for and atone for: it seems to me that he weighed too heavily on Tyrrell and, no doubt with the best intentions, exploited him in a way. It must have been difficult for him to assess the stresses and strains of a temperament so different from his own. But the story of the collision and interpenetration of these two remarkable men must be one of the only dramas on a grand scale in these rather meagre days. Much as I detest the Church's *methods* in excommunicating Tyrrell,

* See Appendix II.

I feel her decision was right and inevitable. Santayana, by the way, wrote a most illuminating and penetrating essay on Modernism and Christianity which I'd like to lend you some day. But we've both got enough to read and do for the moment. Don't bother about von H.'s *Letters*: I have them from the London Library. It was one of our many good 'rapports' that I should have hit on Huvelin's admirable sayings just as you had written to me quoting some of them.

As regards religion, dear Peter, have no fears about me. Doubts and revulsions are inevitable with my nature (you don't need the devil to account for that though I certainly don't deny his existence) but I think they will gradually become surface storms only. The inner conviction grows slowly but strongly, but, as you say and I instinctively feel, quiet and steady practiCe is my great standby. I begin to have what I never had in childhood, when we automatically went to Communion every day, a hunger for the Blessed Sacrament. And I begin to see dimly the connection between accepted suffering and internal peace, joy and light, the cross and the resurrection not successive, but simultaneous. I *understand* now words of St Bonaventure which I repeated automatically for years: 'Transfix me with the most joyous and healthful wound of Thy love.'

When I find this *exactness* in a saint, I do rejoice. My language-sensitiveness is often a hindrance, making me wince and quibble when something is put in feeble or exaggerated words but it also helps me when something is stated in a way I can appreciate. It was the sound of *Sero nimis te amavi* that printed it in my mind for twenty years. And so, until one has learnt to master one's 'fastidiousness', it seems to me a practical notion for a writer to stick to saints who happen to be verbal poets too. The others I salute with all respect, but don't *frequent*.

I sometimes think the surest indication that my grace was a genuine 'gift' was that it led me to Fr Hugh who is so exactly the holy man for my needs that, if I'd specified a director, he would be the ideal one. I rarely see him and only exchange a few words with him but each time I am more struck by his rightness for my particular nature, as well as for many people entirely different from me. He is very lenient with me, yet I know when the moment comes he will be firm and I have enough instinctive respect for him to try and obey him when he is. He sees that I need solid food, but not too much at a time, warns me against 'spiritual indigestion', yet calms my anxieties. I recognise in him a man sensitive to insults, with a hot temper tamed; often tempted to doubt and dryness, but so integrated by love and discipline that he radiates warmth, strength and the simplest, most gentle humour. You would love this man who sleeps on a plank bed and 'does other things of that sort', who is an excellent gardener and 'handy-man', is deeply interested in meta-physics and psychology, and enjoys a Disney film with the serious pleasure of a child. He is also admirable with children. After ten minutes' chat with Susan, he gave me an impression of her character which could not have been bettered by anyone who had known her for years. And I had given him no hints.

One discovers odd things at the beginning of one's spiritual life, doesn't one? I've always felt horror at the idea of a vocation. And I detest physical discomfort. Yet if ever I did become a nun (which I don't think is likely!) the only order I could think of joining would be not one of the teaching or contemplative ones but the Little Sisters of the Poor who go into working people's houses, scrub the floors, cook the dinners and wash the babies. And I loathe domestic work! But I love the poor, and that's an inheritance from my mother who was as flighty and frivolous as myself but who could do things for poor people which I wouldn't have had the strength to do. She was a woman who adored scents, pretty clothes, comforts of all kinds. Yet I remember her going day after day to sit in a filthy room with an old charwoman dying of cancer. And the poor loved her for being pretty and gay and never lecturing them or trying to improve them. Poor darling, she would have been so happy if I'd returned last year before she died. From a very vague Catholic she became a most sincere and fervent one, but she never reproached me, even implicitly, for my defection and never criticised my extraordinary goings-on but always sympathised and tried to understand. With my father, I always felt this impassable barrier between us, for he was a devout, but rigoristic man with no under-standing of people unlike himself. He centred everything on me, trying to force me into an exact replica of himself. I adored him, feared him and was never at ease with him. Remember this in my exaggerated fear of 'loving' authority as I will remember your un-happy experience with your mother when I see traces of 'what would happen if someone saw this?' in your letters.

Well, I had to work till one last night and am tired. B.B.C. is a hair-shirt, such an exacting old job full of tiresome details and difficulties, some due to war, some not—you're on edge the whole time. It's the same for everyone in my particular line there and we all get a bit frayed at the edges.

Thank you for understanding about not writing so often. As to postcards, wouldn't you feel worse if, owing to some accident, one didn't arrive? Is it too much to ask you (for I *might* forget to and

I'd really have to send one almost every day) to trust God that I'm there or not there? I promise someone shall tell you if I am hurt or killed. But truly, dear, I'm exposed only to minimum risks, much less than most of the 10,000,000 (is it?) other Londoners.

I must go to bed now and will pray for you as I always do. Your Madonna is very beautiful and I love her. No rationalising can be as beautiful as the Virgin pregnant with God. That is the one miracle I can and do believe in; I'm neutral about the others. I lit three candles for you to St Joseph last Sunday when, after much doubt and dryness the preceding week, the rigidity melted. I seem to have said only the nasty things tonight. God bless you and don't be troubled by my sharp tongue.

Tony.

8 February, 1941.

Dearest Peter (I'm so happy to write it with my whole heart again),

Thank you so much for your last letter. I hope you will get this soon after mine of last night. Yours shows so much understanding that most of mine will now seem unnecessary. And I hope you'll forgive anything that I put too cruelly or harshly. Everything is now not only 'right' again but *better than before* and I feel as much relieved as when yesterday, after days of murky, colourless weather, there was suddenly a high, clear blue sky again and the sun shone on the melting snow. I love 'double weather' like that— the flowers and snow of the landscape of the Della Francesca nativity. This is one of my very favourite pictures—with its angels who have neither wings nor haloes and who are yet so obviously beings from another world.

Thank you so much for the lovely coloured bird prints which I shall have much joy in sending to S. and L. Lyndall will be primarily interested in the bird, Susan in the technique of the wood-cut. She is, I think, gifted for drawing and one of the few things she's naturally humble about is seeing how much better other people's work is than her own. She does very good drawings and lino-cuts sometimes (chiefly horses, of course!) but usually destroys them in a critical mood. Unlike me, she's very good with her hands and has been ever since she was tiny. I always enjoy watching her handle things. How I wish you two could meet. I think you would instinctively take to each other, and you'd be very good for her. What I should love—though it doesn't at present seem practicable— would be to bring both the children to Portmeirion for a few days at Easter or in the summer. Maybe there's some cheap pub or cottage or farm not too far from you where we could stay, the big fancy hotel would be too expensive. The children are both handy on a farm and can muck out stables, clean pigstyes, look after chickens and so on and are never happier than when doing so. Biggest BUT is that officially I get no leave from B.B.C. (except one and a half days a week) till 1942. Smaller 'but' is money, but I think I could manage that somehow. But wouldn't it be nice? I so long to see you and talk to you, to show you my children, and to walk with you to church and go to Mass and Communion with you.

Thank you very much, too, for lending me your precious *Nova et Vetera*.* I will take the greatest care of it. I can see it is a rich and wonderful book and I shall find a great deal for me in it. I shall begin with the ones you have marked.

I got your Gill autobiography today and am skimming it rapidly before sending it on to you. It is very interesting and I think you'll agree with a good many of his remarks about that perplexing old subject of sex. I may seem to harp on it too much, or rather on the Church's teaching about it as far as I have understood it. But I do feel there is a real need for some clarifying and constructive work on this to be done by our revered instructors. I have met so many people who have found this a very real obstacle either to entering the Church or remaining in it. Catholics in Latin countries seem to manage to remain Catholics while allowing themselves considerable latitude. But the English, with their puritanism and conscientiousness, don't so easily reconcile discrepancies between belief and practice. The usual story seems to be this. A devout young man or woman falls in love and discovers himself or herself to be a sexual creature. If for some reason, money or anything else, they can't marry, they find continence an unnatural strain. Or if they can marry, they can't face the alternative of unlimited children (and, if you know what it costs in the modern world to support even two children modestly, it's not surprising) or almost total abstinence. They feel they can't honestly go to Confession because they can't wholeheartedly make a resolution to avoid this particular 'sin' of extra-marital relations or using contraceptives. And so they drift away from the sacraments and eventually away from the Church. And often it is the more honest and scrupulous who do this. The

* One of Fr Tyrrell's early books, passed by the ecclesiastical censors, its sub-title is 'Informal Meditations for Times of Spiritual Dryness'.

others commit the 'sins' but find some way of squaring their consciences. I'm not talking of my own case, but of very many personally known to me. True, they may return to the Church in later life when the problem has ceased to be a pressing one. But it means that many of their best years have been spent away from it.

This doesn't mean I'm defending promiscuity, which, in any case, is often as pathological as frigidity or impotence. But promiscuity brings its own retribution and, incidentally, it's much easier to 'repent' sincerely between casual affairs than in the course of a serious one. I think the Church's view of marriage is certainly good and right (with slight hesitation about dogmatic forbidding of contraceptives) but wonder if she couldn't modify her rigour a trifle in the case of people unable to marry or unsuited to marriage, which is a vocation. As a woman, I know it is much easier for us to be 'chaste' than it is for a man (as a general rule) but it is very difficult for a woman to refuse a man she loves something that obviously means so much to him. I agree that there is a tremendous amount of truth and sense in what the Church teaches about sexual behaviour but I can't help feeling a little might be left to individual conscience. Anyone whose conscience is at all sensitive knows perfectly well when they have abused sex, in marriage or out of it. Surely there might be some loophole for reinterpretation? I see the extreme difficulty of legislating about this and the self-deceptions and abuses that might result if the Church took a more lenient view. But the rigorous view involves abuses too, as well as great misery in some cases.

I don't, do I, suggest that this in any way alters our own free decision for ourselves about 'chastity'? Because I'm as firm as you are on that. I feel as you do that for us it would be a sin . . . and I think I'd feel it as much, even if we weren't both Catholics. You have a wife whom you love and who loves you and I've more respect for marriage than you might suppose from my past life.

This is my last outburst on the subject. It was glancing at Gill's book (fervent Catholic as he was, he saw the difficulty clearly) that brought it sharply to my mind. You see I feel you and I mustn't be smug just because we've solved our problem and come to a conclusion. Think of all the young people struggling in the net which we couldn't keep out of when we were young. We're expecting them to be much stronger than we were and I feel we're the last people to preach to them. But . . . I admit there's a danger of another sort of 'patronage' here—a presumption that they can't do better than we can ! And how easily one spoils things by softening and diluting them. All feeble 'pseudo-art' comes from that. So maybe the Church

85

is right in her *teaching*. But—I cling to this—she must change her *approach* if she's to be effective. People do heroic things for positive, not negative reasons.

Do you know Donne's 'Batter my heart, three-personed God'? If so, don't you think it one of the greatest religious poems ever written? 'Nor ever chaste, unless you ravish me' is the best statement of *that* case, surely? All his 'Divine Poems' are wonderful themes for meditation. For some reason, I prefer male writers on religion to female ones. It is a profound truth that makes Eve the *Channel* of the fall and the Church's defects may be due to her femaleness. A woman *is* more corruptible, I believe, than a man because of the slower rhythm of her life, as still water breeds scum. And haven't you often noticed, in men, that it is their female side that betrays and corrupts them? It is not for nothing that in no religion is God imagined as female.

Here, if you don't know it, is something I love from Jeremy Taylor:

'We look after white and red and the meaner beauties of the night; we are passionate after rings and seals and enraged at the breaking of a crystal; having no love for anything but strange flesh and heaps of money and popular noises. And yet we are a huge way off from the kingdom of God whose excellencies, whose designs, whose ends, whose constitutions are spiritual and holy and separate and sublime and perfect.'

Eric taught me that one.

My dear, when you say you need my love, I capitulate entirely. I do forget you have your own difficulties and discouragements. Sometimes (perhaps for my benefit) you seem to present such a united front that you deceive me! I know very well you have a nature as difficult to harmonise as mine. But sometimes I have thought you had only achieved a surface harmony, over-simplified. I see now this isn't so. Oh, if you knew how strongly and warmly I feel towards you when you write me such an honest, understanding and yet delicately tender letter as your last.

If I'm any use to you, I'm proud and happy. You help *me* very much, and most of all when you make an effort to hold back a little and give me a freer rein.

I love it so much when we are in harmony and agreement. And we can make a good counterpoint with our differences. Not with the discords in our own natures, weaknesses and vices of various kinds, but our genuine *differences*. I can admire your mastery of physical things and the warm-hearted practical way you try and help other people. I'm no good in groups; I'm only useful to individuals. You are quick and good in debating; I'm dumb and confused and see things more clearly in silence than in talk. Whether we like it or not, we both produce an effect on other people. People of all sorts and conditions respond to your charm. I am, and always have been, violently loved or violently hated (often both by the same person), violently admired or violently despised. I am perhaps subtler, able to hold more things in suspension at the same time. If I had a 'patron bird' it would be the falcon. As an artist I would like to balance and hover for a long time and then fall dead on the prey. Anything connected with falconry has an extraordinary fascination for me. I love Francis Thompson's image of the soul as God's falcon, free, but stooping to the lure at the Divine Falconer's whistle. That is what I would like to be, willing to accept the hood and the jesses and only flying and striking at the Master's word. Sometimes I think there is no better image of the soul than the tamed falcon. I would like to write a poem about it one day. The training of the falcon is like God's breaking-in of the soul: it is starved and kept in darkness till it will feed only from its master. And falcons sulk and sicken, sometimes have to be allowed to return to their natural life for a season and then be lured back. And there is a whole mysterious love language the falconer uses to his bird. I like to think of you and me as potentially the hound and the falcon of the heavenly huntsman. It has just struck me that the hound and the falcon are good images of von Hügel and Tyrrell. But von H. is an old, questing bloodhound, following every scent and you're something quicker and lighter—a greyhound perhaps.

When you see Orion striding across the sky, think of the heavenly huntsman. I wish someone could make us a seal with the hound and the falcon. The hound has more trouble with the flesh, the falcon with the devil!

Good night, my very, very, very dear and God bless you. I can't do without you, however much I rebel and scratch, for there's not a soul in the world to whom I can say the things I say to you.

With love from

Tony.

My dear Peter,

This short note must, I'm afraid, be the last for several days. I go to Bristol on a job tomorrow for a day or two; then I want to dig into my *Horizon* story which will take all my spare time apart from B.B.C. I know you say 'don't answer' in your letters, but you always raise some point on which you need or provoke an answer.

My domestic arrangements are very simple. I don't live alone and I don't live with a 'sound, intelligent woman' whatever that may be. Since I can't afford a flat and a resident housekeeper as I used to in the good old days of 1939, I have two rooms in the house of a man whom I've known for twelve years or so. It suits us perfectly as neither of us wants to be quite alone (no one does in the blitz) and yet, both having cat-like natures, we like to have plenty of privacy. So, as a rule, we only meet at mealtimes. His name is Ian Black and he's an expert on economics and on everything to do with politics and finance in France. We share the kittens and the comfort of Miss Conway, our Irish charwoman who is a peach, a pearl and a poppet. Ian and I, having both been married three times, find this sort of bachelor-spinster ménage suits us very well. As to your 'resident or visiting lover' line, if it's a joke, it's cheap, and if it's serious, it's vile. That is the kind of thing in you (like your suggestion of our writing a novel in letters about our friendship) that makes me arch my back sky-high and *spit*.

As to all this 'modern' business. I quite agree it is very hard for people of two different generations to use the same language and see eye to eye. I often forget the difference. But it is true that, if my father were still alive, he would be only three years older than you are.

But one thing older people tend to forget is how quickly a fashion changes. What was 'modern' in the 1920s is quite out of date in the 1930s. I think you're still judging by the revolt of the 1920s against everything. I assure you that since 1935 or so, those very same people have all been madly hunting for 'frames', pursuing communism, buddhism, fascism, quakerism, etc., etc. And the new young people aren't like my lot at all. So be careful that you're not flogging a dead horse.

I remember our parish priest in the country in 1916 inveighing fiercely against the wicked women of London in their shameless hobble-skirts. As the wicked women had abandoned hobble-skirts at least four years before, it rather missed its mark.

Good-bye for the time being and God bless you. I can't write a story without concentrating and I've been concentrating for four months on *you*. So have a heart and give the work a chance.

Much love,

Tony,

12 February, 1941.

Dearest Peter,

I was rather snappish in my last one and I'm sorry. My annoyance was quite a lot due to my own imagination. But every now and then I do feel a real need for a breathing space. It doesn't mean I've stopped being fond of anyone if occasionally I need time to myself. And anything my demon can interpret as nagging or 'getting at' me in any way always pulls the trigger. You must remember my whole day is spent among people and I hardly have a minute to read, except in buses and crowded restaurants and snack-bars or time to think, let alone to work, except in the evenings when I'm tired anyway. And I've got a good deal to think about just now. I do get a bit tired and when I'm tired I get (not more irritable for I shall be irritable all my life) less self-controlled. And it's really a sign of friendship very often when I lose my temper with someone. I'm studiously polite to those to whom I am indifferent. There are so many nagging jobs to be done apart from the B.B.C. that I sometimes feel as if I'm being pricked to death with pins. You've no idea what a practical convenience a husband is when it comes to dealing with schools, insurances, income tax and all the other nightmares! So with you I like to be able to expand as one does in talk rather than be incessantly answering questions and discussing small points. Do you see?

Your letter was so sweet and I didn't feel you were piqued but hurt and that I am sorry for. There's no question of my 'giving you leave' to write to me. Of course you must write as much as you like. Only I feel a beast if I don't answer at once. If I could be sure you really didn't mind this, then I could enjoy your letters without feeling guilty.

I am still deep in Tyrrell and have nearly finished Vol. II of the *Autobiography and Life*. It is a terrible story. I can't say how much I love that man, in spite of all the contradictions in his nature. It confirms all my worst misgivings about ecclesiastical authorities and does make one wonder a little whether the old bottles will hold new wine. If the Church still has a living seed in her—and there seems a reasonable hope that she has (and Tyrrell and his friends certainly helped to make it germinate if one *thinks* one notices a shoot or two) —thanks be to God. If not, one will probably go down with the old ship since there isn't another to embark on. She has hold of enough eternal truths and she embodies enough of them in her life —in the sacraments and the liturgy—to make it possible to avert one's ears when the screams of aggressors and oppressed become too deafening. She has enough bread, if she'd unlock the cupboard, not to put us off with stones. The life of a *pratiquant* is absolutely necessary to me, as I have long suspected it was. And her great truths are manifest in too many departments of life not to be accepted. But one can only hope that some day they can be re-stated and disentangled from their rigid crust and shorn of their excrescences and *non-sequiturs*. I do pray for the Church, for wise and holy rulers and for living and holy people in every stratum of her society. Surely we want more and more people to be Catholics not from fear or habit but from unforced conviction? Is it a heresy to wish that the rulers were not inevitably fixed for all time in Rome and that they were a slightly more cosmopolitan body? Every Englishman has a dash of the Protestant (and the Nonconformist) and instinctively dislikes 'ecclesiasticism'. Her rigidity has preserved her in the past but surely the time has come for a little flexibility; for more understanding, more charity, more humility and less persecution mania. Surely she must know people's needs, how desperately they are groping for some light, how much their very criticisms show that religion is once more becoming a living question instead of a dead one? I don't mind for myself because I can find all I want in the old frame, but I could never even attempt to convince any newcomer. The strongest indictment, not of herself, but her methods as the onlooker sees them, is in Tyrrell's tremendous indictment of the Jesuits in the long letter to Fr Martin. However, all my intense repugnance to that side of her doesn't destroy my faith in God or Christ or the Holy Ghost and I truly hope that in our lifetime she may give again a clear sign that she is the Church Christ founded.

What happened to Maude Petre?* I presume she is dead. Did she die in or out of the Church? I have a great admiration for her from what I can see in her writing; she seems to have an exceedingly powerful, solid and orderly mind. I should very much like to meet Gwendolen Greene† one day, for quite different reasons. But I would

* See Appendix IV.
† Baron von Hügel's niece.

probably have been able to make more contact with Miss Petre, just as Tyrrell would have more personal appeal for me than von Hügel. His *Mystical Element* breaks my teeth with its fearfully laborious, craggy and parenthetic style, due, I suppose, to his thinking in German. Unless he artfully made it unreadable so that the Holy Office would never have time to wade through it and pick out the heresies. Simply as a writer, Tyrrell must be about the best pamphleteer since Swift? Where can one get the dozens of articles mentioned in Vol. II? There is nothing in the London Library but the autobiography and some letters. Surely there are other works still in print?

Forgive this dry letter, full of questions. I am very much interested in all these recent controversies and developments of which I knew nothing. I go carefully and don't rush to wild conclusions but they make the implications of this religion so much more real and living to me after being fed in childhood on fifth-rate 'manuals'. I continue to read and love the *Imitation* and can swallow a good many 'hard sayings' if I don't get nervous contractions of the throat.

I'm afraid—talking of books—that you'll never really like anything I write except *Frost* but you must just be noble and patient and believe I'm doing the best I can according to intermittent lights.

Don't think, dear Peter, you can lose my friendship. I'm a really tough rock-bottomed friend, however rough my tongue and a much better friend than lover. The few people with whom I have had an intense friendship know that it lasts. Some of them are already dead —one was almost certainly shot by the Nazis last summer as a traitor—two are in America and you and the one or two others of a very mixed bunch of all ages and both sexes are still, thank heaven, over here. But I would like to SEE you and talk to you. God bless you, and go on putting up with me.

Your loving sour-puss,
Tony.

12 February, 1941.

Peter dear,
    I feel the other letter you'll get by the same post will seem too dry in the present circumstances, so just before going to bed here is a tiny postscript to say how generous your letters were after my

long outburst, and how much more *real* and lovable they made you for me.

I've been reading old notebooks of mine—I've kept them since 1921 and marking how many passages refer to religion—surprisingly many. I once made (I had forgotten) a rough forecast of what I thought my life would be, especially in relation to religion and what I thought my vocation might be. I wrote it when I was 22 and it has turned out oddly accurate in result though of course I didn't know clearly the extraordinary things that would happen to me. I would like some day, if I ever, ever have TIME, to make enough extracts to show you the sequence of nearly twenty years of my search for God and God's search for me. I found in the notebook two wonderful things of St Augustine that I had forgotten. 'Manducans Manducatur' and 'Who touch thee, burn for thy peace'. I have been reading a little of St John of the Cross lately at Fr Hugh's suggestion. There is a wonderful and terrible passage in the *Dark Night* where the soul seems to disintegrate and to be swallowed up by a great beast. I know the psychological equivalent. This 'dark night' of St John's is obviously only the experience of the very high and purified soul, but it is things like that that bring home to one vividly the intense reality of the spiritual life lived by a spiritual genius. Nothing ever gave me more strongly the feeling that there *is* another world with tremendous and dangerous laws of its own . . . and the absolute necessity of fitting oneself, very carefully and not presuming beyond one's powers, for living in another *element*. The doctrine of purgatory alone marks the Catholic Church as *inspired* as opposed to any other Christian body. None of us likes to dwell on the doctrine of hell and yet there is, to us, some fearful inevitability in it. One can only say 'Hell exists' and hope that only spirits fallen from a greater height than any poor entangled, muddled, blind human being inhabit it.

One small physical fact interested me. You know how often one is told that saints are raised above the ground in thinking or speaking of God. One accepts it with a grain of salt, perhaps. But in an excellent article on Ellen Terry, Virginia Woolf records how, when Ellen was really absorbed in a part she loved, she actually became so light that a boy could easily lift her.

I felt that passion, madness and all the emotional states can be thought of as transcripts of the spiritual life but that, though psychopathological states can be shown to be parallel with many of the things recorded by and of the saints, you cannot explain the effect by the apparent cause and the result in the outside world *always* differentiates the true saint from the neurotic 'case'. Freud's investigations into the actual workings of human psychology (his facts are most patiently observed and he puts forward his hypotheses in the most provisional and tentative way) back up doctrines which seem to many to be mere myths, such as the fall of man particularly, in the most astonishing way. It is not his province to surmise whether or not religion is 'true' but he says very emphatically that religion is the most important of human creations and activities. It seems to me that the 'natural' explanation and the 'supernatural' one are each true in their own province and run parallel. I am sure that, properly understood, there can be no conflict between 'natural' and 'supernatural'. If one thinks of the supernatural as another dimension, having a relation to the dimensions we know, but transcending them, it all seems more apprehensible, though more mysterious than the old images of 'above' and 'below'.

I am sure that, the more the physical world is explored, the better and truer images of the other world it will give us. More than images it cannot give. I feel every spiritual truth is embedded in the Church but that it can only be intuited and not explained. Dogmas and rules of conduct are graphs of this heavenly mathematics but people tend to take the diagram for the thing itself—the commonest of all philosophical errors and one from which theologians are certainly not immune. We need a new St Thomas to restate our philosophy in relation to our present physics (and that again would only be a diagram, but a contemporary one).

Tyrrell surely was an angel of light and his sins only human ones. For me he sheds so much more light and clarity than darkness and confusion. His 'sins' all seem to me physical and psychological and never spiritual. 'And thine own heart a sword shall pierce that out of many hearts thoughts may be revealed.' He was a great spirit but not a saint. God had mercy on him and killed him quickly when he had done his work and could have endured no more. For the rest, passive suffering without the agonies of choice and doubt . . . and *security* at last. Dante should have written of Tyrrell in purgatory.

Whenever I start, I always get back to Tyrrell. You will forgive me for you loved him so much yourself.

I have, haven't I, made it clear to you how much I value you, dear Peter? If I haven't, you must make it clear to yourself!

Very much love,

Tony.

Dearest Peter,

You do make me feel a beast. You have been so generous about all this. It isn't that I don't want to write or to have letters, but just that I have got to go underground, as it were, for a bit. I don't know the explanation myself but it is something stronger than myself and sometimes it irks and even frightens me. I think it is really that it means a fairly exhausting effort to adapt myself to a new interior life and if a person can be dazzled by darkness, I am that person. I think it is possible that I have some faint, faint inkling of what the mystical life means and as you know, one has got to go carefully and find one's right road. I am terribly shy with Fr Hugh and only see him for odd minutes and have never really spoken much to him about myself, for, as you can see, it is not easy and there are the nervous strains set up by the track of the beast in my mind and these have to be taken into consideration. I don't want to tangle those threads again. I must find some method of living the spiritual life which is in accordance with my nature. It is not difficulties I fear, but strains and confusions. It is vital to attempt something within one's own range and capabilities and not to force oneself into some alien path, however many shining beacons there may be along it. Huvelin's sayings fit me better than anything I have found so far, but they are only fragments. And von Hügel was scholar, critic, philosopher and interpreter, i.e., working on material extraneous to himself, whereas a writer, pure and simple, uses *internal* material. This creates quite a different problem and a tricky one. It is trickier than for a painter or a musician since writing is both more personal and produces more immediate effects on others.

To deny what I have laboriously found out as a human being, to present experiences only with an eye to their being edifying or at least 'safe' seems to me a betrayal of one's function as an artist. And I don't feel strong enough to sacrifice that whole side which would be plucking out my eye and my instinct says it isn't right for me. But it is a very, very hard problem.

Thank you so much for sending me the Tyrrell books. *Hard Sayings* produces a curiously unpleasant effect on me; it seems somehow false, as if the man were saying what he felt he ought to say rather than what he deeply experienced. Hence I find it *un*nourishing. And that slightly syrupy, flowery style is immensely inferior to the admirable clear, nervous style of the later and I suppose 'suspect' works.

As to the necessity for the hatred of the natural world, this is most unequivocally and repeatedly stated in St John of the Cross in his own words, so your argument of 'hagiographers' does not apply. So it is in almost every saint's writing I have ever read. It may be a violent metaphor but they always talk as if they meant it literally. And to what other end is deliberate *violation* of the senses as opposed to *restraint* directed? There is something so profoundly antipathetic to me in all this that I cannot help feeling many of these insistences are morbid, even pathological.

Necessity for restraint, incessant vigilance, mortification and re-direction of one's natural impulses, love of created things, whether plants, people or works of art, *sub specie aeternitatis* and *in* God instead of violently, adhesively and possessively—all this seems to be not only necessary but natural and wholesome. This discipline is equally necessary in trying to *live* any kind of life of the spirit, in art or philosophy, as well as in religion.

Since Christ Himself told us to love our neighbour it seems to me a kind of perversion or spiritual pride to try and be more Christlike than Christ. Of course by a paradox, if you take the proviso 'as yourself' and you aim at hating yourself, it will logically follow that you will aim at hating your neighbour. However this seems to me the logic of hell, not of heaven. Luckily it isn't borne out in the *practice* of the saints. But from their own words you would sometimes suspect that they regarded it as a failure, not a success!

I am sure there is an answer, otherwise to live by a sane, disciplined natural philosophy would be better than to attempt to live by religion. But here, for once, I part company with Eric and feel a conviction which I cannot explain that religion is potentially the deeper, richer and more inclusive way. I feel equally strongly that there *is* a supernatural world and that it is *related* to the natural world and that neither *contradicts* the other, any more than a three-dimensional world contradicts a two-dimensional one. But I can see that the writings of the saints may be interpreted as an attempt to render three dimensions in two and are therefore confusing. The words of Christ, interpreted in the Church's life *as lived*, seem to me the only bridge that miraculously spans this abyss. One has to remember the saints are specialists, heavenly monsters as it were, each exemplifying some particular type of attainable spiritual life, whereas Christ exemplifies them all and is accessible to the meanest as well as the highest. I suspect the saints are highly explosive material and only to be used 'under doctor's orders'.

Thank you very much for the lovely bird and flower books. It was naughty of you to send them, but the whole family will very much appreciate them, especially Mamma, for we have always longed for some good bird books. So I scold you mildly and thank you strongly!

Don't let yourself get fretted and feverish because of a sort of transition I'm going through. It won't affect *us* one bit except for the better—do believe that.

God bless you and make you happy. I pray for you every day, morning and night.

I've just had a new F. *in* M. letter from a girl of 19—an Anglican. How A. is going to answer THAT I don't know. However, luckily this didn't arrive before my reversion so I can tell her I have reverted! Otherwise, having been strongly attracted to Catholicism, she has been slightly shaken by reading me and Bernanos. Bernanos is still a Catholic, I presume? And do tell me if M. Petre died one, if she is dead. It's a sign of these extraordinary times that, if one reads anyone good, one always fears they've either renounced the Church or been condemned by it.

By exquisite irony, having cleared a space for evening work by ruthlessly shouldering away my dear Peter, Ian Black promptly receives a knock-out blow from the outside world with the result that for four evenings I have had to sit up late trying to soothe him, for he was in an awful state of nervous depression and it would have been too cruel to leave him absolutely alone to it.

Very much love,

Tony,

22 February, 1941.

Dearest Peter,

Your letter was so good in every way and raises many, many things I'd like to talk about. But I daren't even look at it tonight. I'm very tired and have to go to Bristol for three days tomorrow on a trying job. At the moment, I can only cling on to 'faith' by my teeth; once I start raising even one question, it leads to an endless chain. So I feel it wiser not to let myself be drawn into any argument, discussion or speculation, however fascinating. In spite of all the things one must admit in Tyrrell, his violence, duality, almost pathological rebelliousness and the unconscious equation of himself with Christ at the end (there is certainly some resemblance between him and Lawrence, as you say) I feel that he had got on to something true and fundamental. I have been trying to read St Thomas. It seems to me all verbiage . . . a wonderful but entirely artificial construction. It is obvious he cannot be read in extracts; you must be trained in the language. I am sure I must simply go quietly and practise, leaving aside all the irreconcilable and puzzling facts and discrepancies, and try to get on with my own job. Once I begin to torment myself with questions, the old beast begins to stir in his sleep.

It was a relief to spend an afternoon among smoke-huts and stirrup pumps, learning how to put out fires. At least I couldn't read, write or think while I was doing it!

Ian's book A *Friend of France* is very interesting. Its appearance next month and his new job will comfort him a lot. I am trying hard to get you Tom's two lovely stories but they're sold out. Tom *is* a writer though he only brings it off every now and again. He's always competent but that's a different thing. But when he can use his odd, special gift, he's really rare.

There's a million miles between competence and that other thing, but I think only writers notice it and maybe it's a good thing. But what excitement we get when we find it anywhere, in any language! I expect you feel the same about printing.

You know your letters get better and better. I believe it stimulates you to be scratched now and then! Now I feel you write me the truth, not what you feel you ought to say or what you think I'd like to hear. And you'll never, never find me *unresponsive* to that even if I don't *answer*.

Bless you and pray for my silly old mind to disentangle itself a bit. There's some grit in the works somewhere.

Tony.

28 February, 1941.

Dearest Peter,

I feel such a brute not to answer your letters which gave me so much joy. But I just can't yet. I am tired to the marrow of my bones and must sleep. Bristol was tiring; sleepless nights, etc. Poor I. B. is still in extreme distress and I have to do all I can in the way of sitting up with him late and listening and trying to smooth things out a little for him. I really am terribly sorry for him for he

97

has had a crushing blow and a real shock and, until his job comes off to take his mind off it, he won't recover any resilience. He is really very brave about it but he's not broken in to unhappiness and is a sensitive, introspective man who can't easily shake it off. And so you must forgive me; I've just got no extra vitality at the moment. Tomorrow I have to dash down to Salisbury to see Susan; I'll take her the lovely bird books.

I am so sorry about your 'crash', perhaps not altogether surprised. You must learn to go carefully, my dear, and be a snail and draw in your horns when the nerve ends begin to jangle. Then one recovers one's resilience quickly. This War Weapons thing sounds a brute to handle: good of you to let yourself in for it but I know the strain that sort of thing involves. I hope you are better again now. Don't, don't fret about me or my problems; allow yourself to feel perfectly calm, happy and secure about me. I feel one shouldn't feverishly clutch one's faith but simply, quietly immerse oneself in it and not mind if the sea closes over one's head. The mysteries are so profound that I think the only thing is to go into them without a torch and not even force one's eyes into trying to see. I think both of us must be content to be in doubts and uncertainties and accept them. We both have restless and practical minds, excellent for certain purposes, but the whole art of life is to use the right tools for the right objects. So, my dear, for the moment, quietness, blankness even, and you'll find yourself refreshed. I believe, if one only knew it, there is a way to sleep in God. The older I get, the more I see reason as a clearing-house and not as a driving force. The springs of life and action are much deeper than reason. I believe one must never force oneself actively, only negatively. Force will clean the windows but it won't make the sun rise. I am sure this is the real meaning of dying to oneself; not really alarming unless one clings to oneself in one's idea of oneself as the most precious thing there is. Even as regards our two selves, don't you find that by 'purging' and 'renouncing' you have truly found something much better than a romantic dream? Two people are never more united than in the contemplation of something loved outside themselves.

Very, very much love,
Tony.

Dearest Peter,

I hope you're better again. I've managed to get normal and rested again with a couple of good nights. On Saturday I dashed up to see young Sue at Salisbury and inadvertently stole your letter to her (which letter gave her immense pleasure) so that, though she has begun one to you, I shouldn't expect it much before Easter. I took her the Coward bird books and the animal book: she is simply delighted with them. Her Lent resolutions (her own idea!) are (1) only one sweet a day, (2) say her prayers *every* night, (3) put her hot water-bottle in the bed of a chillier child. Imposing, don't you think? It was lovely to see her, though we could only snatch two and a half hours to shop, look at the cathedral and eat a lot of buns. She nearly always destroys her drawings. Woodcuts much admired and treasured. I asked her what was the craze in her house this term. Last one was spiritualism! Now it's 'reincarnation and all that'! She says it will be much easier to write to you now she's had a letter from you.

I'm sure St Thomas is a G.O.M. But it's no good in snippets. The premisses I suspect are the main trouble. Spinoza rears the same sort of edifice but takes care to define exactly what he means by each term. No doubt St Thomas does too in any good edition.

I would like to read Tyrrell's *Lex Orandi* for I feel from some hints in the *Autobiography* that it would be illuminating. My own instinct at the moment is that the Catholic religion is a life to be lived, not a theory to be debated about. The hard question of 'literal truth' and 'symbolism' must come up but I am sure there is an answer. I feel there must be truths which are true in the spiritual sphere but which cannot be exactly correlated with the 'truths' of ordinary knowledge and that much misery and self-torture has arisen from a confusion between the functions of the two. It seems to me one must accept, though not too hastily, such things as seem true in ordinary spheres and trust that they can eventually be reconciled with the spiritual truths. It would not, for me and for many other people, in any way affect the value of the Catholic faith if the whole of Catholic theology turned out to be a symbolic rendering of spiritual truths. The oldest of all philosophical errors is the confusion of the *expression of a thing* with the thing itself. And I am convinced that the sphere of religion is something fundamentally apart from philosophy, science, ethics and sociology though it has relations with them all.

I cling to the faith because it is old, organised, tested and my natural language. I do not believe in artificial syntheses or in an entirely private devotion. But I think one must be content to hold things in suspension and not be alarmed by the irreconcilables. If one tries to be honest in all the other spheres—and humble too— and goes on practising dumbly, I think one will get as much light as one needs from day to day. As long as one is always prepared to accept what *is* as opposed to what one would *like to be*, I think one can't go too far astray. This is the 'scientific attitude' and one much more important to human beings than any *finding* of science. The new age of the Church may be the age of the Holy Ghost which has not yet begun and one can only wait patiently, not denying any of the corruptions and anomalies until this new awakening (the thing that Tyrrell hoped for) comes, even if we don't live to see it. Even if there were no heaven and no hell, I still feel it would be worth while accepting the Catholic routine and discipline. But these are personal feelings which are probably exceedingly unorthodox and, even if they groped in the right direction, would not probably make the Church any more acceptable to those who are neither broken in to it nor attracted to it.

For the deliberate falsification and misrepresentation which one too often finds in Catholic 'apologetics' I can find no excuse. It may be due to ignorance (in which case they should go away and make some inquiries) or more likely to a mistaken zeal for propaganda. But if the Church claims to be the possessor of truth, she should fight with the weapons of truth. I don't say there aren't values more important to human beings than truth for there obviously are. A man might know all the truth that human beings are capable of knowing and yet be unable to *live* as successfully as someone crammed with the most fantastic notions about the nature of things. But one must keep one's categories separate and when one is talking about facts one shouldn't deliberately falsify them. It can't be only due to the machinations of the devil and the perversity of men that the Church has such a reputation for hypocrisy, sophistry and distortion of facts. But I can't help feeling she wastes too much time on argument and not enough in putting before the world her real and deep message, never more needed than now.

Yes, I would like very much to meet Michael de la Bedoyère. I don't know any Catholics in London but Fr Hugh, and I only see him for about ten minutes once a fortnight—it is impossible to discuss 'secular' questions with him..

Please don't worry about me and your attitude to me. That's all clear and good now. Of course I was a little 'in love' with you but I do know how easily that leads to a dream which vanishes in a maze of illusions and mutual reproaches. One loses one's true imagination and feeling by drifting on in that. I do wish we could talk: even letters become unsatisfactory when there is so much to say.

Very much love,

Tony.

I hope you're working well but not too hard. I plough on like a snail with my story. But I've always loathed the *act* of writing.

Dearest Peter,

It was so nice to find a blue envelope by my plate again this morning. I am so relieved that you are better. You *are* getting sensible!

I am getting sensible too. I have quite rested myself and creep quietly along with the story, trying not to be too discouraged at the impossibility of trying to fit 20,000 words into 8,000. It may be a physical impossibility, but anyway it is good to have a shot at it and to try and write a little steadily every day, however much loathing and despair I feel.

I find that the best way to deal with doubts and perplexities is to concentrate on the positive side, on whatever really helps and nourishes and does not cause any mental or moral irritation, viz. Holy Communion, the gospel, the psalms and the *Imitation*. I find Communion is becoming a real necessity to me in a way that it never was before. I feel better and calmer all day if I go and the effort of getting up an hour earlier doesn't make me tired. I don't by any means, or even often, feel 'sensible devotion' but I do feel literally as if I had been fed and strengthened. The sacraments seem to me the strongest of all supports to the Church's claims.

I have got hold of an interesting book by Abbot Vonier *The Human Soul*, which is a simple exposé of St Thomas. By some odd chance it was in Ian Black's library. I am trying to read it humbly, checking the impertinent questions. As tomorrow is St Thomas' feast, I think I will go to Mass and ask the saint to clear up my muddled old mind! Obviously one can't neglect the intellectual side of one's faith entirely and I am asked too many questions by interested and sceptical people to be able always to fall back on 'inner conviction' as my only justification. If, on sifting out real difficulties or misunderstandings, I make a list of them, do you think Fr D'Arcy or one of his trained athletes could find time to give short answers? I don't like to bother these busy people but I know no one competent.

Fr Hugh can tell me all I need about one's own spiritual life but he admitted to me quite frankly yesterday that he had no idea people suffered from the kind of doubts I had and had never himself, except for odd seconds, had any of that kind. I told him I thought a great many other people had them nowadays and he said 'it was quite an education for him!' He said he would bring up some of my queer questions at recreation. He said he couldn't answer them but I told him that he and his life were the best answer. I do think for oneself 'foi de charbonnier' is the best but, as one doesn't always move among charbonniers, one needs another line of defence. I told him God the Father was my great stumbling block which surprised him but did not seem to distress him. He certainly surprised me by saying he did not feel at all worried about my soul though he did about some souls. As he probably knows about such things, I accept it. I always feel as small as a pin's head when he says things like that—maybe that's why he does it!

Ian continues to alternate between extreme depression and a kind of delirium. It is rather touching the interest he takes in my return, as having happened under his roof, and he assures me the difference it has made to me is quite astonishing. I can't help feeling that this is an amiable exaggeration for I seem to myself just as moody, irritable, etc., as ever!

I am hoping to meet Bernanos some day. If Ian gets his job, he will be working with Bernanos (this is hush-hush).

There is a very good essay of Tyrrell's in Hard Sayings—the one on 'Discouragement'.

I forget if I said I would like to meet Bedoyère if it's possible.

Dearest Peter, don't send Sue engraving tools yet, please. This is not 'Hopkinsonian pride' but a purely practical thing. She is hopelessly careless and too young to look after them. Good tools are good tools and nowadays probably irreplaceable. Has the little wretch written to you yet?

It really is a penance not to be able to see you for it has become not curiosity, excitement or vanity but a solid need. However, if we're meant to meet, it will be arranged somehow. Please give my love to Sylvia.

Tony.

Dearest Peter,

It's a very long time since I've written to you, I know. But I expect you've been as harassed as I have. I trust you're nearly through with the war weapons by now. I've done the first draft of the story—about thirty-four pages—and shall put it in cold storage till I return from Manchester (I have to go there on Thursday to produce a show) when I shall re-do it from beginning to end.

The B.B.C. continues to be a best-quality hair-shirt though I use all your pious tricks. If you know anyone who is looking for a short cut to sainthood, I recommend them to join our esteemed corporation immediately. It combines every mortification of the flesh and spirit with remarkable ingenuity. Watering broomsticks is a productive occupation compared to it. This is more like watering nettles (which grow at a tropical pace) with a watering can made of solid lead with a large hole in the bottom. I feel a cross between a kitchenmaid at Berchtesgaden and a broken-down usher at Dotheboys Hall. Only a low brutish pride inherited from a lot of dumb, low-class and spec-tacularly unsuccessful Sussex ancestors who 'won't be druv' stops me resigning in one memorable memorandum.

I have not heard a word from M. de la Bedoyère. Maybe you 'oversold' me! I shouldn't have said anything about it if you hadn't more than once asked me if I'd like to meet him. I didn't know it would involve any fuss. But, as things are, please don't bother any more about it. It's quite likely we had nothing to say to each other anyway and I'm growing into a recluse.

I am enjoying Christopher Dawson's book. I did read *The Land of Spices*. Interesting, but for me the climax-scene where the girl finds her father 'in the act of love' with a man didn't really come off. But all the decoration, background, etc., is excellent, as in all Kate O'Brien's books.

My real excitement has been Bernanos' *Curé*. Up to now I've always had to break off about a third through because it was too disturbing. This time I swept straight to the end and was more moved by it than anything else I've read for years. It really is a work of genius—full of risks which never land him in disaster—and one of the most profoundly religious books I've ever read.

Between whiles I'm having a wonderfully mixed and muddled diet—Huvelin, Dill's *Roman Society*, Dawson, Pfleger, the seven-teenth-century English poets and Alain, with the Gospels and à Kempis going steadily all the time.

I would like to do nothing but read and make notes for six

months. I am giving both Tyrrell and von H. a rest for a time; I may return to them later. The more I read of von H. the more I am struck by the immense wisdom and shrewdness of Huvelin's advice to him. I rather suspect von Hügel wasn't a great man, only a large one. Huvelin was great—even from those little aphorisms you get his quality. Von H. is mere *quantity* beside them. And Tyrrell seems to me like the raw material of genius, gold-bearing rock from which very little of the potential pure gold has been extracted. Interesting if Huvelin had been Tyrrell's director.

Bernanos has shown me more of what it is to be a saint and to be a priest than anything I have read.

I continue to pray in a dogged way and to go on battling every day with my innumerable faults and weaknesses—with the same dreary list to recite every night! I don't make any notable progress, but I don't worry. It stops me from getting conceited, anyway. The hardest article of faith for me to swallow is that God loves human beings. That one fact alone convinces me that the gospel *is* a revelation for I don't see how one could ever arrive at such a conclusion by reason alone.

The gospels seem more and more wonderful as I go on. I am in St Luke now, are you? Some things in St Mark seemed mysterious. I wonder if the text is corrupt or mistranslated or if they're just mysterious. One was 'Every victim shall be salted with fire'; the other the barren fig tree which is withered for not having any figs when it *wasn't the season for figs*.

I was thinking the other day of the crucifixion and the garden of Eden. How men ate of the tree of knowledge but not of the tree of life. And that since the redemption we are *commanded* to eat of the tree of life, Christ on the cross, in the Blessed Sacrament— the antidote to the forbidden fruit, the tree of wisdom, not the tree of knowledge.

The garden of Eden is surely the most beautiful and profoundly true of all myths. I love Adam's occupation before the fall—distinguishing and naming the creatures God had made.

And how wonderful the temptation in the wilderness is; the three subtly chosen temptations and Our Lord's answers to them. Of all the amazing things in the gospel, the temptation, the agony in the garden, and the seven last words stand out most in my mind. And the exquisite economy of the miracles, each one separate and inevitable and never worked for the sake of working a miracle. I like best of all the blind man on whose eyes Jesus spits, and at first the man only sees men like trees walking. I would like to say: 'Lord, spit on my eyes that I may see.'

And the character of St Peter: he only says about ten things, but the whole man is there and probably the whole Catholic Church. It's interesting that Our Lord didn't make St John the head of the Church but the stupid one, the one who always got His sayings all mixed up. When I think of St Peter, I feel much less critical of the Church.

Bernanos made me think that perhaps the 'gift of tongues' nowadays is the extraordinary power of divination of souls, the capacity to speak to a soul in its own language that is the gift of the holy man. And that the innumerable languages of the Church—the different '*attraits*' as von H. calls them—are the sign that she is still filled with the Holy Ghost.

St Thomas is wonderful about hell; the idea of a soul perpetually fixed in an unnatural attitude really means something. And so does Bernanos' definition of hell as the state in which one has lost the power to love. The idea of hell is really the measure of the majesty of the soul and the necessity of the Passion. I have always before felt it seemed wanton cruelty or a slur on God's omnipotence. The *possibility* of hell for human beings is one of the grandest doctrines of Christianity though, please God, the possibility will never have to be realised for any individual human being. But heaven, hell and the Passion are all such tremendous doctrines, so out of scale with what a human being seems in time, that they can only be divine revelations or the most insane dreams of *folie de grandeur*. Heaven without hell—without the possibility of hell—is meaningless.

Forgive a letter which isn't much more than stray notes but you say you like to have anything that strikes me.

I must go to bed for I'm very tired and as it is St Joseph's feast tomorrow I want to go to Mass.

Did Sue's letter amuse you? It was disgracefully written (she usually writes neatly and well) but it was long and from the heart. She is deep in *Les Misérables* (her first 'grown-up' book except for *Gulliver's Travels*) and thoroughly enjoying it. They lead a very austere life at her school and the poor child has what she spells 'Chill blames'.

Very, very much love, dear Peter. I've missed your letters badly!
Tony.

P.S. I made a lovely and most honourable plan to produce a show at Bangor. But they took the idea and decided it would be much cheaper to get a Bangoree producer to do it. So, of course, it would. But isn't it vexing?

P.P.S. In the big Saturday raid, Ian and I really thought we were for it. But we were indoors and the bombs fell a hundred yards away. Ten minutes before we should have been in the street. So thank you for your protective prayers.

Dearest Peter,

I am horrified to hear of your accident. My dear, you might have broken your neck or crippled yourself for life. I am thankful you *haven't* 'snapped' anything, but the strains and bruises must be horribly painful. Who could have been such an idiot as to leave a trap unbolted? I should think you might take this as a strong hint to keep off War Weapons and stick to your reconciliatory activities with the Bishop.

I do hope you come to Chichester, in spite of all this. That would be lovely for it's quite easy for me to get to Chichester any week-end and I'm quite prepared to hang about and catch you in your off-duty moments.

I didn't get your pathetic note till last night as I'd been away in Manchester 'producing' some of the Old Vic people—or rather letting them produce themselves. Manchester really is a grisly place but it's distressing to see how badly smashed up it is. The steady pressure of this war certainly is a strain. If I hadn't rediscovered my religion I think I would relapse into hopeless depression.

I have had a note from Michael de la B. and hope some day, if we can find a day that coincides, we shall lunch together. I am sorry I was 'prickly'; you'll laugh when you realise that the prickliness which unwittingly got through was about ten per cent of the prickliness I swallowed! It was childish and touchy, I know, but I was so cross that you'd felt it necessary to explain to someone whom you'd asked *me* if I would like to meet that I 'wasn't a clinger'—and still more that you'd felt it necessary to tell me you had—that it took me twenty-four hours to simmer down! So now you know how absurdly prickly I am.

However I shall write meekly to him and hold myself at his disposal and *not* say I'm probably as busy as he is. For I would like to meet him, partly because his book is interesting and still more because I'm longing to meet someone who knows you.

This is not prickliness, but does it tire or bore you when I put down things that occur to me, what you call my reflections? Up to now I've only put them in notebooks or not put them down at all. I wouldn't feel like writing them to anyone but you.

You make me feel very heavy when you say you're 'not up to my weight'. But I think you only mean we have different types of mind. You can do things quite outside my scope—handle large numbers of people and get them to work together. I am diffident and self-conscious when faced with a lot of people and my mind immediately turns to blotting-paper. But in a sort of way I am reflective, though only in flashes. That is, I can occasionally see a connection between things—it's more an 'intuitive' process than a reasoned one. In close reasoning I am easily tired and distracted and have to begin all over again. My 'reasoning' really amounts to a sorting out of experience, discovering parallels, trying to correct a tendency to distort or exaggerate. In some things I'm intelligent, in others plumb stupid. And it's nearly always easier for me to grasp a difficult point than an easy one. This leads people to think I'm either much more intelligent or much more stupid than I really am. I lack concentration and patience more than anything else and my timing is hopeless; I go in spurts and long spells of laziness so that people who started behind me are miles ahead. I shall probably always be a failure which is probably my punishment for having once so desperately wanted to succeed. My function may be to be a scarecrow labelled: 'Don't go this way if you want to get anywhere.'

I've just finished Bernanos' *Journal of my Times*—a remarkable book. The Majorca business certainly—and rightly—stuck in his guts—and he writes very honestly, but with a controlled bitterness, about it. But he remains a hard-bitten Catholic in spite of it. Bernanos is very much my man. We could do with a few more like him. He knows how to be angry without being peevish. Miss Petre strikes me as a trifle peevish, a bit self-righteous. We want more people with the *tone* of Bernanos and his deep grasp of what Christianity is. Catholicism and *honour*, that is his cry. And it's one of the things I've found hardest to bear in some Catholic behaviour, the lack of honour. It may be a pagan virtue but surely we need it. A Church militant should have a soldier's honour and fight clean. But then you know I wanted to be a soldier when I was a child and, if I'd been a man, I'd have gone into the army. And I'm glad it's the centurion's words we use before Communion. It wasn't the soldiers who betrayed Christ, even if they mocked Him; it was the priests and lawyers. I love the way the centurion spoke to Him, as one officer to another. And (this has nothing to do with it) how perfectly Our Lady speaks to the angel, without false modesty, soberly and so nobly. If that much-abused word 'Lady' means anything, that must be what it means. Her ancestor King David was a guttersnipe compared to her. He was abject, but she was humble. Do you remember the Curé: '*Il est bon de dépasser la fierté . . . mais il faut d'abord l'atteindre.*' It is most annoying that I can't anywhere find a copy of his *Jeanne d'Arc*. I know he would be wonderful on *her*.

I have just read Ghéon's *Curé d'Ars*. I am sure the Curé d'Ars was a very holy man but I can't stomach Monsieur Ghéon. And I can't be very much edified by visions of Our Lady with 'her hands flashing with the finest diamonds' or 'quietly dressed in the fashion of the time but all in white'. Still one's got to remember that the Catholic Church isn't made to one's own particular measure and no doubt lots of people would be edified by a vision of Our Lady in diamonds and white suède shoes. Von H. is quite right when he said one must swallow one's fastidiousness. I prefer the Catholic Church with all the awful Sacred Hearts and Little Flowers and the rest to the still more awful bleak 'tastefulness' of the others. After all we've got Giotto and Dante and Mozart and Palestrina so why shouldn't other people have 'Hark, hark my soul' and the rest? If we all had our own way, we'd leave nothing for the others. Even you would take away those silly little candles for which I have an inveterate sentimental affection. They're symbols that mean something to me and nothing to you and yet you'd probably be sorry to see them disappear from the churches.

There is an old shabby man at the Carmelite Church. When people go to Communion he comes up near the altar and just kneels there on the floor with such a look of illuminated love as I've very seldom seen. It's things like that people remember in their dry and rebellious days. When I was a child I remember seeing an old priest weeping for joy during the Gloria on Christmas Day. Those are things one remembers in spite of C.T.S. pamphlets and the shootings in Majorca.

Well, my dear, I just go on and on as usual and I hope I haven't tired you. I always pray for you . . . every day explicitly and implicitly. I do hope the pain is easing up now. Very, very much love. I wish I could come along and be useful in person!

Tony.

P.S. Ian B. is feeling a good deal better. And he's got a very good and important job with the B.B.C., much more impressive than mine, so I hope I shall behave decently and with not-too-hypocritical detachment. What a pig one is to find it more difficult to rejoice in one's friends' successes than sympathise with their failures!

P.P.S. I'm so sorry—I didn't get to Communion on St Joseph's day after all. It was a very blitzy night and I overslept. I hope it wasn't the day you fell through the trap-door!

P.P.P.S. I am going tomorrow to High Mass at St George's, Southwark. The Polish soldiers are going to sing so I will have my Church militant the way I like it! It's just opposite Bedlam which is now a War Museum. I've seen my old cell with a case of shells in it and a radiator which we lunatics would have greatly appreciated!

3 April, 1941.

Dearest Peter,

I got your sad letter this morning. I'm feeling rather weak myself; had a mild dose of flu but could only take the week-end in bed as I had much B.B.C. work and so drag about in that dead-and-alive way and have to go to bed early. Susan arrived this morning for three days so I won't have a moment over the week-end and on Monday I have to go to Leeds—a five-hour journey to produce a five-minute talk, isn't it silly? All this to explain silence is only silence on *paper*.

My poor dear, I do sympathise so much. Just now I took a *Sortes Salesianae* for you and hit straight on this 'His will is that you should serve Him without attraction, without sensible feeling, with repugnance and with anguish of spirit. . . . You will find that when you are no longer thinking of deliverance, God will think of it. He will make haste to be with you.'

I too have been dry as a bone, full of doubt and repugnance. I go on with the Gospel. I try to resign myself to the doubts. Even supposing our dogmas are not literally true, that our revelation is neither the final nor the only one, the truths that those dogmas symbolise are profound and eternal for human beings. I am sure that much confusion comes from a misunderstanding about the nature of truth. There are truths which can neither be measured nor proved but which can be experienced and lived. There are many approaches to the spiritual life, but all who have lived it deeply, whether in religions or philosophies, come upon the same necessities: the necessity for an incessant discipline for the sake of clarity and detachment, the necessity for self-knowledge without despair or presumption, the necessity for loving the things in nature in the light of eternity. The Catholic Church is, as it were, our grammar of this language and, without a grammar, the language would be useless. One can only go by the light one has though I, heretically, think there are other lights and that the examination of other lights, such as Santayana's, can clear much of the smoke from one's own.

Sometimes I think you and many other good Catholics (possibly including Bedoyère) are too much occupied in trying to found a kingdom of God on earth, which is not the Church's mission. Surely the Church's true mission is to be a link between the seen world and the unseen, the vehicle of a spiritual discipline. I can't help feeling that the sense of failure which has haunted you all your life comes from trying to achieve something which you are not fitted to achieve but which for some reason you have decided is the only thing worth achieving. Nothing is harder to do than the thing for which one was *intended* rather than the thing one *wants* to do. One's true job may be to 'achieve' nothing, but simply to be something.

Your disappointments over me (though you try so valiantly to overcome them) do seem to me to show that you tend to love what you imagine rather than what is. Reality seems dull, flat and tame compared to the dream. I fed for so many years on dreams, with disgust and disillusion on waking, that I never even began to be happy or sane until I learnt a little how to fall in love with what is. You tend to 'presumption', I to 'despair'. They are different aspects of the same thing, and both are sins against the Holy Ghost. The language of theology is a very exact language; the trouble comes when people take the word for the thing expressed by the word. The Holy Ghost is a name for something we can dimly apprehend but not comprehend.

I am very distressed to hear about Sylvia's eye and that they may have to operate. Poor thing, what a painful and terrifying thing for her. I call 'being pretty brave' about that something heroic. I do hope and pray it is curable. The possibility of losing the sight of one eye is bad enough for anyone but far worse for a painter.

Dearest Peter, don't be discouraged. It's often a good thing instead of fighting against it to relax to it, let the water close over your head and then you find the 'destructive element' bears you up.

I am afraid you go back over things and torture yourself. I can be the 'poacher-gamekeeper' here all right for I *know* that while one is doing that and trying to rewrite the past more acceptably, one is losing the present and impoverishing the future.

You must get well, be a rock for Sylvia in this horrible predicament and that feeling of failure will go. Falling through a trapdoor may be a strong hint from heaven that at the moment your place isn't on platforms. You've so often forced yourself too much; one's got to find one's right pace and tension.

I will ask Ian if I may lend you the Bernanos—it's his. Re Stanley Morrison—I feel 'not yet'. I met him casually years ago. Wait until you and I have met first. I still hope you'll be coming to Chichester when you're better.

My heart (leathery as it is!) does go out to both of you. I wish I could help. Sometimes I feel you set yourself ideals *too* high: one has to climb Jacob's ladder, not bound straight to the top. Even that much-debated word 'purity' is something you can't achieve just by making a vow of celibacy and keeping it! Spinoza says you can only drive out one passion by a stronger one. Huvelin says one should *detach* only in order to *attach*. The moral of which is, possibly, that one should be on with the new love before one's off with the old!

Darling, forgive a dry letter. But I'm very, very tired and full of ashes. Let's look forward to Easter. Bless you, dear Peter, I'm very, very much fonder of you than you realise.

Tony.

8 April, 1941.

Dearest Peter,

I returned from Leeds about five minutes ago and v. pleased to find a letter. No secret about my B.B.C. work—thought I'd probably told you about it long ago. I think up, commission or write 'Features' for N. America, Canada, Australia, S. America etc., and produce them. Leeds was my small contribution to Improved Relations, being Martin Browne and the sermon from *Murder in the Cathedral*.

I really shouldn't be writing you even a short note tonight for I'm still in a black, sour and rebellious mood—partly physical for I always get this accidious melancholy with even a whiff of flu. But it's one of those times when I query very much the validity of this 'return' for it was not lack of thinking about the whole subject that kept me away so long. There is something so profoundly repugnant to me in the manifestations of organised religion—something at the same time strained and hysterical and stuffy.

I hold on but I am very critical both of it and of myself. There are plenty of explanations for this revolt—physical, psychological and religious too. I hope it will pass, or rather I hope I'll have the courage and honesty to go whichever way my true convictions go. As regards

111

'difficulty' it's equally difficult to go or stay. The more one reads of Church history the more dubious one feels. As to the history of the development of dogma, it seems to lead one to inextricable confusions by any human standards. Frankly I sometimes wish one could be left as a human being—enjoying the natural pleasures of a human being and bearing the miseries of a human being with as much grace as one can. Church history is *not* pretty reading. I often wonder whether Eric and Sylvia are not much wiser than we are. I don't like things mixed up. A tiger should be a tiger, a lamb a lamb and a man a man, not a bastard angel. It seems to me a man may be more just, honest and kind by treating justice, honesty and kindness as human ideals instead of demanding divine sanctions for them. Often I wonder if religion isn't simply our monstrous vanity, our refusal to accept the limitations of being human and mortal. Von Hügel notes that 'conversions' are usually prefaced by a sense of failure and inadequacy. This in itself is fishy.

I don't deny for a minute there are naturally good and holy people or that there is a spiritual realm. But sometimes I suspect Santayana comes a good deal nearer understanding its nature than the official doctrines.

If I thought anything I could say would shake your faith, I wouldn't say it. But I feel you are firmly established. Bernanos keeps his while seeing all the horrors. But Bernanos took in Catholicism with his mother's milk and I didn't.

I was very much interested by my talk with de la Bedoyère. He said I had drawn the picture of a 'real' Catholic in Léonie. Maybe. But it would be fake for me to try to be that kind of Catholic. I have too much sour puritan blood. On the other hand I can see the charm of taking it lightly—as what Santayana calls 'a warm mystical aureole' round one's ordinary life—instead of being so desperately serious about it.

But I'm quite ready to agree this fit of blackness may be only a reaction after straining too much after light. I could do with a little plain thinking and high living as a détente. You probably know those bad spells when one feels corrupt and poisoned right through, when every spontaneous thought is tinged with vanity, hatred, contempt and bitterness. I hope you don't, though.

Anyway, I'm a bit overworked and definitely overstrained. I miss Eric terribly for I see no one but the B.B.C. people and Ian. For six weeks I had nothing but his troubles; now I have nothing but B.B.C. talk and the French situation. I like him very much but he *is* a bit exhausting.

It's mean of me to vent my spleen on you. Take no notice. I need sleep, sleep, sleep and some country air. London in wartime is sometimes an intolerable strain. Forgive me. I'll be better soon.

I had only one sensible reason for writing—to say how glad I am that Sylvia's eye is better. What a relief for both of you. Sometimes I wonder if God knows the physical and mental agonies people go through. I can understand the doctrine of the incarnation—but the doctrine of the Atonement often seems to me an insult to God and man, a beastly legal profit-and-loss notion. God knows, our natures are corrupt. There's no difficulty in believing *that*. Is there a doctrine that the fall takes place in every human being? That would be credible and then the atonement too might be credible. It's no good, I am more Spinozan than Catholic by nature. It is easier for me to think of God immanent in creation than in the Catholic Church and I can see His hand in a shell or a feather more clearly than in all the theologies and pious manuals. Thank God even the theologians permit us to believe the natural world exists and is not a diabolical illusion.

Your recalcitrant
Tony.

17 April, 1941.

Dearest Peter,

This time I will let you have a word to say I'm all right for last night's raid really was a smasher. I was staying over at Eric's for the night and from 9.50 to 4.30 there wasn't one quiet minute. I really felt as if I'd been miraculously saved from being hurt for I'd just got out of bed and was stooping down to find some slippers when the blast from the big bomb or mine that brought down half the houses in Chelsea Square (about two hundred yards away) blew my windows in and tore a large hole in the wall over the bed. If I'd been standing up in the line of blast I'd probably have been hurled against the wall. Anyway I moved out more quickly than I've ever moved in my life, found Eric, who'd come down to find me, lying in a heap in the passage (but not hurt) and we spent the rest of the night sitting under the stairs while things dropped and crashed and screamed all round. However about half past four I cleared the debris off my bed and got into it again and SLEPT!

No one at the office is working this morning—everyone's had a bad night and a bomb story. Usually we don't take much notice of raids but this was a really bad one—quite possibly the worst we've had and we're none of us looking forward to tonight.

Piccadilly is very badly hit, Marylebone Goods Yard burnt out, Paddington hit, Leicester Square station demolished, Waterloo very bad. etc., etc. Hardly a district seems to have escaped a really bad pasting and fires are still burning all over the town and almost every street you go into is a mass of broken glass.

During the last two days I've been getting back a good deal of faith and confidence, thank God. Eric gave me just the same advice as you and said: 'Make a five year plan. Practise it really thoroughly for five years and then see.' He really is a remarkable man! Some years ago when the beast was at its worst and from violent suicidal impulses I'd subsided into a state of hopeless, blank despair, I thought seriously the most reasonable thing to do was to kill myself deliberately because there seemed no hope of getting better. Instead of arguing against that he said: 'Hang on for six more months. Then, if it hasn't got any better, I think you would be perfectly justified in committing suicide.' And I did hang on and now I'm very glad I did.

Santayana says somewhere that all the things that repel people in Catholicism *are* repellent, but they're only dirt on the skin and not cancer in the tissues. I think that's true and anyway I propose to act as if it were.

Sorry, my dear. I'm so tired I can't write any more just now. I do hope your wrist is better—you must rest it.

Very much love,
T.

18 April, 1941.

Dearest Peter,

Thank you so very much for the beautiful *Imitation*. My birthday was on 31 March (I'm 42 now and gaining fast on you!) so I'll take it for that as a very special present. It is a lovely binding and it's a great treat to have such a beautiful object to look at and handle in these meagre days. I lost nearly all my furniture and nicest possessions in December when the warehouse was bombed, including over three hundred of my most treasured (and largely irreplaceable) books. Of course lots of rubbishy ones weren't damaged at all!

My only 'scruple' is that the present should have been for *you*; it was like your wild generosity to pass it on to me. But I'm so pleased with it and touched and grateful.

It was wonderful to have a calm night last night and to sleep. That was the one thing everyone in London wanted and thank God we got it.

I'm so sorry you're still under a cloud even though the cloud has thinned since Easter. It seems to me that, if one accepts the Catholic point of view, you and I could take the agonising doubts we both suffer from as our particular 'thorn in the flesh' and the raw material which can be turned in the end to our own advantage and other people's. We must be typical of thousands of people today and can therefore enact their problem in a very personal way and possibly find some faint light for them. I've always felt that 'Thine own heart a sword shall pierce that out of many hearts thoughts may be revealed' applied to a great many problems, certainly, for one, the artist's. Also Jacob wrestling with the angel.

I too was profoundly disturbed and influenced by *Portrait of the Artist*. I have not read it for several years but I still remember that terrible sermon. I never met Joyce but one of my best women friends knew him very well and he was a profoundly unhappy man, suffering from persecution mania. Yet he has transformed all his torments, physical and mental, into art. What I think is interesting is the way that, for all his efforts, he never can get away from Catholicism and that all his work could be interpreted as the friction between the *odi* and *amo*.

As you say, the problem doesn't clarify itself by thinking about it. I think it must be clarified in action; never perhaps solved.

I am very much attracted by Santayana's way of looking at things and I think it is possible to use a great deal of his method in dealing with the Catholic life. He is not, I think, dogmatic in his materialism (in the sense of thinking of matter as the base and home of spirit) but merely says that, for him personally, he is not out to attempt to explain the origin of the universe but is content to accept it as a going concern. I think he would say that, starting as he does from purely human premises, he is out to discover what life a man can live in relation to the universe and he is determined to accept no outside agent whose existence cannot be proved by the consensus of ordinary human methods of reason. But I do not think he ever dogmatically asserts that there can be no other reality besides nature, and that one could only know such a reality by revelation and that he personally does not believe in revelation. He admits that man by his nature must live by some faith and he makes his act of faith in the actual existence of the universe, i.e. that 'matter' is what it appears to be and not a mere dream in the mind as the 'idealist' philosophers believe. As to the idea that he is the founder of a new system of philosophy he repeatedly states that it isn't a system and that it isn't new.

I think also that he would say that spirit speaks in many voices or rather languages, all equally valid provided that they have their own organic unity and are not mere scraps and artificial syntheses. He has (although I understand he no longer practises) a profound respect for the Catholic Church and regards it as one of the richest, most complete expressions of man's relation to the universe and the vehicle of a very valuable and authentic spiritual discipline. In fact, I think he would only part company with the most orthodox Catholic on the one (I admit important!) point that he would say it was *poetically* true as a harmony of man's deepest instincts but not *literally* true in the sense of a correct description of man's actual situation.

I have wrestled a great deal and for many years over this problem and I admit that I am greatly drawn to Santayana's view and find it clears up many ambiguities and confusions.

On the other hand, in order to be a Catholic, one has got to make an act of faith and commit oneself to something. For a long time (and often now) it seemed to me mentally dishonest to make that act of faith when one felt the grounds of belief were insufficient. But I think that may come from confusion about the nature of faith. Reading the gospels I have been very much struck by the bold insistence of Christ that one must *believe* in Him. One has got to take the risk somewhere and, if one has taken it, I think one must just do one's best to take the consequences. In a sense the grounds of belief in anything, even one's own existence or that of the world about us, are insufficient but at some point, in order to achieve anything, one has got to make an assumption and see where it leads to.

Even the Catholic faith admits it is full of mysteries and that dogmas can be only rude transcriptions of truths too great to be put into language. I think what one must aim at doing is seeing the system as a whole, with all the proportions and interrelations of its parts instead of taking bits here and there and separating them out for criticism, denial or over-emphasis. And, granted the initial assumptions (which frankly, I think, do require an act of faith and are not 'provable' even by the subtlest theologian), I think it stands the test. Eric was telling me about the 'fallacy of composition' which I didn't know of, i.e. roughly that what is true of a part is not true of a whole and this seems to me to throw some light on our trouble with particular aspects. On mine anyhow, for I expect I tend to identify your difficulties too much with my own.

I can't help feeling (sometimes I get such a feeling of the Church sitting on one's mind like an octopus that one hardly dare have an opinion, much less utter it!) that the Church is too timid about saying: 'I demand, in my founder's name, *faith* from you first and foremost.' It is perhaps the Church's own concession to the scepticism of the time that makes her keep insisting (erroneously I dare to think) that reason alone could lead one to such extraordinary conclusions. I do not see how the existence of God can be either proved or disproved. Where she is safe in asserting that she does not demand unreasonable compliance is in the inner cohesion of the logical dogmatic structure she has built up on the premises . . . or revelations. The *whole* of religion cannot be dealt with in the same strict formula as the kind of knowledge which deals with exact relations in the physical world and whose truth or falsity can be proved by results. Even by 'righteousness' one cannot prove the Church's teachings right or wrong: as 'good' a man by human moral standards may be produced by totally opposite beliefs. Perhaps, therefore, one must make one's act of faith (supported by some moment of internal conviction which one *believes* to be the touch of God on the soul) and, having put one's hand to the plough, try not to look back.

It's just occurred to me that if one thinks 'faith fruitful in good *work*' instead of 'faith fruitful in good *works*' one gets a clearer picture of what one's own function should be. I know, personally, 'good works' calls up inevitably the picture of someone perpetually bustling about with baskets of medicine and leaning over sick beds!

I am determined to get on with the book. I have with much labour got the first draft of the story done. I'm not at all satisfied with it and it needs heaps more revision, but having done the best I can with it, I shall let *Horizon* have it. The theme really needed 20,000 words and I can only have 8,000 so it will be a compromise and I shan't be pleased with it. But it was important to break the ice somehow to get going again. Then I can begin the book again for the fourth time!

Well, I suppose we have to work out our own salvation, in the Church or out of it. I think one must hold on humbly to whatever one feels to be true, allow an immensely wide margin for error and for psychological peculiarities and try to live by what little light one has. Personally I'm pretty sure I need an actual system, such as the Catholic one, which has *points d'appui* in the real world and an external practice as well as an interior life. Humility, detachment, recollection and discipline are extremely necessary for the artist—as necessary as for the saint—but whether or not the realm of religion and the realm of art are two aspects of the same thing, I don't know. Santayana would probably say 'Yes'; the Church emphatically says 'No'. Meanwhile, as a human being, one has to make what one can of one's life. I can in my heart renounce neither religion nor art: I can only try and combine the two in some mixture that suits a mixed nature.

I'll have to keep John VIII for another letter. I have seventeen dull but necessary letters piled up to answer.

It is *wretched* not being able to see and talk to you. I too have 20,000 things to discuss with you apart from a strong desire to *see* you and hear your voice. Is there no hope of your coming to Chichester? I fear there's none of mine being transferred to Bangor.

You talked about the fantasy picture one makes of one's beloved —that time in connection with the things that repel one in the Church. I think there is an important difference between fantasy and true imagination. The fantasy is projected from oneself on to the object and so distorts its nature. But true imagination, proceeding from the single eye, the 'naked heart', waits with expectation and love and is rewarded by a moment of perception in which the clear *essence* of the object—in eternity as it were, and free of the distortions and accretions of time—is revealed. This is what artist, lover, and saint all strive for and sometimes do see; and surely it is the true meaning of the beatific vision. I hope to have *that* vision of the Church one day . . . and of you as I once had it in that queer dream. For me heaven would be to see this whole universe through the eyes of God. Hell might be to see it through the eyes of Satan.

Do you know Hans Andersen's *The Snow Queen*? I remembered it the other day when I was inflamed and darkened with pride and bitterness. The boy with the fatal splinter of glass in his eye who sees everything distorted—the boy scorning love and trying to build everything up by reason (he is trying to make the word 'eternity' from icicles in the palace of the cold-hearted and perfect Snow Queen)—seems to me to have a very real meaning. And he is only saved from being frozen to death by the child who loves him and by regaining his own childhood. In heaven the saints and artists must understand each other; here they are mutually hostile and suspicious. Yet I believe the truth they contemplate is the same. The great artists, the great scientists and the great saints seem to me like three nations speaking different languages and sometimes quarrelling like children because the object they are contemplating is not the *word* '*hund*', '*chien*' or 'dog' but some object validly labelled all three. One can learn one language and the rudiments of another but it's no good mixing them up in a hideous Esperanto. And the Church, thank God, is a language and not Esperanto.

Very, very much love, dear Peter. It's a funny thing but what you call your 'costive' letters are often to me the most stimulating.
Antonia.

P.S. I love the *Imitation* as a book as well as an 'object'. After the N.T. I find it much the most nourishing and solid.

P.P.S. Might I have my letters (e.g. *your* letters) back some day?

20 April, 1941(?)

Dearest Peter,

I haven't time to write because I'm in the middle of a 'Production' rush. I just want to thank you for your admirable letter which I have read several times. I certainly shan't 'bite' you for your advice but try to follow it. I had come to the same sort of conclusion myself.

As you say, one has to make one's own fight. I can't even explain the real problem to myself for it goes so deep and is so instinctive, this recoil which may be due to a misconception of the whole thing. I do feel that buried in the mass of rigid dogma is a living truth but whether or not the Church is the best or only exponent of that truth I simply don't know. I pray in a blind way and try to find some spot of dry land on which to rest. I go on with the New Testament in spite of all and thank goodness still find that full of freshness and life. But the Church seems to have coated the New Testament over so thickly. Maybe it's preserved it but sometimes it seems as if it has preserved it rigid and embalmed with all the flexibility and vigour of Christ's own words spoilt. I do believe in Christ so I suppose that's something.

I like your Pascal 'cry'—but Lord, how I hate Pascal. I'm afraid I prefer the artists to the 'religious' and find a lot more edifying in them than in the saints.

One glimmer of hope is *Lex Orandi*. If they really passed that (I know they didn't want to) I'm jolly well going to take it as official. After all I'm a poor ignorant creature who believes in an *Imprimatur.*

Love and thanks

T.

24 April, 1941.

Dearest Peter,

Your lovely letter came this morning and was a nice compensation for horrible cold and east wind. Are we ever going to have any spring?

I mustn't write you a long letter now as I'm at the office (unusually early) and soon the wheels will begin to go round. So this is only to thank you and to tell you I survived Saturday's raid all right. It was nothing like as bad as the Wednesday one but I was alone at Linden Gardens (Ian was away for week-end) and I felt decidedly nervous. However I went down and slept in Ian's room which has sand-bagged windows which muffle the noise a bit and has also some kind of shoring-up arrangement. I laid out by my bed your *Imitation,* the New Testament, my rosary, torch and gas-mask and with a comforting cat curled up on my shoulder passed not too bad a night.

My lurching faith does begin to steady itself a bit. By keeping very close to the ground, as it were, and observing one's thousand starts a day towards malice, pride, dishonesty, envy, etc., etc., one's dispositions become calmer and firmer. I agree with you that the Church's very lack of 'accommodatingness' is a strong point in her favour. No, it really seems to boil down to the fact that if one is going to be a Christian, one has got to be a Catholic. And as, however I may squirm, Christ has got his hook into me, I am caught in Peter's net whether I like it or not.

Allowing a wide margin for obstinacy, pride, 'spirit of the age', love of one's own way etc., it still did seem to me that the Church demanded the sacrifice of such intellectual honesty as one had. But last night it occurred to me that she demanded the sacrifice, not of intellectual honesty but of intellectual pride. And that, in theory anyway, one is quite willing to make—or attempt to make.

As to Catholic philosophy I don't attempt to grapple with it yet, though perhaps I may try some day. The Catholic intellectuals keep saying (not, I can't help feeling, without a certain snobbery) that an understanding of it is vital for a proper understanding of one's faith. It may be so but from what little I know of it there seems a wide gulf between the faith as *practised* and the faith as *formulated*. For example Vonier (who should know) says that God is a pure spirit and therefore inaccessible to feeling of any kind. Yet faith in practice, speaks of the wrath of God, the love of God, etc. The latter is anthropomorphic if you like (or you can say a human being can only *apprehend* God in a human way); the former would seem to make God an abstraction like Pure Being. However, don't worry, I'm not going to plunge into all that. I prefer to be with the 'Guardees' and take Christ's word.

My poor Peter, if you suffer from accidie, you have my deepest sympathy. People who don't, don't realise the awful stale misery of it. I do agree that it's the foulest of all afflictions. I still have bouts of it—though not so prolonged or so acute since I was psycho-analysed—but I think I will suffer from it to some extent all my life. It is a fearful thing, ashes in the mouth and mud in the mind and without the liberating power of a sharp pain. To me it is much more remarkable that you should write me such admirable letters under that cloud than that I should write 'serenely' after a blitz. I don't like blitzes but I much prefer them to accidie.

I am sometimes puzzled by your constant cry of: 'Was it all illusion and self-deception?' A feeling, no matter of what kind, surely cannot be an illusion. It may have been inordinate or attached to an object about which one has illusions, but the feeling *itself* cannot be an illusion. While one had it, it was what it was . . . like pain, laughter or tears.

To my great joy B.B.C. will give me a fortnight's leave this year. I feel I must spend it with the children but I'm wondering if we can't compromise. If I could bring the children up to Wales from 11-25 August (my leave time provisionally) and you could find us some cottage or farm accommodation near you, I would be able to see quite a lot of you and yet be with them too. Do you like the plan?

I must stop now. God bless you and lift your horrible cloud of accidie.

Very much love, dear Peter
Antonia.

My dear Peter,

It's unpardonable of me not to have written long ago to thank you for all your plans. But I can't make a decision yet. Since I last wrote, so many things have happened to upset plans. My B.B.C. department is in throes of reorganisation and I'll probably be shifted to another with a different holiday rota. Also Lyndall's school is beginning a month late and not breaking up till September. And as she looks (from X-ray) as if she's broken her arm from a nasty fall from a horse a month ago she may not want a riding holiday. Everything's in such a muddle that maybe I'll take a long week-end in a few weeks' time and come up to Portmeirion on my own for a few days.

This isn't a letter, my dear, only a note. I've been very low lately, physically and mentally. Every kind of confusion in the head and a series of colds which are not just quiet snivels but violent physical assaults so that I can't think or read but am reduced to a miserable dislocated Organism.

You've got a birthday this month I know and ages ago I got you a tiny present which I can't summon up the physical energy to pack. I'll be all right as soon as we get a little thawing warmth; it is still cold as winter.

As regards religion I worry about it day and night till I've worried myself to a standstill. I think there is a way in which I can accept and practise Catholicism sincerely but I don't think it's your way. I get hints from Tyrrell whom I've been reading again with great interest. I know you want to help me and you often do but fundamentally our types of mind are very different. It is no good my bothering you with problems which you strain yourself to see but cannot *feel* as they don't concern you or arise for you. Roughly speaking you are what psychologists call an 'extrovert' and I am an 'introvert'—you work from the outside in and I from the inside out. You are perfectly at home in the outside world, can work with your hands, be active in work with others, are interested in sociology, reform, etc. I have to get my mental and emotional world in order before I can tackle the external world. I am beginning to find a way, but very slowly. I can only follow my own clues and those of people who have had the same sort of experience. We meet, you and I, at many points but approach them from different angles. I forced myself too much to try to think in your way which is sometimes, for me, sterilising.

Much love,

T.

My dear Peter,

It was very nice to get a letter today. I can still only write a note. I meant to write one after the Saturday raid but was feeling too ill and tired on Sunday after a nerve-racking night, expecting to be finished off every minute. You feel more helpless in raids when you're feeling ill and dog-tired anyway. It certainly was a brute and the damage is probably the worst to date. Two whole wings of Bedford College where we work since being bombed out in December were completely destroyed by fire and H.E. No one killed, thank heaven, or even hurt there but we are exceedingly disorganised; several sections homeless and quantities of papers burnt. I haven't seen the rest of the damage but Ian says it's sensational. I felt so ill on Monday that I finally got the doctor and have been sent to bed for a day or two. My ill-advised efforts to cure my cold only drove it in and made it much worse and gave me sinusitis so now I'm condemned to incessant inhalings. Eyes, ears, nose, throat and BRAIN all feel as if they'd been put through a mangle or filled with lumps of hot lead but I'm much better today though I feel so heavy, flat, depressed and sleepy that I can't remember how it feels to be awake and alive. I guess everyone in London feels tired and low after the last three months; weather, food and circumstances are all depressing. A week's sunshine would make all the difference.

I don't propose to discuss Freud with you. But, with due courtesy, I don't imagine you have studied him very deeply. So why pounce on a couple of innocent words (not even invented by Freud) and start barking about 'fashionable jargon' and 'dogmatism'? Any new technique has got to invent some sort of language. You would be angry if anyone talked about the Church's 'jargon', but theology, like anything else, has to have a language—a language meaningless for those who haven't studied it. And Freud never asks you to believe his 'dogmas' which he in any case would only call tentative hypotheses. The Church is dogmatic all right and asks you to believe her dogmas on pain of loss of salvation. You may, with or without knowledge, think poor old Freud all wrong but at least, in fairness, admit he doesn't demand your assent to his theories! I fly off the handle about this, not in defence of Freud whom I'm not competent to defend though I owe very much to the technique he discovered, but because it is just that uncritical, sneering attitude towards any new discovery or exploration that makes people dislike Catholics so much. It's the tone of C.T.S. pamphlets which you've often agreed with me are very inflammatory material.

I continue to go battling about faith, or rather not battling but plodding on in a perfectly blank desert, going through all the motions *as if* I believed. I was impressed, oddly enough, by a second life of St Thérèse of Lisieux for whom, as you did once, I cherished a peculiar aversion. But this did impress me—I felt that here was a really heroic and austere soul, holding on in spite of darkness and fear—a very masculine soul under all the frills and a passionate one. At the moment the only saints I can pray to are this St Thérèse, Jeanne d'Arc and St Clement of Alexandria. I am relieved to find that the last *was* a saint, I was afraid he was too much of a Greek! I am just beginning Chateaubriand's *Mémoires d'Outre Tombe* which I've been saving up for a year. This seems the right moment though my head's been so sodden this last fortnight I can hardly read sensibly. Chateaubriand is very good in spite of all the florid bits. And his religious life is exceedingly interesting.

I don't think I feel any doubt that Catholicism is the richest and deepest religion for anyone brought up in the Christian religion. Its absolutism, its claims to literal and exclusive and universal truth are much harder nuts to crack. Yet whether belief in Christ (which I have whether I like it or not) necessarily leads one to belief in the Church as she is, isn't by any means clear to me. I know all the stock arguments so don't tire yourself by setting them out. They will be conclusive for some people, not for others. It may be a matter of temperament, training, or Newman's 'illative sense' whether they seem conclusive or not. You can't appeal either to 'intelligence' or to 'goodness' for equally intelligent and equally good people will disagree over this. It looks as if there were a religious faculty like the faculty for music, painting or mathematics, and that the final appeal is to that. But here again you get endless disagreement as to the form the religion is to take.

I don't think I can ever be a Santayanan like Eric, admirable as I think S. is and unanswerable if you take the flux of nature as your only ground. I have too strong a sense of another world for that. But that may be pure illusion and is certainly not susceptible to proof. I could much more easily be a Spinozan; Spinoza believes in God and has a very fine conception of the relation of God to the universe which, if I'd never been brought up a Catholic, I think I should have accepted as the most satisfactory solution suggested.

I suppose it comes down to 'faith'. And I pray for faith. But a quiet voice which the Church would say was the devil whispers: 'Of course, if you pray hard enough for faith, you'll get faith. You will have suggested yourself into an attitude of faith and will be simply believing what you wish to believe.'

The only thing I suppose is to continue to pray, to reject nothing through impatience or darkness and to try and live like a Christian. One may never find, but one is not to be excused from honestly *looking*.

Forgive this monologue which will be meaningless to you. I wish I were a naturalist. When I feel strained and giddy from reading and puzzling out things it's an exquisite relief to read about birds and insects; to find out any little *fact* such as that bees can only see blue and yellow or that bats and fishes have nerves that tell them when there are obstacles in their way.

Well, Peter dear, this has turned out, not a note but an arid and disappointing letter. Many happy returns of your birthday on Sunday! I would give a lot to know what I'll think and believe when I'm your new age. But there seems a good chance that I'll be killed long before I've made up my mind. I often find myself wishing to be dead just to end this torture of uncertainty and that is a great sign of weakness from every point of view. But if one is weak, one must admit one's weak and not adopt the attitudes of the strong out of vanity.

I want to come to Portmeirion when I'm feeling better and will be livelier company.

I am waiting for this for three things: (1) health; (2) cash; (3) the departure of one of my best friends who is off to the east with the R.A. and will be having his last leave at any moment.

(3) is a sad reason and one contributory cause of my depression. This war has separated me from everyone I am fondest of, the children and my nearest friends. And a 'good-bye' is a good-bye these days. Still, the wind is tempered to the shorn lamb and I have my new-old friend Peter for whom I am deeply grateful. But the people with whom one has a past in common leave a big hole and at my age one doesn't go out and look for new friends. You do, my dear Peter, but I always told you you were much younger than I am!

Thank you for your snuff advice. I will try it as a prophylactic next time I feel a cold coming on. I doubt if I can make a habit of it yet, though it would be grand to have a new vice to replace smoking!

Well, good night, my dear, and forgive my megrims. Pray for me: I need it.

I am still wrestling with my beastly story: final draft now and *must* finish it this week.

Much love,

T.

P.S. I hope your arm is better.

Dearest Peter,

Here is one half of a very small birthday present. The other half is Ian Black's book, which I thought would interest you, and which Cape's are sending you direct so that it won't arrive too long after the birthday.

This is the nearest approach to a N.T. of the type you asked for long ago. I have hunted quite a lu but this was the simplest, clearest I could find. I'm afraid it's not the Catholic version but you said you didn't mind.

I do wish you, dear Peter, a very happy 'new year'. I wish I could be more effectual to you as a friend. I am not the ideal companion for Tyrrell's 'mercurial T——'. I have been through a difficult time lately. You have been kindness itself but the very real differences between our approach to things and our true pre-occupations are very much accentuated by our never having met. The things you pick out and the things you ignore in my letters show the differences most and you find the same with mine, I am sure. If you could accept the difference instead of, as I think you sometimes do, being disappointed because I am not a feminine counterpart of yourself, it would be better for both of us. I warned you of so many rocks in myself in my early letters and my dear, hot-headed Peter has run his nose on so many of them!

Bless you, dear Peter. And may your accidie finally lift.

I haven't time for more than a note as I want to catch the post. I am much better but v. tired this morning. It wasn't a noisy night but raids begin to affect me a little since those two bad ones and I couldn't sleep till 4.30.

I am very happy. I have finished that story I've been wrestling with for three months and it will be out in the next *Horizon* or the one after that. This is the first serious story I have written for seven years. You won't like it so I shan't show it to you. But, for myself, it's the best I have managed to do so far, though far, far below what I would like it to have been. But I know you will share my pleasure in having been able after all these dry years to have done some work again. I do truly thank God for if He'll let me use my faculty for writing again I feel I can bear anything.

I think Black's book will interest you. The misprints are frightful but I suppose that is wartime proof-reading.

Again, bless you and be happy.

Antonia.

21 May, 1941.

Dearest Peter,

Thank you so much for your sweet note. It isn't possible for me to come just yet as I'm in the middle of being transferred to another department. You must not worry about me. I have been through rather a bad patch, mentally and physically, but I'm very tough and pretty resilient. The last few days I have been much better and with plenty of sleep and an efficient tonic I shall last quite well until I get some country air and sun (if any). I can't say just when I can get away: I hope in June some time. When one gets a bit low and overstrained the war sits like a nightmare on one's chest but in the intervals one comes to terms with it. I look forward very much to seeing you and Sylvia. One of the hardest things I find to put up with in the war is the boredom and monotony and I just long to see you and let us talk our heads off. My old job was exquisitely pointless but my new one will at least have the charm of irony. I am to be the B.B.C's prime publicity booster in the Overseas Press. However, from now on, I simply propose to make myself comfortable, to work regular hours, and get on with my book. My new chief is a pleasant man, from the rough outside world like myself, and not afflicted with the typical B.B.C. manias and neuroses. So you may sing with me:

Thank heaven the crisis is over,
Our Annie is better at last.

I now sit like a housemaid in an attic, with my little tin trunk corded up and my references in my shabby purse, waiting for my new master to drive me away in a four-wheeler to the Langham Hotel. This last is a favourite dumping ground for staff: presumably on the principle that having been bombed twice it will probably be bombed thrice and save our keep.

Curse your accidie. Isn't it enough that poor wretched human beings should be afflicted outside without having permanent fogs and east winds in their minds too?

I could do with a bottle of champagne, couldn't you?

Love,

T.

26 May, 1941.

Dearest Peter,

No time to write you a proper letter which I badly want to do. Your last long letter was so good, I took it away for the week-end to answer it but had no time. I was so tired, I slept all Sunday afternoon as well as two long nights.

This is only to say, as I want to catch post, that I am planning to tack two days on to week-end of 21 June and COME UP to the White Cottage!

I think this is the earliest I can safely hope to get away with. Whitsun is too soon and I must get the new job taped and running smoothly. I have already got provisional permission so all should be well unless something extraordinary happens. I am very excited and anticipatory.

I suggest, therefore, that I take the 8.20 on Saturday morning 21st. It is lovely if you can meet me in Bangor. Actually I think it would be rather nice to have a pause in Bangor before proceeding to Portmeirion. On the other hand, if journey is much quicker by car, that *does* recommend it. Ideal of course would be if you came in by car and the driver would wait while we went and had a 'cup of' to wake me up after my journey and also to rub off our first strangeness. But that belongs rather to the old régime than the new dispensation! All things considered, I expect train plan is best.

Anyhow, main thing is that on Saturday 21st you collect from 1.51 (approximately) Bangor train a battered female with a suitcase. You may have some difficulty in recognising me as during the last few months I have become more and more unlike the photograph you approve of. Go by the worst one and you'll be safe. I shan't have any difficulty in picking you out.

It is very sweet of you and Sylvia to take me in. But please as a P.G. and not as a G. It's difficult to get food here other than one's rations so I don't know if I can bring any supplement. But I will try.

I am scribbling this with some difficulty in my new room at the Langham. My colleagues are very nice, but there are five of us in one tiny room, and two typewriters clack the whole time and my opposite number dictates his articles at the top of his voice straight on to the machine. So far I haven't tried WORKING here.

You won't have to lend me pyjamas etc. as I shall bring the bare necessities of life. Among these I don't include a mackintosh because I haven't had one since I was 16 and don't intend to start one at 42. I've got a husky tweed cape that I can do everything but bathe in.

I'll write in a day or two properly, but I've rashly undertaken ANOTHER story. Keep your fingers crossed!

Very much love,
T.

2 June, 1941.

My dear Peter,

I have stupidly mislaid the letter I wanted to answer. So you must have a little non-answering letter instead. Not a long one because I'm still stupidly tired and flat and because soon it looks as if we will at last be able to Talk. All is so far going well about the 21st and I don't *think* there'll be a hitch. I certainly agree about the car; it would be much nicer, especially if we can have our cup of tea first.

I believe somehow that I shall manage to cling to my faith. The alternations between faith, sometimes dim, sometimes less dim, and total blankness, darkness and emptiness are violent and often very sudden and they are difficult to bear quietly. They are, I know, partly psychological and therefore one needn't be too much upset by them. I do try to be as humble as possible and I do pray all the time to the Holy Ghost. But I am tormented sometimes by miseries or scruples and by the awful old fear that it is my fault if I can't see . . . that I'm fundamentally perverted. This is a very bad state if I want to preserve the sanity I've built up with considerable labour and pain. I can only say to God: 'If you damn me, I accept it. I wanted to find the truth. If I cannot take it in the only form you prescribe it, then damned I must be and I won't complain. But if you want me to see what I don't see, however much I strain my eyes, you must either do something about my eyesight or convince me if I've committed the sin against the Holy Ghost in which case I'm damned already.'

The trouble is that there is no Catholic who knows enough of my mental history to be able to give me relevant advice. I can therefore only put my case before God as honestly as I can and leave it there. I would give so much to have known Tyrrell who was, I feel, a real priest who could instinctively understand and calm people with a bias towards despair. But unfortunately, in his later letters, the ones which seem to me to show the deepest insight into human beings, he was presumably becoming more and more unorthodox. I like to think he was only a little in advance of what the Church herself will one day come to admit, but the stiff fact remains that he *was* condemned. I want to ask you a great deal about Tyrrell.

I have been reading Bernanos' *Journal* again. I admit it's violent, even hysterical. But to me that shout, that imprudent, spontaneous shout of rage and indignation shows much more true faith in the Church than the smooth, prudent syntheses of the wary boys. It makes me at any rate far more inclined to hold on to the Church than all the Watkins, D'Arcys and Dawsons. I always feel the apologists are dangerous to certain types of mind, far more dangerous than the attackers, and that any premature synthesis is more dangerous still. As Bernanos said—and as I think Tyrrell felt—it is not her errors that drive people from the Church but that we splinter on the rock of her pride. And if the Church really is infected with pride, she's as near the gates of hell as she's ever been. If she'd be humble, we'd kiss her feet. Nothing will convince me that Bernanos is not a true Christian and a real Catholic, no matter how much he may annoy the clergy.

I've been reading Spinoza again a little. So much of what he says is true and useful for Catholics and is so cooling and clarifying after some of the theological contortionists. But, thank God, this terrible Catholic exclusiveness does seem to be loosening up and one is almost allowed to believe officially that the Spirit bloweth where it listeth.

My soldier friend is still standing with one foot in Woolwich and the other in mid-air waiting to be planted on some ship bound for the east. We manage to snatch meetings and to have not entirely fruitless talks. He is an ex-communist and is trying very hard to understand my return to the Church. In trying to explain, not defend, my position it grows a little clearer to me. It is when one is with people one loves and who are searching hard for a way of life that one most longs for a clear conviction to share with them. Will you pray for him? I feel more and more that we are all so much our brother's keeper and inextricably bound up together. I pray to Péguy, the 'good sinner' who said: 'What would He say if one of us came to Him without all the rest?'

Sorry, my dear, I must go to bed. I am so looking forward to seeing you.

Much love,
Tony.

13 June, 1941.

Dearest Peter,

I'm sorry I haven't time to answer your last letters: I hope I'll answer them in person! I'm very busy at the moment, getting everything cleared. Only a major catastrophe can prevent me from coming. It's exciting to think I'll be setting off a week tomorrow.

It's sweet of you and Sylvia to insist on my being a non-P.G. I'll collect all the food I can. But I don't think Sylvia should give up her room to me. I'm quite healthy again now and I know how horrid it is being turned out of one's own surroundings.

No time for more than a note and much love.

T.

My dear Peter,

I do hope I didn't leave you too exhausted. I am afraid your desire to pack a year into three days wore you to a shadow. And I am also afraid that I enjoyed my visit a good deal more than you did and that the alternation of being stimulated and paralysed was very nerve-racking for you. I am sorry I was often snappish. I didn't want to be and tried to control it. But I found it difficult to accept what I know perfectly well and have often experienced, that if one person doesn't 'get' another, no amount of explanation is any use. I tried to make it clear to you that the way to get anything out of me was *not* to ply me with questions but you were too strung up to hold back and let things develop. All this doesn't worry me but I'm afraid it may worry *you*, knowing your tendency to brood over things and wish them undone or re-done.

I did enjoy myself so much. You hadn't given me any idea of how enchanting your house was and how beautiful the country round.

I am pretty tired today after a hectic rush round Bangor studios, all separated by long steep walks, and an interminable hot sticky journey back last night. Also it is so hot today that we are all sitting in the office with our tongues hanging out like thirsty dogs. I'd give a lot for the sight of your lily pool and the sea and the mountains.

I'm not sending you the book on psycho-analysis for the moment (a) because it's over at Eric's house, (b) because I'm rather doubtful about sending it at all. It may seem to you meaningless and possibly disgusting or you may find it 'disturbing' in other ways. I'm inclined to think you're needing peace more than anything else just now.

I was sorry we couldn't go to Mass on Sunday. I never miss it in the ordinary way but it did seem more sensible that particular day. Sylvia obviously thought it would be too exhausting for you.

I have thought about you almost continuously since I left. Whatever you may feel, I am very glad for my own sake that I came. You were kindness itself to me and I feel I made you a very poor return. I wish you did not live so far away. Many things are difficult to write and a short concentrated visit is full of possible misunderstandings. I found it so much easier to be natural with Sylvia, mainly because she took me as I was and hadn't got into any state of nervous apprehension about what I should be like or how she would appear to me. I felt instantly at ease with her though I was worried because she was tired and ill and my being there meant so much extra work and discomfort for her just when she needed rest.

I found a charming letter from Susan to you when I got home. I forgot to bring it up with me to the office but I will send it tomorrow.

Seeing you confirmed a lot of things I had guessed and also cleared my mind considerably about much which had confused me both about religion and life in general. After a period of muddle and anxiety, as often happens, the irreconcilables reconcile themselves.

Why I can sympathise with you—and also one of the reasons why I seem harsh with you—is that you have much in your disposition that is like mine. I have been much more fortunate than you in having perhaps been driven harder up against the consequences of that disposition and so having been forced to come to terms with it or disintegrate altogether. I wish I could hand you the results on a plate for your own use, but that is not possible. There is no magic formula. Your restless drive to action, admirable in itself, doesn't give you time to keep still and see what happens. You don't give time for the corn to run into the mill and the result is that the wheels go on grinding in a vacuum which is one of the most horrible experiences one can have. I am perfectly sure everything you need is in the Gospel if you would go back to that and simply brood over it and live it instead of trying to fit it in with this or that Catholic doctrine. The Church means *nothing* without the Gospel. Why not try really leaving your nets for a time? If you could do that, I believe you'd get your miraculous draught of fishes when the moment came. Trying to do everyone else's job for them (I know your active fingers itch) means you don't do your own and I imagine that is what one is judged on.

Well, God bless you, dear Peter, and DON'T WORRY. If I seem hopelessly puzzling to you, don't try and worry it out. Forget about it and you'll wake up with the solution one day.

With love and thanks for having given me a lovely week-end.

T.

My dear Peter,

I must just write you a little note: your letter sounded so very sad. I feel guilty for it seems I've hurt you considerably and I certainly didn't mean to. My coming to see you appears to have had no pleasant results at all for you—you find it an 'ordeal'; you are miserable for twenty-four hours, and your belief in the devil is confirmed! Yet over and over again I've warned you that I'm tough, harsh and impatient and it surely shouldn't be such a shock to find that I have told the truth.

What you say about how much I owe to Eric is absolutely right. For twenty years the poor man has been patiently trying to teach me how to think and above all how to look at things and I'm still only at the beginning of being able to do either. It certainly is a tremendous advantage to have a master and I've been lucky in finding one who is not only extremely rare but the one right person for me. You were unlucky in losing Tyrrell who was probably the right one for you.

I don't think for one minute that you were responsible for not having been able to make full use of your many gifts. Nor should you make yourself miserable with 'vain regrets'. But there's a difference between vain regrets and looking a fact in the eye which is the only way of coming to terms with it. I could, I think, have told you some things which might have been useful to you but I don't think you were in a mood to listen. I think you had made up your mind beforehand what you had expected me to say and do and because I neither said nor did those things you were too busy being hurt and disappointed to be able to get anything out of me at all. I'm really sorry you were made unhappy for I feel much fonder of you after seeing you than I did before, though also, from your point of view, much more 'useless'. It is terribly important that you should not think of your relation with me as a 'failure' as I suspect you are inclined to do. For this sense of failure and fear of failure that you have is the most paralysing thing there is. I can't help feeling that you think far too much about results. In your various 'crafts' you are absorbed by the work itself but in your 'public' activities I would say you are too much driven by thought of the results and that blinds you to the best way of achieving them. I am sure that, say in carpentry, you know exactly what can be expected of every tool and how to achieve the best work with it. I guess that in many other things you rely too much on your own personality which naturally breaks down under the strain of doing the work of two. Even in the Church you seem to me to be trying to do the whole work of the Church instead of co-operating with it and using it which is presumably what it's meant for.

It's a pity you had only a Catholic education. It is good as far as it goes and it teaches you things you don't learn elsewhere but in these days it is rather thin soil, generally speaking. If one is at all quick-minded one absorbs it all very quickly and feels one knows all there is to know, but one has no standards of reference by which to find how little one does know and how much there is to be known. Merely beating one's breast and trying to be humble doesn't have much effect; one has to find out in practice. Your mind is, I am sure, fresh and supple enough to learn a great deal but your temptation is to teach before you have learnt. That's your presumptuous devil. But your despairing devil whispers to you that your mind is superficial, your memory bad and you're too old anyway. You shouldn't listen to him. Auden, who is very good on the devil, says he may not tell us lies but only half-truths. The Devil's very useful . . . in the right place. On the assumptions of theology, God must have known what He was about when He permitted the Devil to tempt man. And in every legend (I think you get your rationalism in the wrong place when you deride legends; there's a reason why good fairy tales survive) you have only to see through him for him to vanish. Do you notice how he always promises a concrete reward on easy terms? Our Lord (and every spiritual master) never does that. He and they always stress the fact that it's very difficult—the way—and that there is a reward but that any particular person would be extremely unwise to bank on getting it. I have an odd feeling that in religion you sometimes work from the outside in instead of from the inside out. If you went more to the roots, I believe you'd find your surface difficulties seemed irrelevant.

I've tracked down the fourth dimension book. It's quite an old one but I'm sure it's the one you mean. And it's admirable and very clear. I have been reading it most of the week-end and begin, by analogy, to imagine the unimaginable. The hypothesis of a fourth dimension, if it could be proved, would clear up all sorts of troubles about religious questions and make all sorts of theological paradoxes and apparent absurdities perfectly coherent. In fact I'm not sure it wouldn't make the best possible case for Catholic theology. All the things people are so busily trying to explain away, the resurrection, the ascension, etc., etc., would be seen to be historically true. Still the fourth dimension remains only a hypothesis. Apparently you can get practical results and confirmations in mathematics from assuming it but of course that doesn't prove its existence. I found the glove image puzzling (the editor admits it is and points out that several of the contributors have misunderstood it themselves) but one's own image in a mirror gives one a much better idea. Try as you will you can never put yourself in the position of your mirror image which is identical with you except that its right hand is your left and yet is obviously not turned inside out. If you were 'turned round' in the fourth dimension, that's how you would look when you returned to

3-space, just as the triangle $\underset{A \diagdown C}{\overset{B}{\diagup}}$ turned over in the third

dimension becomes $\overset{B}{\underset{C}{\diagdown}}\!\!\!\blacktriangleright A$ in 2-space. What I've always been told

of the orange being passed through its own skin or the man passing through the closed room apparently *is* true in 4-space if it exists. Flatlanders can't get through the circumference of a circle without breaking it; we can. Four-dimensional beings therefore would have no trouble in passing through our solids just as we have no difficulty in stepping over the Flatlander's bounding circle.

Now, I must go to bed. Give my best love to Sylvia *and* to to yourself.

T.

10 July, 1941.

Dearest Peter,

Thank you so much for taking so much trouble about trying to find us lodgings. I am afraid it doesn't sound awfully hopeful as it is too expensive. It would work out to sixteen guineas a week just for board and lodging, apart from fares and all the various odds and ends and I'm afraid I can't possibly manage it. I'm so sorry, because I should so much have liked to bring them up to see you. Money is sure a bore sometimes! I'm trying at the moment to 'borrow' my own cottage for a fortnight and take them there. I do wish you didn't live so very far away.

I think your 'retreat' idea is probably a good one. From every point of view it's good to cut one's cords sometimes and quietly take stock of one's situation.

You disconcert me when you talk of my 'giving you counsel'. Because really, my dear Peter, I don't feel qualified to do so. I'm much too ignorant and too unstable myself. I couldn't, at the most, do more than drop a hint here and there for you to pick up if it sounded useful.

As to 'problems', it seems to me perfectly legitimate to drop them if they seem too difficult or if they don't interest one. Provided that, afterwards, one doesn't behave as if one had tackled and solved them.

I suppose you never think it worth while to state your problems to *yourself* in writing without showing them to anyone? I was thinking of your 'indictment'. The mere statement of exactly what is worrying one, without reference to other people and stated as oddly, even as shockingly, as one likes is often a great help.

I sometimes feel as if you're often too much concerned with what you'd like to be or feel you ought to be instead of quietly trying to find out what you are really like. So many people give themselves such useless misery because they decide they ought to be oak trees when nature intended them to be elms. I don't believe anyone could or should aim at all the virtues, only at the ones appropriate to themselves. It's like trying to be Shakespeare, Dickens and Hopkins all at the same time. Any other 'humility' than the often distasteful one of accepting one's own limitations seems to me false and very likely to lead to inverted pride. Everyone, I think, is given their own particular problem to solve in this life and that is the only one we shall be examined on. But the first step is to discover what the problem is and it's usually written in invisible ink !

I don't, by the way, mean that the Catholic religion is 'thin soil' for it is very rich soil. I only meant Catholic *education*, the secular side of it.

I've been having a look at Catholicism from the negative side, i.e., looking into other versions of 'mystical' religion. All this increases my respect for the soundness, in principle, of the Catholic version. Probably no two people take the Catholic thing alike: the fact that it is, in practice, flexible while maintaining a rigid outline seems to me in its favour. I certainly feel it's badly preached today and is far too concerned with picking holes in other people and defending its exclusiveness instead of letting its light shine. It makes me mad that the French Canadian cardinal has banned Bernanos' book. If the Church is going to keep up this attitude of blind complacency, it's going to have a nasty shock one day.

Sorry—it's too hot to write properly. My head's like a dry sponge.

Love to you both,
T.

26 July, 1941.

Dearest Peter,

I'm terribly sorry about your obstinate accidie. I wish I knew a cure. It is a curse and all I know is that it does eventually lift as suddenly as it descended.

I know well how you feel about 'our queer Church'. So much of the outside is so repulsive and so apparently at variance with facts and findings that one is extremely tempted to reject the whole thing. But underneath are very deep, old, and *human* truths, by no means unknown in all the great religions and I am sure those are the important truths, however clumsily expressed and wickedly exploited. I believe, once you've got a hold on them, you won't much care what your 'label' is. They've always been difficult and seemed to contradict nature but only on the surface. Lao-Tze said: 'When in doubt, empty yourself of everything and remain where you are.' I am sure the only thing is to relax, accept the emptiness and the horror, and expect *nothing*. Your instinct not to try and break through the barbed wire is sound. It is very hard indeed to stand still and let the sea close over you but I'm pretty sure it's the only thing to do. It's like drowning: struggle and you exhaust yourself. Keep still and the chances are you'll come to the surface and float. But accidie is the hardest mental trial I know and you have all my sympathy. Often when it goes you find you have moved on without knowing how. But when you're in it it is impossible to believe that you were ever in any state but this stagnation or will ever emerge from it. The only thing is to go on mechanically with one's daily routine—if one can. I am terribly sorry for you. Hold on to whatever you feel *in your bones* to be true, no matter whether it's a Catholic doctrine or not and try not to be frightened even if the most extraordinary thoughts come into your mind. One's true self, one's human nature, as opposed to one's desired or fanciful

138

self, has its own wisdom and will right itself if you leave the reins slack. And look at the outside world, not in the mass but in detail —a flower, an animal—and you may find it a point to steer by when everything is in sick confusion. Dear Peter, I'm so sorry. By the way, when it's past, you might notice *in what circumstances* these bad bouts arise. You may find they're connected with the same sort of happening, perhaps a real or imagined frustration. Didn't you have one after you had to give up your public efforts because of your accident to your wrist? And haven't you been inclined to depression since my visit which did not go just as your imagined picture of it went?

> Very much love,
> Tony.

5 August, 1941.

Dearest Peter,

I'm so relieved that the cloud is breaking up. Your letter was so good that I felt, in spite of clouds, confusions, despair and reaction that you'd made a definite new step. I do believe that, once one gets a taste for 'The Moment of Truth', you find it has a quality far more exciting than any romanticism, however fervent and charming. It is sad when you say I'm the only 'critical and instructed' creature you've met who didn't despise the Catholic religion. I know this isn't literally true, for you have your 'learned priests'. Also, though 'critical', I'm only 'instructed' up to a very, very limited point. Yet I know what you mean and it is alarming that the 'intelligent' Catholics use all their brains and ingenuity in defence rather than in examination and understanding. The 'suppression' policy is so widespread and so disastrous that there must be hundreds of people like ourselves who wonder if it's mentally honest to stay in the Church. I do not know a single priest or layman (it's true I know very few of either) with whom I could talk perfectly sincerely and naturally about difficulties. One defers to holiness, of course, but holiness absolutely unaware of what has been going on in other fields for the last thirty years and being serenely unconscious that there *are* difficulties for the non-holy is rather disconcerting. The Buddhists teach still—and we once taught—that insensitive stupidity is one of the deadly sins.

139

Now it is considered almost a virtue, or at least safer than any kind of intellectual curiosity. Everyone knows that intellectual curiosity may lead to pride and a dozen other ills but the Church seems not to *want* to know facts, even simple physiological, sociological and psychological facts. How can she cure us if she won't even listen to our symptoms?

As to the content of the faith, I know how deep and rich that is, but how it seems to be distorted and overlaid with irrelevances. All the accents are put in the wrong place. Christ asked for free faith and service: the Church seems to give a formula and say: 'Apply that and don't ask questions.'

However, I continue to 'practise' to the best of my ability and to believe I can find under all the coating the real stream of life in it. I can only pick my way by finding what I wholeheartedly respond to and ignoring the rest. But how much 'the rest' is, alas! I am reading a good deal about Buddhism. Much is admirable and seems superior to 'ours'. But it has its dangers, I think, as being more inclined to develop self-complacency and not being so rooted in the external world as Catholicism. Being inclined to coldness and conceit myself, I think 'ours' is better for me, it's so mixed, so earthy, so despised and unfashionable. Huxley's *Ends and Means* I find extremely interesting and think you would too. If only Catholics would realise that books of that kind are far more help in confirming their faith than all the sugary books of devotion or the arrogant defences. If the Church fears mental inquiry it can only be because her own faith is shaky. However St Peter denied Christ three times and nowadays looks like one of them. So if she is what she claims to be, she should soon be weeping bitterly. I often feel many priests make 'The Church' an idol and Christ is forgotten.

I can't give you any light . . . I wish I could. I'm too busy looking for it and may lead you up wrong alleys! But I'm your very firm friend, dear Peter.

Love to yourself and to Sylvia,

Tony.

Dearest Peter,

I must send you a little note before I go away from 16th-30th with the children to Cornwall. During the last week, I feel as if, after so much oscillation, confusion, doubt and questioning, I had at last reached firm ground. It is as if an eye opened inside me. I don't mean, of course, that I see anything at all clearly, very little indeed except the necessity for much prayer, self-discipline and some fairly hard study. I look on this entirely as an operation of grace to which I have contributed nothing but knocking very importunately on the door and asking, none too courteously, if there was anything behind the door. And, perhaps for the first time in my life, I felt a definite certainty that here was everything I could ever hope or wish for, every object of knowledge, love and desire, the one quarry to which heart, mind, imagination and will could address themselves for life. And I know it means incessant struggle against oneself, one's desires, one's vanity and one's laziness. Also that this glimpse will almost certainly be withdrawn and one will have to work most of the time by blind faith. But what I must hold on to is the memory of it.

I have often written to you very impetuously—raising difficulties impatiently and struggling violently in the net. But now I want to conserve energy as much as possible and use my mind less restlessly though more actively than before. I have at last got hold of some really good Catholic books, I just have to have solid food. Dom Butler's *Western Mysticism*, Fr D'Arcy's *Thomas Aquinas* and *The Cloud of Unknowing*. I am convinced everything I am looking for is to be found in the Church, and in orthodox dogma without any chipping or dilution. Once I can get on firm ground in that, I shall feel solid and not febrile and the surface difficulties can be dealt with later. It is only applying the principle I've found best in secular things, to immerse in a writer or a new subject until you have really got the hang of it and brush off one's swarming questions like midges at that stage. Nervous attempts to reconcile apparent irreconcilables are fatal at the beginning of anything, even though the buzz of modern life makes one frightened of leaving any questions unanswered even for a day. So for the moment I must just be content to appear a fool to nearly everyone I know. I shan't like it but that's quite irrelevant.

I do hope you have emerged from your cloud. Did you know St John of the Cross said 'Aridity is the thirst of the soul for God'? But I doubt if aridity is the same as accidie. I'm pretty sure it's not for there is a muddy, clogging quality about accidie very different from dryness.

Much love,

Tony.

My dear Peter,

I had half expected a letter and hope that its non-arrival doesn't mean that you are ill or suffering from accidia. I am terribly sorry that Sylvia's eyes are bad again and that you are having these giddy fits. Have you seen a doctor about them?

I could not bring myself to write from St Ives. I'm bad at hotel life and feel lost without a desk of my own. Also the place, though lovely, didn't suit me and I felt tired the whole time. However the children loved it and that was what the holiday was for and I did a good deal of useful reading. I also met a very nice Benedictine priest whom I could talk to a bit: I find it easier to get on with priests than I did. I have been reading mainly the mystics, some Maritain and Bishop Hedley, an excellent man. There are several gaps in my doctrinal education which no book fills satisfactorily and I shall have to write for information. One of the best books I have read lately is by an Anglican bishop—Gore—*Belief in God* which you can get in Penguin. I've no hesitation now about believing in God but feel there must be some better proofs of the existence of God from reason than the usual ones—design, order, conscience, etc.—which don't convince philosophers nowadays. Since I'm up against atheists all the time I need to have the facts. So I shall write to Fr D'Arcy or Fr Christie when I've made a short list. I don't want to bother them unless I can't get the information I want elsewhere. Fr Hugh doesn't pretend to be an 'intellectual' and I'm thrown a good deal with 'intellectuals'. The last fortnight has been very useful to me: I begin to feel the whole thing taking shape in my mind but want to get my rational foundations firm both for myself and for the people who question me. I'm pretty sure I'll have to go back to St Thomas as the fountainhead of the philosophical side. Since he wrote prayers which I use all the time and might have been written especially for me since they ask for everything I need, I ought to be able, with patience, to get a faint idea of his system. The more I feel drawn to the mystics, the more I feel the necessity of a very firm and orthodox doctrine. I have got to accept, embrace and understand, not fuss and criticise. In fact the house must be built on a rock and not on sand. I have a lot of hard work ahead but the work is a pleasure and a nature like mine absolutely needs activity if it is not to disintegrate.

I am very grateful for all you have done for me for you certainly stimulated me to go into all these questions. You must forgive my irritability and impatience. I have to admit that your last note worried me rather. Is it so hard for you, dear Peter, to give up a curious dream of yours? What exactly do you mean by 'losing me physically'? Why talk as if we had been lovers since we never were? It makes everything, to me, false and sentimental this way you talk as if we'd ever had a physical relationship. If you won't —or perhaps can't—give up these fantasies, how are we ever to communicate as real human beings? If I'm harsh, I'm sorry. I do, I know, tend to be blunt and brutal. But I'm not sorry for wanting to be truthful, however often I fail in being so. If I could only make you feel that even a glimpse of the truth is so much richer, more exciting, more varied than the most charming fantasy. All real imagination is rooted in truth and when Rilke said 'Nothing is more monotonous than fantasy', he knew what he was saying. Believe me, I know all the seductions of fantasy and only too easily yield to them but I know that every time I do I make my life poorer and not richer.

Very much love,
Tony.

12 September, 1941.

My dear Peter,
I can't write you a proper letter because I'm about 'written out' —my correspondence seems to have grown enormous lately and if I'm to get going properly on my book, as I must do this autumn as soon as the children are packed off to school next week, I'm afraid I won't be able to do more than wave an occasional hand-kerchief at my friends. I love having their letters but there's no doubt that answering them 'properly' takes a good deal of time

143

and energy—leaves one stale for writing a book. I know you'll understand and forgive this.

I'm very glad indeed to know that you too have had a 'light' on the religious question. Having had mine, I now feel I needn't exhaust myself puzzling over controversial questions for some time. I shall clear the decks as much as possible and try to get on with my job. The last nine months have been feverish and fretful but having reached a point and a firm ground of acceptance I shall cut down this reading campaign and get back to writing.

Forgive this scribble which comes with much love. I must go underground again now as the book needs endless reflection and I have to try and give myself the illusion of leisure which it not easy with an all-day job and many ties and bits of duties.

Yours always,
Antonia.

12 October, 1941.

My dear Peter,

I know you very sweetly don't mean me to answer but you write me a letter which makes me feel very churlish if I don't. But I can't deal with all the points you raise for I am really very busy and have not managed to get in any work on the book all this week. So you must forgive me and not doubt my friendship if I answer very inadequately.

It was most kind of you to send Susan those tools and she is delighted with them. Most kind too to offer me books on typography. But just now typography doesn't come into my sphere and I must concentrate on the things that do.

I'm afraid it's no good asking me for proofs of the existence of God. I doubt if there are any which would be considered incontrovertible by all schools of thought. It is a question you should ask a priest or a Catholic philosopher, not me. Even Bishop Hedley admitted he could not find an absolutely watertight presentation of the official 'proofs'. I've simply decided not to worry. I believe in God and that's that and I am pretty sure no one was ever converted simply by the official syllogisms. They might make the existence of 'God' highly probable but I doubt if they would lead anyone to believe in a personal God of the kind we believe in on the testimony of the gospels and the Church . . . and our own inner response to it.

I do truly think it is far more important to try to live one's religion than to argue about it. You have to remember that the proofs were constructed *after* the event and no religion came into being by disputation in the first instance.

I don't see that we can guess how St Thomas would have handled his speculations if he'd lived now instead of in the middle ages. His faith would have been the same but he might have presented his philosophy entirely differently. We live in too much of a tower of Babel world, I think, for there to be any universal language in philosophy. In science, mathematics and religion in the widest sense, a universal language does seem possible.

I'm sorry you still feel such a chill. It's by no means easy for me always to understand you though I sympathise very much. I know a great many of your difficulties are outside your control; I think you blame yourself too much for things you can't help.

You have the will to serve God and surely that is what counts. Of course it is an endless battle but I think (on good authority!) that one should judge oneself as little as one *tries* to judge other people. One is weak, full of faults, constantly backsliding and revoking one's promises but perhaps God asks no more than our incessant feeble *direction* towards Him. Once we turn in on ourselves, despair and presumption are always waiting to pounce. I am sure this constantly renewed direction of the will, even when one feels no spark of 'devotion', is the important thing, and that the effort should not be strained and violent but quiet and constant. It isn't easy but I think it achieves more than the flogging up of oneself to good intentions, followed by the inevitable reaction. I certainly find it works much better for me, though it is very slow. Spinoza says you can only drive out one passion by another and Huvelin told von Hügel to *de*tach himself only in order to *at*tach himself. Maybe, in the spiritual life, one has to be on with the new love before one can be off with the old and if one could patiently, strand by strand, weave God into the very core of one's life some of the things that seemed so important and so impossible to give up might lose their fierce attraction.

But lately, my dear, I've realised more and more that I can't be of any real help to you in your particular difficulties, whether 'personal' or 'religious'. Fond as we are of each other and firm friends as I'm sure we shall be for the rest of our lives, we belong to different species and don't speak the same language.

I feel that what we both need now is to get on with our own

peculiar jobs in our own peculiar ways, encouraging each other and praying for each other but not wearing ourselves out trying to achieve a mutual understanding of a kind which, through no fault of our own, isn't possible. At least we can console ourselves with this—however unlike we are, we are after the same thing and though horribly conscious of being 'unprofitable servants', working for the same Master. But, just at the moment, Peter dear, I think we must stop deafening each other with our own voices and listen quietly for our particular words of command.

Very much love,
Antonia.

A few months after our vast correspondence which had lasted almost exactly a year, Peter and I met for the second and last time; on this occasion in London. It was a much easier and happier meeting than our first, rather disastrous one in Wales. Now that the tension between us was relaxed and he had finally dispelled his romantic illusions about me, we could meet on a natural basis. Though we never saw each other after 1941, he remained the faithfullest and kindest of friends and we kept in touch by letter till his death nearly twenty years later. For many years he continued planning new 'projects'—religious and political discussion groups, controversial pamphlets, lectures and classes in woodwork and typography, crusades in speech and writing for social reform; but what he called his 'demon' invariably attacked him as soon as he got anything under way and prevented him from pursuing it further. Later, increasing ill-health made it impossible for him to continue these activities, but he never lost his passionate zeal for 'causes'. Some of his ideas for promoting them were excellent, but it would have needed a more plodding type of mind to bring them to fruition. He often told me that the 'broken head' which he said many Jesuit novices besides himself developed under the strain of going through the Spiritual Exercises of St Ignatius—and, for his mercurial temperament, the strain must have been considerable— was partly responsible for his inability to concentrate long on anything.

As he grew older, his mind became more and more easily fatigued but it never lost its resilience. Though he lived well into his eighties, it was difficult to think of him as an old man; there was something unquenchably youthful and buoyant in his temperament which defied physical age. The only noticeable change was that he became very peaceable and touchingly humble. In fact all the fundamental sweetness of his nature came out in old age and I think I appreciated him more truly then than ever before. The fact that he had never been able to make full use of his talents might have made a less generous-minded man turn sour and embittered and grudge others their success. But Peter had one of the rarest of all human qualities —complete lack of envy—a virtue as positive as it is unusual and which ought to have a positive name.

In her letter telling me of his death, Sylvia said that he had suffered very much in his last weeks but that his faith seemed to have given him strength to bear his sufferings with extraordinary patience. Though she had never been able to share his faith, she respected the sincerity of his belief as he respected the sincerity of her scepticism. As she wrote to me recently—for she and I are very old friends now and our friendship began on that strange visit to Wales in 1941 which was such a bitter disappointment to Peter— 'I have no religion. I am an agnostic. But happy are those who "believe".'

When the publication of these letters of mine, written so long ago to her husband, was first suggested, I naturally asked her whether she had any objection to their appearing in print. She knew all the circumstances in which they had been written and, though it is obvious to anyone who reads them that she had no cause for jealousy since the woman by whom Peter was temporarily attracted was not a real woman but an ideal creature who existed only in his imagination, it is typical of her own rarely generous nature that she replied unhesitatingly: 'Of course publish the book.'

I may say, in conclusion, that the same old doubts and difficulties that I brought up in the letters still afflict me, at times, to this day. But I have learnt from experience, though even now I sometimes forget the lesson, the wisdom of St Francis of Sales' advice to St Jeanne de Chantal: 'Do not philosophise about your trouble, do not turn in upon yourself, go straight on. God could not lose you so long as you live in your resolution not to lose Him.'

APPENDICES

APPENDIX I

A Letter to Cyril Connolly

When I unearthed the letters to Peter, I found in the same file several loose pages of scribbling block in my handwriting for which at first I could not account. They were numbered, and when I began to sort them, I was still more puzzled to find that page 1 opened with 'My dear Cyril'. It was only when I read them through that I realised this must be my first attempt to do something for Horizon about my return to the Church. I had entirely forgotten having written this imaginary letter to Cyril Connolly but, reading it through after more than twenty years, it seemed to sum up fairly accurately my reactions to my reconversion. So I decided to send it to John Guest along with the Peter letters and he thought it should be appended to them.

I cannot date it exactly but it must have been drafted in the spring of 1942 as, in a letter to Peter (not included in this book) dated 9 April 1942, I wrote: 'I have got to write an article about my return to Catholicism for Horizon—about the most difficult thing I have ever tackled. I'm wondering if it would help at all if I consulted my letters to you since I made hardly any notes at the time. I hate the idea of bothering you to send them and I tremble at the thought of reading through what must be hundreds of pages! But I believe you marked a lot of passages which deal with my religious problems and I might get a few ideas from them. I find it fearfully difficult to do this piece since I oscillate as much as ever. I despair of ever stating my problem clearly which is all I set out to do. For I'm still definitely conscious of a dislocation somewhere. I can't feel at home in the Church. I understand Tyrrell so well when he felt the Church like a great octopus sitting on his chest! . . . Yes, I know I have got to try and work it out quietly and pray about it. But this state of incessant doubt and dislocation is exceedingly painful.'

April 1942 (?)

My dear Cyril,
   Your saying to me the other day 'Why don't you write something about Catholicism?' has haunted me so much that I can't

settle down to the short story I promised you. At the time I shuddered and said 'No', explaining that I was in too much mental confusion about the whole subject to be able to say anything coherent about it. I have, in the course of the last fifteen months since I was reconciled to the Church, said a great deal about it in letters and in conversation because I am so preoccupied with the subject of religion in general and of Catholicism in particular. If those scraps could be reassembled, they would, I know, be violently contradictory and present such a beautiful case of ambivalence that they would be better material for the psychologist than for the student of religion. I am writing this to you therefore with no records at hand of the different phases I have gone through, though I think that if such records could be recovered they would only be a précis of the interminable dialogue I had with myself during the fifteen years in which I did not practise my religion at all.

Frankly, I feel very hesitant even now—so hesitant that my hand is shaking as I write—at attempting to state my position or my predicament to you. I am trying to do it partly because it may help me to clear my mind, partly because I cannot help suspecting that there are other Catholics in the same predicament as myself. The language of Catholicism and the whole Christian idiom is, I believe, repulsive to you. But in talking to Catholics (I know very few) I have up to now found the same attitude of dislike and hostility towards many things which you and I have no difficulty in accepting. I can talk to Catholics in their language and I can talk to you, E. and others of what I suppose one must call the 'intelligentsia' in yours. But so far I have not found anyone who understands both languages.

As a matter of fact I did find one and recently spent a whole night talking to him. The prelude to that conversation shows that I am not the only Catholic in a predicament. I had met this man casually several times in the course of the last two years but had never talked to him at all. I knew nothing about him except that he had three passionate interests, religion, philosophy and music and that he had become a Catholic. He knew of me only as a writer and a 'renegade'. A few weeks ago we met in the street and he asked me to come and have a drink saying: 'You are just the person to help me. I want to know how one gets out of the Catholic Church.' I explained that I was the last person to advise him as I had returned to the Church and was attempting to practise my religion. He then told me how, soon after his own conversion, he had written to a friend, a pupil of Maritain's, who had considerably influenced him towards Catholicism, expecting to receive delighted congratulations. Instead, the friend wrote back that he must expect no enthusiasm from *him* as he himself had come to the conclusion that Catholic philosophy was radically false and that he had abandoned his religion without a qualm.

At the risk of being boring and personal, I want to try and explain how it is that Catholicism is for me the one subject *par excellence* which it is almost impossible for me to treat objectively. The facts are simple but a modern psychologist and a Catholic would give entirely different and equally coherent interpretations of them. It is quite possible that both these interpretations are correct in their own realm and not mutually exclusive. Frankly, I don't know. I am not attempting here to suggest solutions: I am only trying to state my problem.

My position in the Catholic Church must always, I fear, be ambiguous. I was neither born a Catholic nor did I become one through intellectual, emotional or spiritual conviction. My father, who was a classical master in a minor public school and a tolerably good Greek scholar, became a Catholic at the age of thirty-five, thus cutting himself off from any possibility of becoming a headmaster and exposing himself to much criticism and ridicule. He remained an unswerving and extremely devout Catholic to the end of his life and I am sure that, at the time of his conversion, he was so intellectually and morally convinced that he would have made any sacrifice rather than not follow his light. He had at the time gone into the question with his characteristic thoroughness and convinced himself that the Catholic claims were unanswerable. But the impulse which had finally made him take the step came from another source. He had been kneeling in a Catholic church and had suddenly felt a definite sense of a Presence on the altar and the words 'I am the way and the truth and the life' formed so vividly in his mind that it was as if someone had spoken them.

Only once, in a very rare moment of confidence, have I ever heard him betray the slightest doubt. Seventeen years after his conversion (he was then 53 and I 24) we managed for the first and only time, for the space of a few minutes, to talk naturally to each other on the subject of religion. He said that he was glad that he had become a Catholic but that if he found himself once again in the position of hesitating between alternatives, he was not sure that he would make the same choice. After that the shutters came down again completely between us and I was never able to talk frankly to him again.

My mother was received into the Church on the same day as my father and, I think, entirely through his influence. It was not until some time after his death that her religion became really important to her. At the time of his conversion I was seven years old. I had been baptised into the Church of England but I never went to church except occasionally with my grandmother and my religious instruction consisted of scraps picked up from the servants, pious books of my grandmother's of the 'Ministering Children' type, which I thoroughly enjoyed, and occasional bible stories read to me by my mother and my great-aunts. My father, being definitely non-religious at that time, had been teaching me the Greek myths and the Homeric stories ever since I was four, so that when I came to be instructed by Fr Sidney Smith S.J. I knew all about Artemis and Aphrodite but I had never heard of Our Lady. As seven is 'the age of reason' I could not be conditionally baptised as an infant but was instructed for several months by this old Jesuit, just as my parents had been, before I was received.

Technically, I suppose I could have refused to become a Catholic if I had been dissatisfied with Catholic doctrine. But, even if I had been, it would never have occurred to me to go against my father's wishes: I adored and revered him too much. In any case, I thoroughly enjoyed my instruction, found it all extremely logical and extremely interesting, supplemented it by reading any pious book I could get hold of and learnt my catechism with speed and pleasure. It may sound nonsense that a child of seven should have the faintest understanding of Catholic dogma but I am sure that you will find that hundreds of small children absorb the broad outlines very clearly and do not just learn it parrot-wise. The 'invincible ignorance' from which I now suffer did not appear till many years later.

The effect of a strict convent education on a child who, though technically a Catholic and trying to live its religion as well as learn it, had none of the background and the easy grace of the bred-in-the-bone Catholic, you know already from Frost in May. If I were to re-write the book now, I would delete very little but I would add a good deal. It is sincere as far as it goes, but it is superficial. Perhaps it could not be otherwise for to give a true picture of a convent school one would have to have some understanding of the spiritual life of the nuns themselves and its relation to their teaching activities. With a child's egotism I had no notion that nuns might have conflicts and difficulties of their own; they hardly existed for me in themselves but only in the effects they had on me.

The shock of being sent away from Roehampton, unjustly as I felt, did not in any way shake my faith as a Catholic. Nor did I feel any great bitterness against the nuns. They seemed to me to have behaved very much more reasonably and humanely about the whole thing than my father did. To the end of his life he refused to discuss the matter or to let me state my side of the case. Thus for fifteen years there was a cloud between us which was never entirely dissolved.

I continued up to the age of 22 to be a fervent Catholic, often finding the Church's discipline galling, but never questioning the fundamental truths of the faith and defending them fiercely against all comers. It was not till I had married and left home that I began to be worried and to question the Church's claims to be the one infallible repository of truth.

The general climate of the 1920s, the scepticism, the almost idolatrous devotion to art got under my skin. I began to meet painters, writers and the minor intelligentsia and to find that to be a practising Catholic was considered, at the worst, mentally dishonest and at the best an amiable eccentricity. I certainly did not cease to believe in God or in the teachings of Christ and I was perpetually preoccupied with the subject of religion. For weeks I would not go inside a church though I continued to pray in a floundering way: this would alternate with bouts of orthodox practising.

Gradually the artists came to replace the saints (I had always found the saints a little repellent) in my private pantheon.

In 1922 I had a long and severe mental breakdown and was in an asylum for nine months.

When I recovered, the fever seemed to have gone out of my religion. I continued to practise but in a more conventional and tepid way and no longer suffered extremes of attraction and repulsion. I would envisage dropping it altogether without paroxysms of guilt and terror should I find something more satisfactory. In practice I remained loyal to it and went through the tedious and extremely unpleasant business of having a marriage annulled in the ecclesiastical courts. This process certainly opened my eyes to some peculiarities of Church administration which I had hitherto indignantly denied. But I will not go into all that as it would be merely a criticism of a method and not a principle and, as such, irrelevant.

Soon after, I was married again to a man who had no religious belief but who had a very definite philosophy and lived according to it with as much disinterested devotion as any Catholic might live by his faith. He accepted all the conditions of a 'mixed marriage' which non-Catholics usually find so preposterous; we were married in a Catholic Church and he did not in any way discourage me from continuing to practise my religion. But gradually, from association with a person whose mind was not only so much better than my own, but seemed to be of an entirely different quality from any mind, Catholic or non-Catholic which I had met, I became aware of all sorts of possibilities which had never occurred to me.

E. had not merely read Santayana, but he had soaked himself in Santayana's philosophy and made it his own. Now, for the first time, an alluring yet frightening prospect opened up. Suppose that the whole of religion should be considered exactly as one considers art or poetry, not as literally true, but as having its own inner laws and harmonies and values not absolute, but relative? Suppose that the Catholic Church had fallen into the fundamental Platonic error of hypostatising ideas and attributing independent existences to them? Suppose the destiny of the human soul was not to strive desperately to be acclimatised to some other life and state of being but to learn to be at home in this one, to use nature as the raw material on which the spirit operates? Thus the function of spirit would be to distinguish and contemplate things as they are in themselves whenever it can rise above the animal necessity to regard them as objects of desire or alarm. In the realm of art I could perfectly understand this attitude. Indeed it seemed to be inevitable. The artist who paints an apple is not regarding that apple as something to eat or as something that may be thrown at his head; he is contemplating it in eternity and expressing it in time. Nor does the person who looks at the picture imagine he is looking at a 'real' apple. The pleasure he derives from the picture is of another order, though none the less 'real'. To apply this canon to religion seemed both an immense relief and a daring blasphemy. To adopt the Santayanan attitude was to sweep away all the old terrors of religion, the fear of hell, the agonised preoccupation with conduct, the heavy yoke of Catholic exclusiveness and rigidity. Yet it entailed a discipline quite as severe as the religious one. Certain habits of mind, sometimes loathed and sometimes embraced, had to be ruthlessly broken. The belief in a personal God, the sum of all perfections, in the beloved and living figure of Christ, in immortality, must all be renounced. Whatever flashes of illumination the spirit might receive were conditional on the existence of the body; in other words, spirit depended on matter, not matter on spirit, and could only be called eternal in the sense that matter itself could be relied on from time to time to fall into conjunctions favourable to spirit. The vexed question of the origin of matter did not seem to trouble Santayana as it has troubled Catholic theologians and philosophers; he seemed to regard it as a flux without beginning or end and either to posit it as eternal in itself or to dismiss the question of origin as irrelevant or unsurmisable.

What made Santayana still more formidably difficult to oppose was that, born and bred a Catholic, he had assimilated with great precision the whole of Catholic theology and philosophy and had immense respect for the Church. In his last book *The Realm of Spirit* he uses, with masterly subtlety, the whole language of its theology to express his philosophy. I have never seen more than his name mentioned—and that remarkably seldom—in any recent Catholic book and he seems to me the most difficult of all to refute. You may wonder why, having been introduced to the best of teachers, to this rich and subtle interpretation of human experience which preserved all the values I had discovered by experience to be really valuable to me and which disinfected religion of every superstitious, repulsive and sentimental aspect, I did not permanently adopt it. By freeing myself from the fears connected with Catholicism I could have enjoyed it as a rich and complex essence, a wonderful work of art of the human spirit, as one may enjoy the statue of a Greek god without feeling impelled to propitiate the god by sacrificing a goat to him.

There are many possible reasons why I have not adopted the Santayanan philosophy or have only done so in spots. One likely one is that I am too uncivilised. E., who has patiently taught me what little I know of Santayana is, as you know, the most civilised of men and much more at home on the banks of the Ilissus than by the waters of Babylon. But, though superficially civilised, I am a barbarian and a lunatic. I am naturally attuned to mysteries, hieroglyphs, symbols and what you call 'beautiful muzziness'. I am also a prig, but that does not radically affect my interminable mental wranglings about to be or not to be a Catholic since one can be a prig anywhere. Also I am a schizophrene, which in practice means that, apart from alternations between elation and accidia, I cannot with the best will in the world maintain a consistent attitude about anything for more than a few days at a time. No sooner have I committed myself to any form of belief or action than the opposite immediately seems the only rational one.

But, ruling out these personal peculiarities and neuroses, there remain two other possibilities. One is that there is a flaw somewhere in the Santayanan view of things which I should be the last person to be able to detect. The other is that the Catholic view of things, however curious, is true. Even E. admits that, curious as it is, it is not intrinsically impossible or ridiculous. In fact he says that he could easily become a Catholic tomorrow but he prefers, as

157

he says, to have the whole realm of essence open to his exploration rather than confine himself to one segment of it, however beautiful.

After a progressive loosening of my ties with the Church, I finally 'lapsed' altogether, from belief as well as from practice, in 1926. Again, I can't give specific reasons. Perhaps, if you cease to practise a religion whole-heartedly, it becomes meaningless to you. Certainly I found nothing nourishing and much that was both puerile and repulsive in contemporary Catholic books, pamphlets and sermons. I hated the shallow cocksure tone of both old Catholics and young Catholics, the assumption that if you were not a Catholic you were a 'materialist'. And by 'materialist' they did not mean, as Santayana does, that you believed in the existence of matter, but that you were completely blind and deaf to all interests other than money, sex and 'having a good time'. I was in a mood, I admit, to find the Church's attitude to sex infuriating and I welcomed the idea of being 'free'. It took me several years to discover that a person's own unconscious attitude to sex is quite as infuriating and frustrating as the Church's and however 'freely' I behaved, I was no freer in my mind and quite as hag-ridden as when I accepted the Church's rules.

Nor, by abandoning my religion, had I got it out of my system. I had just as much difficulty in keeping it out of my mind as I formerly had in keeping it in. I still found myself furiously defending it to non-Catholics while with Catholics I furiously attacked it. Over and over again I would be drawn as if by a magnet into a Catholic church; bursts of religious feeling alternated with long periods of loathing and occasional welcome ones of indifference during which I could regard Catholicism as one of many interpretations of life. Sometimes I felt immense relief at having escaped from it all; sometimes I felt the whole core had gone from my life.

My father, who was year by year becoming more ardently, even more fanatically Catholic, was fearfully distressed by my defection. I was sorry to hurt him but nothing he could say produced any effect on me. He died soon after my definite breach with the Church. I had masses said for his soul because I knew he would have wished me to but I was not troubled by guilt nor did I have an impulse to return. Shortly after, I remarried. My third marriage was, of course, from the Catholic point of view, invalid. Though T. and I were both atheists, his father, a clergyman, insisted on marrying us in his church, much against our wills. I knew that I was technically living in sin but it was not till more than ten years later I discovered that by the act of being married in a Protestant church I had automatically excommunicated myself.

All during those ten years I continued to hunt feverishly for clues on which to found, not a philosophy for I have absolutely no philosophical capacity, but a way of life. I found plenty, in Spinoza, in Nietzsche, in Keats' letters, in Lao Tze, in Rilke, in Blake, in what I could pick up about Buddhism. I filled notebooks with sentences from here, there and everywhere that seemed to ring my particular bell. I picked up a great many valuable practical hints from Joanna Field's A *Life of One's Own* which supported me through a bad patch of suicidal despair. I flirted with the Quakers, with Bertrand Russell's neutral monism, and, much more recently, with the communists and came away from them, exactly as I had come away from Santayana and the Catholic Church, feeling with all of them that something very important—I could not give it a name, except in the case of the communists and Bertrand Russell—had been left out.

Meanwhile, another mental breakdown was threatening, this time creeping on far more stealthily and with much more distressing symptoms including not only the old depressions and terrors but a sense of the whole mind not only disintegrating but putrefying, and also strong impulses to suicide. The result of this was that after one or two bungles I was sent to an extremely competent Freudian analyst. I will not bore you with a description of the process. I will only say that it took three and a half years, that it was remarkably successful in removing the agonising obsessions and fears and making me capable of managing my life at least tolerably reasonably and that I can never be grateful enough either to the analyst himself or to Freud who laid the foundations of analysis.

It is open to Catholics to say that if I had practised my religion I should never have got into the state of mind which needed analysis. To which I can only reply that before my first breakdown I had never even remotely considered ceasing to be a Catholic, however I might occasionally have choked on various points of dogma or discipline, and that for several months before my collapse I had been practising with fervour. During analysis I was usually headed off when I attempted to broach the subject of religion. About a year after analysis was finished, I had an impulse to become a practising Catholic again. I plucked up courage to go to confession, only to be told I was excommunicated and that I could only be reconciled by a complex process involving the authorities at Westminster and signing a document accepting all the articles of the faith and presumably renouncing my errors. The priest was no doubt a good and conscientious man but I do not think he was very good at dealing with human beings in difficulties. At any rate he showed not the slightest sympathy or understanding and dealt with me so harshly that I regretted my impulse and decided that the Church was as rigid and inhuman as I had for years represented her to be. He recommended me to read a certain book—I forget its name, something like *Rebuilding a Lost Faith*, I think—and to come and see him. Realising that from his point of view I *did* need chastising and knowing myself to be vain, touchy and obstinate, I swallowed my pride and went straight off and bought the book. It turned out to be the feeblest set-piece of Catholic apologetics on the familiar lines that 'nowadays people prefer a spin in a motor-car to hearing the word of God' and it was definitely not a book to impress anyone either by its appeal to the mind or by its spirituality. I am afraid I threw it across the room and felt that once and for all I had proved to myself that the Catholic Church was not the place for me. Fifteen months later I was back in the Church, since when I have, in spite of my inevitable attacks of doubt and repulsion, tried as sincerely as I can to live as a Catholic.

I suppose for some time I had been realising that I definitely needed the external practice of a religion. I am, I think, incurably religious by temperament. I wanted to be *pratiquant*; what I found exceedingly difficult was to be *croyant*.

The Catholics and the psychologists would presumably give very different explanations of my return. The psychologists would presumably say that Catholicism was one of the factors in my life with which I had failed to come to terms, as I had failed to come to terms with money, sex, and writing. Obviously the Catholic Church would be very much mixed up for me with my father, who was directly responsible for my becoming a Catholic in the first place. Analysis convinced me without any shadow of doubt that my ambivalent attitude of unconscious love and hate towards him was one of the prime factors of my neurosis. Therefore I would naturally project into my attitude towards the Church, particularly such a very authoritative Church, the same mixture of love and hate, submissiveness and rebellion. In rebelling against him I would naturally rebel against the Church too, and also feel guilty about it. I remember during analysis, when, as a great gesture of defiance to the Church, I gave the blessed sovereign I received when I married E. to the Spanish Republicans, I had such a convulsion of guilt that I nearly fainted. Years later, having finished a fairly successful analysis and discharged quantities of aggression and fear, I was free to approach the Church, like everything else, more rationally. Having disentangled myself at least partially from my fantastic notions of my father and, though he was dead, 'forgiven' him and reconciled myself to him, reconciliation with the Church became a possibility. I could return to my religion disinfected of my morbid fears about it and acceptance of the Catholic way of life, so satisfactory to many neurotics, might be as practical a sublimation as I could hope to find. The return to the Church might, on the other hand, be a regression in face of a conflict too difficult to sustain alone or it might be yet another stage in the cure—a situation to be faced and dealt with, in spite of squirming and repugnance, just like the other situations which I had been forced to face up to.

How would the Catholics describe the process? Something like this, I imagine. Through my father's courageous conversion to Catholicism, I was given the great grace of being received into the Church and being educated as a Catholic. But, through my own perversity, I was not humble and submissive enough to the divine will and the Church's authority and eventually, through love of my own will, unchecked curiosity, self-indulgence and association with infidels, I renounced my faith. After long years of wandering, in the course of which I suffered a great deal, partly as the result of my sins, and during which in a blundering way I did grope after what truth I could assimilate, God took pity on me and gave me the great grace of returning to the Church. The doubts from which I still suffer so constantly are partly the result of my obstinacy and the intemperate habit of mind I cultivated during my 'apostasy', partly an affliction from which many whole-hearted and devoted Catholics, even saints, have suffered and do suffer. They may also be attributed to the devil. In any case they are my penance and my cross and must be born. The only way to deal with them is to brush them aside and pray incessantly for faith. The truths of faith are not contrary to reason, but transcend reason, and reason cannot dispel them.

Possibly both explanations are valid in their own sphere.

One of the great difficulties about getting to know the Catholic Church is that her practice is often so much wiser than her apologetics. To read up the apologetics side, from the crude C.T.S. pamphlets to the expert dialectic of the Jesuit Thomists, one might think the whole emphasis nowadays was on the appeal to reason. In practice this is not so. I have confessed 'doubt' to priests of many types: Oratorians, Servites, Carmelites and to ordinary parish priests who don't profess to be learned. With one exception, they have all given me the same advice—that argument with oneself or others would never convince one and that one must pray and continue to practise, though one was riddled with doubts, nervous of insincerity and entirely without any feeling of faith. One priest said to me: 'For

161

every doubt you mention, I could probably suggest a hundred that have never occurred to you.'

Returning to confession after an absence of fifteen years has been an interesting experience. I usually 'take my chance' and so have confessed to a number of different types of priest. They nearly all seem much kinder, wiser and more humane than the priests I remember when I was young. And I have been struck by how often I have received an impression of real sanctity and deep sincerity in the few minutes spent in confession to an unknown priest, picked at random. I have often received absolution when I should not have been surprised to have had it withheld. And that did not give me an impression of laxity or casuistry on the part of the priest; often those whom I should have expected to be most severe, such as the Carmelites, have been the most charitable. I felt that they had a very remarkable power of intuition and that they exerted it dispassionately in trying to assess the relation of the sin to the character of the penitent.

People have an idea that to return to the Church is to cut the Gordian knot, to abandon all intellectual curiosity or personal responsibility and to receive in exchange complete mental security. Personally I haven't found it like this at all. On the contrary I am more violently harassed by doubt, insecurity, ambivalence and rebelliousness than ever and to be once more in St Peter's boat is to be subject to such violent seasickness that every few months I am tempted to throw myself overboard. My non-Catholic friends—including yourself—are extremely kind, as they would be to someone suffering from a distressing illness or a mental aberration. And frankly I don't like a lot of the company I find myself in any more than they like me. But that is irrelevant and not a serious difficulty. In fact if the Church is what she claims to be, she *should* be full of the most mixed, incongruous and mutually antipathetic human beings.

One of the most important practical aspects of the Church for me is just this necessity for breaking down one's fastidiousness. It isn't hard, of course, to feel an 'even-Christian' with whores and homosexuals, with the poor, the dirty, the ignorant and the stupid. But it is far harder to feel the same bond with the spiritual fascists, the sour old *dévotes*, the cocksure apologists, the hearty tankard-thumping Bellocians, the pilers up of indulgences, the prurient defenders of 'holy purity', the complacent and the snobbish. Nearly all the intelligent, the witty, the tolerant seem to be on the other side and one looks rather wistfully over the walls sometimes, longing for them to come in; sometimes longing to go back to them.

But those are not the real difficulties. One's return is put down to all sorts of reasons—to 'escapism', to desire for security at all costs, to laziness, to intellectual dishonesty, to fear, to the war, to middle-age, to failure, to the decay of one's sexual attractions, to misplaced emotion, to habit and to neurosis. And all these explanations, so galling to one's vanity, find an uncomfortably convincing echo in one's own mind. Any or all of these and similar causes may, even if they do not provide the whole explanation, be contributory to the result. I do not for one moment deny it.

Why then do I continue to cling precariously to it in spite of prolonged periods of questioning, distaste, total lack of religious feeling, doubt, restlessness and rebellion? Because I wish it to be true? In many ways it would be an immense relief if I were convinced it were *not* true. I am not one of those who if the existence of God, of Christ and of the supernatural world could be completely and permanently disproved would feel that the whole meaning had gone out of life. I do not feel instinctively that truth, beauty, justice and other human values are meaningless without divine sanction. Nor am I appalled at the thought of being totally extinguished by death. I don't even think it is the gambling instinct that there is a chance that the Church's teaching is true and one may as well take a sporting chance. In fact the more I think about it, the more I am inclined to feel that it is much less true that I am trying to find something than that something is trying to find me. The more I try to confirm faith by reason, the more it eludes me. And I believe that I am all the time trying to find certainty, which one cannot find, whereas what I have to live by is what is the most difficult of all to someone as sceptical, obstinate and nervous of committing myself to anything as I am—faith. Every time I read the Gospel I am struck by Christ's incessant emphasis on the necessity for faith. It is the most difficult of all gestures for a person of my nature to make and probably that is exactly why it is demanded of me. For weeks at a time I can't make it except by a mechanical act of will and often, when I have managed to do so, I immediately set to work to undermine it and destroy it by self-questioning, by frantic reading-up, by feverish efforts to reduce it to *certainty*.

The violent fluctuations will, I think, continue all my life. But every now and then, especially after a bad period, I get a moment of faint light. I will quote one of them as I wrote it down at the time though I know how hopelessly vague and unsatisfactory it will seem to you.

'During the last week, after months of oscillation and mental confusion, I felt I reached firm ground for a moment. I can only describe it by saying it was as if an eye had opened somewhere inside me, an eye very filmed and feeble but just able to make out a dim outline. It was not the same thing as shutting the eyes of one's mind and forcing oneself to say: "I believe". Nor was it the sudden rational perception which sees the solution of a problem. It was as if, with the eyes of the mind wide open, seeing all the loose ends, all the contradictions, all the gaps to be bridged, this inner eye perceived that the surface was not quite opaque and that an infinite perspective opened out beyond it. It was as if a two-dimensional creature realised for a moment the possibility of a third dimension. Or as if some part of one's being one did not know was sensitive had been touched with exquisite delicacy and precision.'

I may add that there was nothing resembling 'beautiful muzziness' about this odd experience. It was accompanied by no feeling of warmth or 'devotion', only by a peculiar sense of conviction. I would hesitate even to call it faith. It was more like a perception of the necessity for faith, not in a body of propositions, but in what they represent, as a map represents a country.

The conviction that another order of being exists, beyond the temporal and visible one, is not one that one can pass on to anyone else who does not have it. Still less that the Catholic Church provides more reliable clues to their interrelation than Buddhism or any other mode of interpreting the universe and man's relation to it. What makes Catholicism, for me at any rate, the most satisfactory 'map' of that unknown country, is that it is, so to speak, drawn perfectly to scale. No dogma can be isolated; each one has to be seen in relation to all the rest as part of an opaque mass of 'propositions', but a kind of Mercator projection of—forgive me, Cyril!—the spiritual world, which makes it possible to know things about it that we could not know otherwise. *Credo ut intelligam* sounds nonsense perhaps—but that really sums up my position.

This is a most unsatisfactory letter. I started out by saying I was going to state a predicament, found that it would take a whole book to state it, and abandoned it. I started one or two hares and never pursued them. I have said nothing which could conceivably convince you or anyone like you that what I believe has any rational basis. In fact it is altogether so inadequate that I doubt if I shall have the courage to post it. It was your suggesting that I should write something about my return to the Church for *Horizon* that started me off on the subject and the simplest approach seemed to be a letter. But now I've re-read it, I feel it's far too personal, far too subjective and not at all the kind of thing you wanted. So I think I won't send it you after all but put it away in a drawer. Maybe in ten years or so I'll fish it out and look at it again. If I'm still a Catholic, I may laugh at my absurd qualms and queasiness in the early days of 'returning to the fold'. If I'm not—the laugh will be on your side.

Antonia.

APPENDIX II

Fr Tyrrell

Father George Tyrrell (1861-1909) was a Jesuit who was associated with the 'Modernist' movement which involved some of the most intelligent and influential of Catholic scholars and theologians, both lay and clerical, in France, Germany and Italy. Broadly speaking, it was a revolt against ultramontanism and a plea for the Church to renew and reinterpret her thinking in the light of modern Biblical scholarship, scientific knowledge and the social needs of the modern world. He was a brilliant writer and published many books while still a member of the Society of Jesus, although only the first three received the *Imprimatur* and his work became increasingly 'unorthodox'. Although such a controversial figure, it was not till 1906 that he was dismissed from the Society. Soon after, he was suspended by the Holy See from saying Mass and in 1907, after criticising Pius X's anti-Modernist encyclical *Pascendi* in *The Times*, he was excommunicated. In 1909, at the age of 48, he died at the house of his staunch Catholic friend, Maude Petre. He never abandoned the Catholic Church, as the Abbé Loisy and many other Modernists did, and he received Extreme Unction on his deathbed. As he had not officially retracted his heretical views, though three Catholic priests had attested that he was too ill to make any statement, he was refused Catholic burial. After fruitless attempts to obtain permission for this, Miss Petre arranged for him to be buried in the parish cemetery at Storrington, Sussex. Intimate friends, both Catholic and Protestant, including Baron von Hügel, were present at the funeral. A Catholic priest, Abbé Bremond, said prayers at the graveside and, as a result, was suspended from saying Mass by the Bishop of Southwark who also imposed diocesan excommunication on Maude Petre. As requested in his last will, made a few months before his death, his tombstone bears the inscription 'George Tyrrell, Catholic Priest' and the usual emblematic chalice and host.

Father Tyrrell left a highly interesting autobiography, not intended for publication, which covers his life from 1861-84. After his death, Miss Petre took up the narrative and produced an excellent and richly documented biography covering from 1884 to his death in

1909. The two large volumes, *Autobiography and Life of George Tyrrell* by M. D. Petre, published by Arnold in 1912, give not only a vivid picture of this remarkable man but also of the ferment going on in the Church during the latter part of the nineteenth and early part of the twentieth century, when many of the most zealous and intelligent Catholics, both priests and laity, were pleading for a new attitude in the Vatican—in fact for something by no means unlike the '*aggiornamento*' proposed by the late Pope John XXIII.

APPENDIX III

Baron von Hügel

Baron Friedrich von Hügel (1852-1925), a German Catholic scholar and theologian, lived in England from 1873 till his death. He was a student of natural history as well as of philosophy, religious history and literature and keenly interested in the work of the new school of Biblical criticism. Although deeply involved in the 'Modernist' movement, he did not go to the theological extremes of some of its leaders and escaped condemnation, though he was under a certain cloud with the ecclesiastical authorities. Far more prudent than Fr Tyrrell, he drew back in time and kept silent when the storm broke over Pope Pius X's denunciation of Modernism as heretical. There were those who thought that von Hügel had, to some extent, exploited Tyrrell, urging the younger, more reckless man, a far more brilliant and effective controversial writer than himself, to express views in print that von Hügel was too prudent to express openly. Nevertheless, though disassociating himself from Tyrrell's suspect opinions, he remained his friend and was present at the funeral which resulted in the diocesan excommunication of Abbé Bremond and Maude Petre. He was a great scholar and a deeply spiritual man who has had great influence on religious thought, an influence which still persists. Though a convinced Catholic himself, he had the greatest sympathy with Christians of other denominations. Besides the most popular and widely-read of his works, *Letters to my Niece*, a series of admirable spiritual counsels, his books include *Eternal Life*, *The Reality of God* and, what he considered his most important work, *The Mystical Element in Religion*. Almost the last literary labour undertaken by the excommunicated Fr Tyrrell was the revision of the vast text of the *Mystical Element* for publication. No acknowledgement could, of course, be made by the author for the mere name of Tyrrell would almost certainly have caused his book to be condemned.

APPENDIX IV

Maude Petre

Fr Tyrrell's loyal friend Maude Petre did not die until December 1942, at the age of 79. In the last year of her life I was privileged to know her. She died, as she had lived, a devout Catholic. Her excommunication was only a 'diocesan' one, i.e. she was not allowed to receive the sacraments in the diocese of Southwark to which Storrington, where Fr Tyrrell died and was buried, belongs. Her other house, in Kensington, where she lived after his death, was in the Archdiocese of Westminster, so she was able to go to daily Mass and Communion at the Carmelites in Church Street where Fr Hugh was one of the monks. The Prior had great affection and respect for her and she was indeed a most remarkable woman, highly intelligent, deeply religious and never embittered by the savage and unjust attacks made on her by many of her fellow Catholics to whom, for years after Fr Tyrrell's death, she was an object of scandal. She was a friend and great admirer of Père Teilhard de Chardin S.J. and possessed the typescripts of his works which, now published, have become famous. At that time they were only allowed to be circulated privately.

APPENDIX V

Three Poems

EPITAPH

By man came death;
Not by my love, my single sun,
Did this seed ripen to its monstrous bloom
But by the moon's unquickening breath
I was undone.

Bury me deep
Lest my love look on me asleep
And see the time-stained face with which I died.
This hasty, swollen mask of yellow wax
Which fear, the clumsy workman, botched me up
Blasphemes death's patient marble.
Calmer my living brow,
Purer my cheek that flushes now
With dark decay like rouge.
I wear the face of one who could not stay
For heaven's slow marriage day
That stamps me as death's whore and not his bride.

And from that greedy coupling, hour by hour,
My bastard death grew like an iron flower
Transmuting blood to metal, bone to ice
Between the abhorring thighs.

But my eternal travail is not yet.
Not till this waxen mommet turn to flesh once more
Shall I my true-born death beget.
Not yet, not yet may I put on
Majesty and corruption.

Disown the casual mouth with courtier tooth
And gudgeon lip that can no bait resist:
Cherish the hand; neglected on the wrist,
Hooded and fasting sits the falcon Truth.

THE CREST
(for N. H.)

Under the tree, tasselled with bleeding flesh,
The phoenix builds herself a nest of ice;
The condor struggles in the spider's mesh,
The feather grinds the crystal in a vice.
And, like a rose impaled upon its thorn,
The fox is spitted by the unicorn.

If you would like to know more about Virago books, write to us at 41 William IV Street, London WC2N 4DB for a full catalogue.

Please send a stamped addressed envelope

VIRAGO
Advisory Group

Book Tokens

Give them the pleasure of choosing
Book Tokens can be bought and exchanged at most bookshops.